On the ROCKS

Felicia,

XOXO

Sawyer Bennett

Sawyer Bennett

On The Rocks
By Sawyer Bennett

ISBN: 978-1-940883-12-0
Interior Design by NovelNinjutsu.com

Find Sawyer on the web!
www.sawyerbennett.com
www.twitter.com/bennettbooks
www.facebook.com/bennettbooks

CONTENTS

Acknowledgements

As always, I am thankful for the love and support of my family and friends. I am so blessed to be surrounded by so many wonderful people.

Two people I want to mention in particular. My fabulous, PA, Lisa Kuhne. You have been my best cheerleader and have alleviated so much stress from me, that you've made me a better writer. I am so thankful that we met and look forward to you being by my side for the rest of this journey.

Darlene Ward Avery... you are a constant source of inspiration to me. You always make me smile... one of those warm, down low smiles that just stays with me throughout the day. I'm proud to call you my friend and you, more than anyone in my life, give my writing purpose. You know what I mean by that.

Love you girls both.

PROLOGUE

Five Years Ago

Gabby

Oh My God!

He's kissing me, and it's the best feeling ever. I don't want to forget a single detail, so I commit everything to my memory.

The way his lips are soft but assured against me. Roaming and testing. His tongue is demanding... leading me toward my deepest fantasy.

I'm dying.

Dying of pure, sinful pleasure that my eighteen-year-old psyche just may not be able to handle.

I'm not sure if I can handle it because I've been in love with Hunter Markham since I was just shy of ten years old. For eight long years, I've pined after him.

It didn't help, and certainly only fanned my flames, that I'm best friends with his sister, Casey, and I practically grew up in his house. He was always teasing me, as a boy four years older will often do. That only made my crush that much stronger, because surely... the reason he was teasing me was because he liked me.

Right?

And tonight... things couldn't have been any more perfect.

Casey and I graduated high school not but five hours ago. When I walked across the stage to accept my diploma, my eyes scanned the audience. I passed briefly over my parents, who I love and adore beyond measure. They sat right beside Casey's parents, beaming with pride. I vaguely acknowledged both set of parents, who are the very best of friends, clapping enthusiastically.

Then my eyes landed on Hunter. He was smiling at me, bright and cheerful, his teeth dazzling against

On the ROCKS

his tanned skin. I love the way he's wearing his hair longer, all shaggy brown and streaked with pale blond from the sun and salt water. He flew in just last night from Fiji, where he had competed in the Volcom Fiji Pro as part of the ASP World Championship Tour. That's fancy talk for saying Hunter is a professional surfer, and he's quite good. He placed second in that tournament, but he's ranked number five in the world.

In the entire freakin' world, which yeah… makes him that much hotter in my mind.

And tonight… Casey and I made our rounds to the normal beach parties that were going on around Hatteras Island. I'm riding high on the fact that I'm an adult, I'm graduated from high school, and Hunter Markham gallantly offered to shuttle Casey and me around while we celebrated the time-honored tradition of getting drunk on graduation night in our tiny, North Carolina hamlet. So as not to be completely bored with high school parties, he roped his best friend, Wyatt Banks, into riding shotgun with him, which is funny in its own right. You see, Wyatt just started with the police department up in Nags Head, but tonight he was off duty and turning a blind eye to our underage drinking.

Not that Hunter and Wyatt were going to let

Casey and me get out of control. In fact, they strictly monitored our beer intake, insisted we drink a bottle of water every time they drove us to a new party, and hovered over us like protective mama bears.

Not that I minded said hovering in the slightest. Any chance for me to be next to Hunter was a chance I was going to relish. He's more than just a celebrity in these parts. He's practically a god, and said god-like status brings about a certain amount of fawning and swooning by the female persuasion. I can't tell you how satisfying it was to watch as Hunter turned down pass after pass by blonde surf bunnies because he was taking his chaperoning duties seriously.

Now... back to the kiss.

It started out innocently enough, even though I may have provoked him a little. I'd had five beers over a two-hour period, and I'm not gonna lie... I had a good buzz going. We were just leaving Troy Bean's party, which was really quite good. His parents were uber-cool and didn't mind the underage drinking that was going on. They had built a huge fire pit down on the beach, just below the deck of their oceanside house, and had a band playing. It was getting late and, even though we had responsible chaperones, my parents insisted I be home by midnight, fully aware that Hunter and Wyatt would probably be bringing home two very drunk girls.

My parents were cool like that, because I have been, in every sense of the word, the perfect daughter. I graduated top of my class, had never done anything stupid, and got a full ride to the University of North Carolina. My parents trusted me—or rather Hunter—to be safe and smart, even if I was doing a bit of graduation celebration.

When we had less than half an hour to make the approximately ten-mile trip home, Hunter grabbed onto my elbow, bending down near my ear to whisper, "We need to get going, Gabs."

I couldn't help the shudder that rolled through me at the nearness of his lips to my skin or the way he called me Gabs. He was the only person in the world that called me that, and thus it was special.

Turning around, he uttered a small curse. "Where the hell did Casey go?"

Shrugging my shoulders, I scanned the area filled with buzzed and frolicking teenagers, but I couldn't spot Casey. She was most likely off in a dark corner making out with a cute boy. Casey was high-octane wildness times ten, and she owned her sexuality. She made no apologies for the trail of broken hearts she left behind, and always had at least three condoms in her purse at any given time. Casey had it tough the last year, what with her brother and Hunter's twin, Brody, being sent to prison. She's been sort of acting out ever since then, and I spend much of my time letting her cry on my shoulder or listening to her shout out curses to the heavens for taking her older brother away.

"I'll look out here for her," Wyatt said with a grin. "You look inside on your way out, and I'll meet you at the car."

Hunter nodded, his teeth gritted. "I hope to God you find her, man. If I catch her with someone, no telling what I'll do."

I shivered again, this time from the menace in Hunter's tone, because it was just plain hot the way he was so protective. Grabbing my hand, he said, "Let's go, Gabs."

And yes, I shuddered once again because of the way he said my name and the feel of my hand in his.

Hunter led me through the house, weaving his way among the indoor partygoers. He nodded at several people, fist bumped a few guys, and gently removed the hand of one whorish girl that tried to grab him by the neck to pull him down for a kiss. I muttered the word "skank" under my breath as we walked past her, and I heard Hunter chuckle.

We never did find Casey inside, so we assumed

she was out on the beach somewhere and Wyatt would find her. Hunter led me down the front steps, and we walked along the narrow beachfront roadway to where he had parked his parents' car a few hundred yards down.

As we walked in the dark on the uneven pavement, Hunter grumbled, "I swear... Casey better not be..."

He trailed off, not wanting to voice what he hoped Casey wasn't doing. The disappointment rang clear in his voice.

"Give her a break, Hunter," I said, stumbling slightly over a crack in the road. Luckily, he still had a hold of my hand and steadied me instantly. "She's having a hard time because of Brody."

I could feel the tension in his body when I mentioned his twin's name, and he practically growled, "It's no excuse."

He pulled me along faster, and I doubled my pace to keep up. "I'm just saying... she could use some understanding from you."

Hunter immediately stopped and spun around on me, and of course, I barreled straight into his chest. He released his hold on my hand and immediately gripped my waist to keep me upright. The beers I had swimming in my gut and clouding my head caused me to sway, fortuitously, in closer to his body. My hands came up of their own volition and rested against the hard muscles of his stomach, and I internally sighed over the fact I was touching Hunter Markham.

The moon was bright, and I could see its reflection in his blue eyes as he looked down at me in anger. "I don't want her to do something stupid. I'm traveling so much that I can't look after her."

Yes, he was angry, but I also saw something else. He was scared for his little sister. Scared she would become lost and he wouldn't be able to reach her, and my heart broke for him at that very moment.

I'm sure it was the alcohol that made me daring enough to do it, but I pressed in closer to him and whispered, "I'll watch out for her. You don't have to worry."

He stared at me hard for a minute, and then his features relaxed a little. He even raised one hand and tucked a lock of my hair behind my ear in a move so tender... so loving, my heart at that very moment decided that it would never belong to anyone other than Hunter Markham.

I could no sooner stop myself than I could stop a herd of gazelle stampeding the Serengeti to get away from a ravenous lion in hot pursuit. My hands smoothed up his chest and wrapped around his neck.

I felt him flinch in surprise, and his eyes widened with uncertainty. It didn't stop me though. I stood on my tiptoes and brought my lips up, gliding ever so softly over his.

When I pulled back, I saw an array of emotion filter through his irises. Shock, dismay, and maybe a little bit of disgust. My heart sank, and I started to pull out of his grasp. But just as quickly, I saw something else fill up his gaze and it slammed into me hard.

Lust.

There was no warning... nothing that could have prepared me for what happened next.

Hunter's arms wrapped around me tightly, and he brought his mouth back down on mine with a groan that was carnally seductive and had my stomach tightening with desire.

His lips pressed in hard and opened up, causing my mouth to follow suit. His tongue immediately filled me, and he tasted of spearmint and cherry Chapstick. I thought my heart would burst out of my chest it was hammering so hard.

So yes... here I stand on a darkened road with Hunter Markham kissing the hell out of me, and I never want to forget a single detail of this magical moment. It is the best thing that's ever happened to me in my life and can only be surpassed by his continued kissing and his fervent declaration that he feels about me the way I feel about him.

I'm inexperienced... a virgin, but I can't help the way my body wants to now know all the things I never thought I'd be considering this very night. Images of Hunter naked, his body moving over mine... in me... flood my head and before I even know what I'm doing, I press my hips inward.

Hunter is taller than I am by a good six inches, so when my body comes up flush against his, I'm stunned, exhilarated, and even a bit nervous over the thick erection I can feel pushing into my stomach.

Amazement washes through me that he is turned on, and he's turned on by me. It makes me bolder and wanton so I rub up against him, hoping to induce him to take this even further.

But I get a completely different reaction.

Hunter jumps back from me as if he's been burned and curses, "Fuck, Gabs!"

I immediately feel cold when his hands fall away. I watch the way he stares at me with a wild look in his eyes, his chest heaving. His hands are clenched at his side, and he looks like he wants to murder me.

"What the hell was that?"

"I... I... I thought it was a kiss," I mutter lamely,

my heart now sinking down into my stomach. I'm confused. How could he be kissing me with such passion, such fire, just mere moments ago and now, he's looking at me in horror?

"That's wrong," he says sternly, and he actually wipes his mouth with the back of his hand. It makes me feel dirty and cheap, and sorrow lances through me.

"Wrong?" I ask in confusion.

"Yes," he says, like I just asked the stupidest question. "You're like a sister to me. We can't do that. *You* shouldn't have done that."

Okay... now I'm starting to get mad. He's making it sound like this is totally my fault, and while yes... I may have instigated the kiss, he certainly participated in it one-hundred percent.

Narrowing my eyes at him, I say, "I shouldn't have done that? You kissed me back."

His mouth falls open and he starts to argue, then he snaps it shut because he knows I'm right. I can't help the smug look of triumph that overcomes my face, but I realize immediately that it's a mistake to gloat because he stiffens his spine.

Taking a deep breath, he says in a much calmer voice. "I'm sorry. I shouldn't have done that either. This was a mistake."

What? Mistake? No way.

"It's not a mistake," I assure him and take a step closer. He takes a step back, which makes me even madder.

I start to open my mouth to lay into him, when Wyatt calls out from the dark. "I found her, Hunter."

Turning around, I see Wyatt walking into the glow of a streetlight, pulling Casey along behind him. She doesn't look too happy, and neither does Wyatt.

I feel Hunter take a step up behind me and lean down to whisper, "This was a mistake, Gabs. I'm forgetting it. So should you."

Then Hunter is walking by me toward Casey. "Where the hell was she?" he asks Wyatt.

Releasing Casey's hand, Wyatt reaches out and claps Hunter on the shoulder, turning him back toward the car. "It's all good, dude. She was just in the bathroom."

The devious smile I see curling Casey's lips upward tells me she was most definitely not in the bathroom and that Wyatt was covering for her. She grabs my hand and pulls me toward the car, opening the back door and pushing me in. She climbs in behind me, enclosing us in darkness. I can vaguely hear Wyatt and Hunter outside talking, and although I can't hear the specifics, the calming tone of Wyatt's voice tells me that he's assuring Hunter that Casey is fine and all is right with the world.

Casey grabs my hand and squeezes. "Holy shit, Gabby. Fucking Tim Miller had his hand down my pants when Wyatt caught us. I thought I'd die."

Normally, I would raise my eyebrows over Casey's sexcapades and give her a chastising glare. But I can't even find it within myself to care enough right at this very moment. I'm still reeling from the hot kiss and cold smackdown I just underwent in the last five minutes.

Of course, my failure to act like my normal self puts Casey's bestie radar on full alert. "What's wrong?"

"Nothing," I say hastily, and a little too loudly, although my mind is racing over the implications of what just happened between Hunter and me. It's pressing down heavily that the feelings I have for him are most definitely not returned, and now... he probably thinks I'm a big whore of a person, too.

"Bullshit, Gabriella Ward. Spill it," she demands.

I squeeze her hand reassuringly and even my voice out. "I'm fine. Just a little sick to my stomach is all."

That's all it takes... the prospect that I may barf, and Casey's attention has been diverted. She reaches past me and rolls down the window. "There... you can throw up if you need to. I'll hold your hair."

It's at this moment that Hunter opens the driver's door, and the overhead light comes on. My eyes snap to his as he gets in, and he's still wearing that look of disdain on his face. I'm not sure if it's for me or for Casey, but it's probably for both of us.

Wyatt gets in on the other side but before they close the doors and the overhead light goes out, Hunter says, "Let's get these girls dropped off, and head over to Salty's. I'm supposed to meet Mindy over there."

Hunter looks in the rearview mirror at me, maybe to gauge my reaction over the fact he just blatantly made it clear that I've been forgotten. He's hooking up with the biggest slut in the Outer Banks, and he said it to make sure that I'm not disillusioned about how he feels.

It's weird... but just moments ago, my heart was filled with many warm feelings for Hunter. Love, care, friendship, desire.

Now?

It's like ice, pushing out all of my gooey feelings and replacing them with bitterness and loathing. I'm so mad at him, and mad at myself for ever thinking there could be anything there. All those years I had

fancied myself in love with him, I realize in one startling moment of clarity that I am the world's biggest idiot, and Hunter Markham is the world's biggest asshole.

As of this moment… he means nothing to me.

ONE

Gabby

I pull into the parking lot of The Sandshark, an old, dilapidated building that sits on the Roanoke Sound just outside of Nags Head. I meet Casey and Alyssa here every Monday morning for breakfast. It's been our tradition for the last two years since Alyssa moved permanently to the Outer Banks.

Turning the ignition off, I wait patiently while my

dad's old '79 Ford truck grumbles and sputters, trying desperately for some reason to keep running even though I've cut it off. When it finally goes silent, a moment of sadness overwhelms me as I think of my dad. This weekend will mark the third anniversary of his passing, and I miss him just as much today as I did the day he died.

Laying my head against the steering wheel, I take a deep breath and try to push away my sorrow. Today's a big day. I'm going to put in a bid on a construction project that will, if accepted, put Ward Construction in the black and make me an honest-to-goodness, bona fide, general contractor. It's what I've been seeking since I took over my dad's business when he died.

I never thought my life would end up here... with me running a construction business.

The self-doubt and uncertainty plagues me daily, but I always remember my daddy telling me that I could do anything I set my mind to. When he died three years ago, I never thought twice about leaving college at the beginning of my senior year at Carolina and returning to the Outer Banks to take over his business. Mom thought I was crazy, but she supported me. I think she hated to see Ward Construction die along with my dad just as much as I did.

I knew the business well enough. I'd been riding in this old truck to construction sites with him since I was old enough to walk. By the time I was fourteen, I was working every summer with my dad, laying sheetrock, pouring concrete, and learning custom carpentry from him. It never seemed odd to me… being a girl and doing a man's job. I was a natural at it, and there wasn't anything I couldn't build or repair as long as it had a nail, screw, or joint holding it together.

I've struggled the last three years, barely making ends meet. At first, I thought everything would be okay. Most of my dad's work was on the commercial side, and some of his repeat customers didn't have a qualm with hiring me whenever they had new projects. They had seen my work over the years and felt I was trustworthy. However, I wasn't succeeding very well in landing new business. No doubt… the fact that I'm female and only twenty-three years old is a limiting factor. And it doesn't seem to make a damn bit of difference that I have my general contractor's license and can do the same quality work as others. I'm constantly struggling uphill to prove myself day in and day out.

Yes, there isn't a day that goes by where I don't

consider closing down Ward Construction and heading back to school to finish my degree in early childhood education. While being a teacher was my first love and passion, I have an equal passion for building things. I'm just not convinced that I can be very good at it in the long run.

A horn honks beside me, and I turn my head to look out the window. Alyssa is sitting there in her own Ford truck, although it's a tad bit newer than mine is. She shoots me a lopsided grin and a cutsie wave. I return her smile and get out of my vehicle.

Alyssa greets me with a strong hug, which says a lot because she's the tiniest thing. Barely topping five foot, she's waif-like and delicate. She wears her light brown hair in a super-short pixie cut that makes her large brown eyes pop against her fair skin. She's classically beautiful, sinfully rich, and the most down-to-earth, unassuming person you will ever meet in your life.

It doesn't matter that she inherited millions upon her twenty-first birthday, compliments of her being pharmaceutical royalty. Her grandfather founded a small drug company in the fifties that now has a position securely on the Fortune 500.

Alyssa spent her summers on the Outer Banks with her socialite mother, while her absentee father stayed in New York perpetuating the family's billions. She preferred to spend her nights over at my house or Casey's, and shunned the designer clothes and fancy sports cars her parents bought her. She also shunned their desire for her to attend an Ivy League school, instead shocking the family by enrolling at UNC with Casey and me.

Out of the three of us, she was the only one to graduate. Casey and I both dropped out. But rather than taking a seat on the family throne, she once again thumbed her nose and moved to Nags Head permanently, where she promptly put her inheritance to work by opening the islands' only no-kill animal shelter, simply called The Haven. She funds it entirely and works tirelessly helping homeless and abused animals have a second chance at life.

Alyssa has a halo permanently mounted over her head, and I only hope God remembers I try to live up to her impossible goodness when I'm knocking on Heaven's door.

"Ready for the big day?" she asks as she loops her arm through mine, and we walk through the front door of the restaurant.

"As ready as I'll ever be," I tell her, immediately spotting Casey at our regular table as soon as we enter.

On the ROCKS

I slide into the booth next to Casey. We fist bump, and then wiggle our fingers at each other. It's our thing... ever since we were six years old. Alyssa sits opposite of us and pours herself a cup of coffee from the waiting carafe and empty mug sitting before her. Our waitress, Babs McAlvee, a permanent fixture here since we were kids, shoots us a wave and yells, "I'll have your grub up in a flash."

Yes, we come here so much... that the order was pretty much put in for us as soon as we arrived, no questions needed to be asked as to what we wanted.

I pause to rake my gaze over Casey.

"You look different today," I muse. "What could it be?"

Alyssa shoots me a grin, and I return it. Casey rolls her eyes at us and takes a sip of coffee.

"Oh, I know," I continue with a look of keen understanding. "You look like a newly employed woman."

Casey lifts her chin, shooting a haughty look down her nose at me. "I am indeed employed. First day on the job at Dunes Realty."

Alyssa holds up her coffee cup, and we all clink our mugs together. "Here's to Casey... the best damn realtor that coastal North Carolina will ever see."

"Here, here," I agree, and we all start giggling.

Casey has drifted from job to job since dropping out of college. She was the first, lasting barely a year before she flunked out, too intent on partying and not intent enough on studying. She'll tell you until she's blue in the face that she was just homesick, or that she just didn't like college, but the truth of the matter is… Casey has just been so lost since Brody got sent to prison five years ago.

It was only on the prospect of him getting paroled that she decided to buckle down and try to stick with something. That something ended up being a career in real estate… although, I didn't bother to tell her that the market sucked. I was just happy she was excited about something.

Today was her first day on the job, and she looked beautiful in a navy blue suit that may have shown a bit too much leg and more than enough cleavage, but she looked professional and sophisticated. Casey Markham has to be the most beautiful woman I've ever known. She would put a Victoria's Secret model to shame, and there's not a man that gets within her vicinity that doesn't have his tongue hanging out of his mouth.

She's classic… long, blonde hair hanging in loose waves to mid-back, cornflower blue eyes, and the face of an angel. She also has a slammin' body that is usually encased in a bikini in the warmer months, causing perpetual hard-ons up and down the east coast.

"I've actually got an appointment this afternoon with some English dude that wants to buy oceanfront. He sounded incredibly pompous on the phone, but hey... his money's just as good as the next."

"That's awesome, Casey," I tell her, and Alyssa nods in agreement.

"Thanks," she gushes, and it warms me to see her so excited about something. It's been a long time since I've seen Casey care about something other than getting a buzz or an orgasm. "Then I'm meeting Brody for lunch. We're going to drive up to Duck."

The mood turns somber around the table, because while it is indeed a happy occasion that Brody is home now, none of us quite knows how to act. He's been incarcerated up in Raleigh for the past five years, and while his family has been incredibly supportive of him and have been dying for him to get back home... we can't all help but wonder how he'll have changed.

I only remember a carefree and perpetually happy man of twenty-two that made a terrible, terrible mistake. I wonder what type of man will come out from behind those prison bars.

"How is he doing?" Alyssa asks, her tone worried and sympathetic.

Casey gives a small smile. "He's fine. I mean... he's quiet... introspective. But I'm sure he'll be fine. Hunter offered him a job at Last Call and I think once he gets into a normal routine, he'll open up a bit."

Brody has only been home a week, and Casey was just over at my house the night before last, crying that the brother she knew and loved was gone. She said he was distant and moody, and she just didn't know how to talk to him. My heart broke for her, and it broke for Brody as well.

Reaching beside me, I grab onto her hand. "Give him time, Casey. And love. That's all you can do."

Putting on a brave face, she gives a tremulous smile and changes the subject. "Enough of that... So, let's hear your pitch. Today is the day my girl is going big time."

Just the thought of making my pitch causes my nerves to fire into overdrive, and my heart starts beating erratically.

Because yes... today is the day I'm putting in a bid to do a huge construction project and, if it gets accepted, it will help to change the course of my future. I need this job to solidify my resume and show that I can work in the big leagues. I need someone desperately to take a chance on me... to give me a shot so I can prove that I can compete with all the men in this industry.

And the thing that really has me freaked is that it's none other than Hunter Markham that I'm going to submit my bid to. The man who I once thought I loved and now still loathe with most of my being.

Why am I going to Hunter Markham with something so important? Well, let's just call it lack of options at this point. I've been repetitively outbid and overlooked by every major project that I've submitted to in the past three years. I'm hoping the fact that I'm best friends with Hunter's sister, and that our families have been close for years, will give me a leg up.

I have no clue though, what to expect. I haven't really spoken that much to Hunter since our "encounter" five years ago. He left for Australia just three days after that disastrous kiss and essentially trotted the globe for the next five years, competing on the ASP World Tour.

At twenty-eight, it was a bit of a surprise that Hunter decided to retire from the sport. He was surfing the best of his life and just last year had become the number two-ranked surfer in the world.

He was swimming in cash, swimming in women, and swimming in fame. I never asked, but Casey always kept me updated, even though mention of him caused a tiny pang of hurt to lance through me each time.

Without any warning or reason, he retired from the surfing world and returned home to open up a beach bar. He purchased Salty's, a popular oceanfront bar in Nags Head that had started to get rundown and neglected, mainly because poor Salty had a coke habit that sucked up all his money and time. Hunter came in, did a quick refurbish, and had a grand re-opening last month. He renamed it Last Call, and it looked like it was going to be quite a success. He also had big plans to expand onto the existing structure.

Of course, it didn't escape my notice that his return home coincided with Brody's return home, but it was just my guess that he wanted to be there to help his twin acclimate to the world. And yes, that made my heart pitter-patter a tiny bit, but then I hardened it up again. Hunter Markham didn't deserve to have my heart doing anything other than sneering at him in the future.

So, even though it made me nervous to do so, I pulled out the binder that I would be handing over to Hunter in about three hours, and opened it up to show Casey and Alyssa. I spent the next thirty minutes going over my pitch with them and explaining the budget on the bid. I also showed them the architect's plans that Hunter had given me, including a few potential design changes that I wanted to suggest that would help keep the bid low but would functionally be better suited for what he had planned.

When I was finished, Casey whistled between her teeth. "Damn girl... I have to tell you... that's just hot the way you talk all those numbers and construction terms. I'd do you in a heartbeat."

Chuckling, I punch her lightly on the arm. "Thanks, Case. Leave it up to you to turn my bid into something sexual."

Laughing in that husky, sexy way of hers, she says, "Hey... if 'sexual' will help you land the bid, I'm all for it."

"Eww," I groan. "This is your brother we're talking about. This is professional, not sexual."

Casey gives me a small flick of her finger on my nose. "Lighten up, Gabs. It's just Hunter. It's not like he's going to jump your bones or anything."

Even after five years, the mere fact that she called me Gabs causes my stomach to tighten at the memory of Hunter calling me that. I'm surprised that Casey does so now, because that name was only used by Hunter. He had been calling me that since I was a kid.

Shaking my head, I turn to Alyssa. "Let me get a serious opinion. What do you think?"

Alyssa gives me a confident smile. "It's wonderful, Gabby. Truly. I think Hunter is going to be very impressed."

"Really?" I ask, hopeful that I truly have a shot at this. "You're not just saying that?"

"Really," she assures me.

"Absolutely," Casey chimes in. "Hunter will be blown away. Plus, he's always had a soft spot for you. He'll give you preference just because of that."

I can't stop myself from practically sneering. "He most certainly doesn't have a soft spot for me."

Casey raises her eyebrows. "He does, although I'm not sure why. It's like the minute you turned eighteen, all of your friendly joking around with him took a nosedive, and y'all are just at each other's throats whenever you're around each other."

That much is true. While Hunter traveled much of the year, he was always home for a few months during his off-season between December and March. I always tried to stay out of his way, but seeing as how Casey and I are best friends, it was inevitable I would run into him on occasion. During those times, I will admit... he tried to be nice. But I was always snapping at him, or saying something condescending. He would be surprised at first, but then he'd give back as good as I gave him. Before you knew it, we were always fighting like cats and dogs. Over the years, it sort of became natural, and while we did our best to avoid each other, when we couldn't help having contact, it was never very pleasant for any involved.

The only interaction that didn't involve spiteful words was when my dad died. Hunter surprised me by coming home for the funeral, even though he was heavy into the tour. My catty comments sort of stuck deep in my throat when he came up to me at the funeral and pulled me into a hug. He rested his chin on top of my head and quietly said, "I'm so sorry, Gabs. I loved your father, too."

I couldn't help the tears that formed in my eyes over his kind words, and I wanted to hate him in that moment, but I just couldn't. Instead, I pulled away without saying anything, walked over to my mom, and never left her side after that. Hunter never approached me again, and then he left the next day. After that, we were back to fighting like normal.

Breaking into my thoughts, Casey says, "I know you two don't particularly care for each other, but he always asks about you. Every email or time he's ever called, he always asks how "Gabs" is doing. He does care for you, even if he doesn't know how to show it."

I mentally snort to myself, and then throw in a mental eye roll just for good measure. Gah… if Casey ever knew the depth of my anger toward Hunter, she'd be stunned. But she would never know that because I would never admit to her that I used to love her jackass of a brother and then had my heart broken by him.

That would be my secret until I went to the grave.

Now, all I had to do was be nice to him for the potential hour it would take me to make my bid and answer any questions he might have. It would kill me, but I would be polite and professional. I would make him see that I was the best person for the job… my lack of a penis be damned.

TWO

Hunter

I sit at the bar and watch my brother as he carries case after case of beer from the storeroom and stocks the coolers. He's methodical yet efficient as he stacks bottle after bottle.

He's also quiet.

So fucking quiet.

Closing my eyes, I try to remember the Brody that left for prison because he killed a man. Happy, funny, and lighthearted. I wonder if I'll ever see that man again, and my heart shrivels just considering the possibility that he's gone forever.

I want to get him to talk to me, but chances of that happening right this very minute are slim. We just had a major fucking fight, causing me to yell at him. He didn't engage... just quietly told me that he was sorry, and turned around to stock the beer.

I thought I was doing the right thing. I thought it would make him happy. I know it would make *me* happy.

Foolishly, I met him at Last Call first thing this morning, excited about my proposition.

"Brody," I had told him, a warm smile on my face. "I'd like you to be partners with me. Fifty-fifty ownership of Last Call."

Foolishly, I expected him to smile at me. The first smile I would have seen on his face... the face that was identical to mine, for the first time in five years. Instead, he stared at me blankly for a moment and then said, "No thanks."

What the fuck? No thanks?

No amount of begging, pleading, or cajoling could get him to consider. He just quietly... so very fucking quietly, thanked me but said he was happy just having the job that I gave him. He didn't want to be partners with me. Said he didn't deserve it.

On the ROCKS

It didn't matter that I yelled and cursed at him, calling him an ingrate, which I instantly regretted. I immediately apologized, and he just nodded his head at me and grabbed the first case of beer from the store shelf.

Now I watch him as he's lost in his own thoughts, while he stacks a case of Budweiser. I wonder what he's thinking. Is he remembering that night? When he killed that man?

Or is he remembering what it was like to live life in a six-by-eight steel and brick box?

Does he ever think about what his life was like before? Because he surely isn't giving much thought to what his life could be like now.

Sighing in frustration, I glance down at my watch and see that Gabby Ward is due here in a few minutes. Just the thought of her causes my stomach to clench, and not in a good way.

I'm nervous as fuck about seeing her… about trying to carry on a normal conversation with her, without one or both of us snapping at the other. It's been our pattern for the last five years. Ever since she blew my mind with that hot-as-fuck kiss, and I metaphorically slapped her in the face with my rebuff.

God, if I could go back and change that day, I would. She threw me for a loop when she kissed me, and I responded the way I had thought about kissing her for the longest time. For a few seconds, I engaged in the best kiss I've ever had in my entire life… a kiss that has never been equaled since. Then I reacted horribly and put hurt in her eyes that has never left. Because while she hides behind mockery and condescension, I still see the pain that lives just below the surface.

I'm not stupid. I know the reason Gabby acts so vile toward me is because she's bruised and angry. And she has every right to be. I behaved badly, and I wounded her deeply. There's not a doubt in my mind that Gabby had deep feelings toward me, and she was expressing them that night. It's why that kiss was so fucking good… because of the depth of feeling behind it.

It certainly didn't help that for a few years prior, I had noticed with keen awareness how beautiful she had become. How sinfully sexy she was. She was forbidden fruit, completely fucking tempting me at every single turn.

Not only was she Casey's best friend, but she was indeed like a sister to me. I cared for her a lot… still do for that matter. But more than that, I couldn't have a relationship with her because my life was all kinds of fucked up crazy, with me being on the pro surfing circuit. I traveled ten months out of the year, and a relationship was just not feasible. It's not something I wanted, even with someone as amazing as Gabby. And there was no way I was ever going to let Gabby settle for something less than a devoted partner. She deserved way better than what I could ever have given her.

So our relationship changed... morphed into a constant state of bickering and snide comments when we were around each other. Except for that one time, at her father's funeral... where I got to hold her for no more than five seconds, and all the past was forgotten.

But then we went back to our feuding state, and now I'm getting ready to see her and hopefully have a calm sort of interaction.

As if on cue, the front door to the bar opens and I see the silhouette of Gabby framed by the noon sun behind her. Even her outline looks stunning and, as she steps into the gloom of the bar, I can see her features a little more clearly without the sun distorting her image.

She still wears her chocolate-brown hair long, cut in loose layers that frame her face. It's her face that makes Gabby... well, Gabby. She has some Cherokee somewhere deep in her line, at least that's what her mom says, but it must be true. Her cheekbones sit high on her heart-shaped face, and her hazel eyes are exotically slanted. Her skin is golden with light freckles across the bridge of her nose. She has the most amazing lips… full, generous, and as I remember, so very soft. Even now… dressed in a plain white t-shirt, boy-cut Levis, and a pair of worn work boots, she's without a doubt the sexiest woman I've ever known.

And probably ever will know.

She's starred in many fantasies I've had while in my shower jacking off, and just the thought of that causes a stirring down in my pants.

Mentally shaking my head to get my thoughts out of the gutter, I stand from the bar stool and make my way over to her. But before she acknowledges me, she glances over and sees Brody behind the bar. She doesn't even spare me a glance but turns his way, walking right up to him.

"Hey Brody," she says in that soft, southern voice, giving him a huge hug.

I see him jerk with surprise over the contact, his body stiff for just a few seconds. Then he remembers that this is Gabby… like a little sister to him as well, and he returns her hug for a brief moment.

I hear her softly say, "I missed you," and I watch

as his arms tighten around her just a bit, while he stares at me with an impassive look over her shoulder.

My heart hurts so badly as I see the way he struggles with personal contact and kindness. My heart also expands at the same moment when I see how softly caring Gabby is to my brother. I've seen plenty of people over the last week turn their nose up at Brody, completely bent on considering him a murderer and nothing more. I'll be forever grateful to Gabs for making him remember that he's her friend and always will be.

Turning to me, Gabby gives me a polite smile. "Hunter... good to see you."

I raise my eyebrows, amused by her show of aloof professionalism. There's certainly no warm hug for me... no words of how much she missed me.

But then again, I didn't expect any, and it sticks in my craw for a delusional moment that she can be warm and caring toward my felon of a brother, but have a cool politeness for the guy that kissed her senseless.

No, that won't do at all.

I step up to her and grab her in a hug, trying hard not to laugh when she yelps in surprise. "Hey, Gabs. I'm sure you got a hug in there for Brody's brother, right?"

I feel her body stiffen against mine and her hands come up to rest on my biceps, not to return the hug but to push me away. I let her struggle futilely for a moment, and then I release her from my hold. Sneaking a glance at Brody, I see that he's watching us with the briefest hint of interest before he returns to stocking the bar.

"Well, let's go back to my office, and you can show me your bid."

I turn around, but not before I relish the confused look on Gabby's face. There... that will teach her to show indifference to me.

Opening the door to my office, I motion her in before me and follow behind. She stops halfway into the room, and I can't help myself from walking up right behind her and stopping just inches from her body.

She's not immune to my nearness, because even I can feel the heat that swirls between us. Her spine stiffens a little, and I watch with amusement as she pushes her shoulders back so her head lifts tall and proud.

I literally can't help myself when I bend forward just a bit and softly say, "You look beautiful. But then again... you always did."

I'm even more amused when she takes a quick

step forward to get away from me, and I almost want to laugh out loud when I hear the way her breath comes out all shaky. Keeping a neutral look on my face, I walk past her and sit behind my desk, motioning for her to take a seat. She does so, sitting on the edge of the chair, completely ill at ease in my presence.

While it strokes my ego to know that I still have an effect on her, I don't want this to be unpleasant, because I know how important this is for her. So I give her a reassuring smile and say, "I'm excited to see your bid. Casey made sure to text me this morning to tell me how impressed she was with it."

Far from putting Gabby at ease, her face turns slightly red and she snaps, "I don't want you giving me this job just because Casey is my best friend. You need to leave that out of this."

I'm surprised by the vehemence in her voice, and I hold my hand up. "Easy now. I was just pointing out that Casey is proud of you. But don't worry... I make my own decisions, and I'll be choosing the best bid for the job. Our *personal* connection won't have a damn thing to do with it."

I make sure I put a world of innuendo in the word "personal," and it has the intended effect. Gabby's face goes even redder, and she swallows hard. I know her mind immediately went back five years to that kiss, and yeah… I'm thinking about it now as I stare at those lips, which were like heaven against mine.

"How about showing me what you got?" I gently prompt her, and she moves quickly into professional action.

Handing me a binder, she directs me to open to the first page and then she walks me through her proposal. I'm stunned right off the bat to see that she's done something that none of the other contractors did. She actually questioned the architect's plans that I had drawn up, pointing out some areas that she felt could be improved with a few design changes. Amazingly enough, even with the changes, her proposal is significantly lower in cost than the next lowest bid I received.

"This looks really impressive," I tell her sincerely. "But I'm not quite sure how you can do it for such a low amount."

I don't mean to sound skeptical, but frankly… it doesn't seem possible to me. I'm relieved that she doesn't take offense to this but actually gives me a confident smile. "That's easy… I'm going to be doing a lot of the carpentry work myself rather than sub it out."

"And you can do all of that in the proposed timeline you gave me?"

I see a small kernel of doubt filter across her face, but then it's gone. She nods and says, "I promise I'll keep to schedule. I mean... I'll be doing some of the work after hours, and I won't interfere with the running of your business. But yeah... I can meet the deadlines."

I glance back through the entire bid again, making sure I don't have any other questions. It's professionally done, and I'm truly impressed. I am a little bit leery of her taking on the carpentry work herself, not because I doubt her talents. I've seen enough of Gabby's work over the years, including a custom-built china cabinet she made for my parents' twenty-fifth wedding anniversary, that I know she can deliver a good product. I'm worried about her being able to do this all on her own, within the time frame specified.

"Gabby... are you positive this isn't too much? I'm not saying I accept your bid, but if I did... I could work with you on the timeline."

I watch with dismay as Gabby's full lips flatten, a sure sign she's not happy with me questioning her abilities. Her eyes narrow, and her voice is icy. "Did you pose that same question... make that same offer, to the *men* that submitted bids to you? I can assure you the fact I don't have a dick swinging between my legs won't hinder my abilities."

Holding both hands up, I say, "Whoa, whoa, whoa. Hold up there just a minute. I wasn't questioning your abilities, and I most definitely appreciate the fact that you don't have a dick swinging between your legs. It would have made that kiss we shared a little awkward. I was just making sure, is all. As your prospective employer, I'm allowed to have these concerns."

Rather than being chastised as I thought she would be, she seems to get even angrier. Standing up from her seat, she slaps her hands on my desk and leans toward me. "Don't. Ever. Mention. That. Kiss. Again."

Holy shit, she's pissed. And God, she's utterly fucking gorgeous with her eyes flashing at me like that, and I cannot help that my eyes stray down to her breasts, which are pulling against the material of her thin t-shirt as she bends over my desk. She doesn't miss my look, and I actually hear her growl.

I let my gaze travel up slowly to meet hers, and those hazel eyes are practically green with rage. I can't help the lazy smile that takes over my face. "Listen Gabs... if I accept your bid, you're going to have to

curb that temper of yours. We'll have to work together, and honestly… it's a bit depressing having you so pissed all the time."

I had thought a gentle reminder that we are still here to talk about a job that she desperately wants would cool her off, but she gets even madder. "Fuck you, Hunter. I don't need your fucking job."

She reaches over, snatches the binder back, and spins toward the door. I'm utterly stunned by her reaction, but it only takes me a second to yell out, "What the fuck, Gabby?"

It doesn't stop her though, and she wrenches the door open with such force that it slams against the wall and rattles some of my surfing pictures that are hanging there. She doesn't miss a beat and stalks out of my office. I hear her call out a goodbye to Brody, and then I hear the front door slam as she leaves.

I think about going after her… grabbing her and making her listen to me. But I'm afraid if I do… if I put my hands on her, they are going to want to keep touching every part of her.

And I don't think I'll be able to stop.

Walking slowly out to the bar, trying to think how to salvage this, I'm brought up short by Brody growling at me. "What the fuck did you do to her?"

My head snaps up, and I look at him in

amazement. This is the most emotion I've seen from him in years, and while it's white-hot anger directed at me, it makes me deliriously happy to know that he has feeling inside of him.

I shoot him a huge smile. "I didn't do anything to her. She's just a little prickly right now, but she'll be fine."

Brody must accept my word as true because the anger on his face melts away, then I'm met with the bland look that I've come to recognize as Brody surviving in a post-prison world.

God… what I wouldn't give to have my brother just give me one smile.

Just one tiny fucking smile.

But right now, that seems almost as impossible as Gabby giving me a smile.

THREE

Gabby

I finish my second cup of coffee and rinse the mug out, laying it in the drain rack. The extra surge of caffeine isn't doing anything to improve my mood. Yesterday was a freakin' disaster. I ruined any chance of getting the bid for The Last Call project because I couldn't keep my fat mouth shut, and then I had the date from hell last night.

I relented to go on a blind date with Kevin Zulekis, thanks to the evil machinations of Casey and her matchmaking ways. I'm going to kill her for setting me up with that bonehead.

"He's a dentist," she said over breakfast a few weeks ago. "He's perfect for you."

I went home that day and examined my teeth in the mirror. Two years of orthodontics and regular cleanings gave me a fantastic smile. I'm not sure why Casey felt I needed to date a dentist.

The date started badly and got progressively worse throughout the night. It started by him showing up at my door with his fly unzipped which, in hindsight, I'm sure was intentional. I tried to ignore it for as long as I could but by the time we pulled into the restaurant parking lot, I had to tell him so little Kevin didn't make an unintentional appearance. He didn't even have the grace to look embarrassed and sort of leered at me as he zipped up his pants. I swear he even flexed his hips outward as he made himself presentable.

During dinner, he had a hard time keeping his eyes off my chest and kept repeatedly licking his lips. That wouldn't have been so bad, except he had a dab of steak sauce on the lower right corner of his mouth, and he kept missing it every time that slimy appendage made an appearance. I finally had to point it out as well, and he sort of smirked at me while he

licked it off, then leaned closer to me and asked, "Did I get it all?"

I shudder even thinking about it.

Finally, he insisted on walking me to the door. I was calculating how to best get inside as fast as possible when he went in for a kiss. He caught me off guard, but I managed to snap my lips shut and gave him a firm push away when his tongue popped out and licked against my mouth. I had to struggle not to say, "Ewww... gross," as I quickly thanked him for dinner and locked myself in my apartment.

Like I said... I'm going to kill Casey.

What's even worse than the creepiness of my date, was that all night through dinner, when I wasn't being repulsed by Kevin, I kept thinking of Hunter.

Oh, not about all the ways he pisses me off.

Rather, I thought about all the ways in which he still attracts me.

His easygoing style, his humor, the way he flirted with me at the bar yesterday. My thoughts stayed with me as I went to sleep that night, and then I ended up having a full-blown orgasmic dream about him. It was hot... I mean, really hot. But it was also appealing to my heart, because in my dream, he gave me everything I wanted.

It started out as a repeat of the night of our kiss,

except he didn't push away from me. Instead, he deepened the kiss and his hands touched me in all my forbidden places. He whispered words to me about how much he wanted me, and that he had been secretly lusting after me for a long time. Then he laid me out on the hood of the car and stripped me bare, proceeding to use his hands and lips to push the boundaries of all sleep orgasms. I kept telling him to stop, that someone would see us, and he said the words that caused pleasure to skyrocket through me.

He said, "I don't care if anyone sees us. You're mine, and I want you too much to ever stop."

My climax was so intense that it woke me up. I sat straight up in bed with the covers clutched to my chest, my breathing heavy and labored, and my skin moist with sweat.

It wasn't so much what he was doing to me physically in the dream that caused me to break apart, as it was his words... words that I had been dying to hear that night long ago.

So yeah, I'm in a really bad mood because, apparently, all these years of muttering Hunter's name along with choice curse words really doesn't mean that much. I still have some residual feelings there that I need to get rid of, and I can't continue to walk through this life letting Hunter affect me this way.

"Good morning," I hear from behind me.

I turn and give my roommate, Savannah Shepherd, a quick smile as she walks into the kitchen. "Good morning. Busy day?"

Savannah sets her camera bag on the kitchen table and checks the contents. "Yeah, I have to head down to New Bern and get some photos of the new bridge they're building on Highway Seventeen. Exciting stuff, right?"

"Totally exciting," I tell her with sympathy.

Savannah is a photographer, and she's really, really good. She does some freelance stuff for wildlife magazines and such, but her main job is with our local newspaper, which doesn't pay all that much. She's struggling but determined to make her way.

I met Savannah when I moved back home after dropping out of Carolina three years ago. The obvious choice was to move in with my mom, but I really wanted to be out on my own. If I was going to take over my dad's business and make a go of it, I wanted to really make a go of it. I wanted to prove to myself that I could be a successful business owner, and that meant being able to fully support myself.

But I really couldn't afford a place on my own and Casey was unemployed and living with her parents, so I put an ad in the paper and Savannah responded. She's a year older than I am, and she wanted to relocate to the Outer Banks in order to explore the amazing wildlife and scenic opportunities the beach held. Luckily, we hit it off wonderfully and were content as roommates, although she's a little bit shy and withdrawn.

"I won't be home until late tonight," she says. "After work, I'm going to go help Alyssa out at The Haven for a bit, and then I'm doing some wedding portraits tonight."

Savannah is one of the busiest people I've ever met. She never slows down and spends most of her time trying to pick up extra odd jobs in order to help pay her bills. I grimace in distaste at her mention of doing wedding portraits tonight. She started working part-time as an assistant for this sleazy photographer who keeps trying to cop a feel on her. Luckily, she's been able to rebuff him, but I don't like her being in that position.

"Just be careful around that douche," I warn her. "Don't get stuck there with him alone. I don't trust him."

Giving a small laugh, Savannah slings her camera bag over her shoulder. "I don't trust him either. I'll be careful. See you tomorrow, okay?"

"Sure," I tell her with an encouraging smile as I

watch her walk to the door. Glancing over at the wall clock, I note it's getting close to eight AM and I need to get moving. I'm working on some custom bathroom cabinets for one of my mom's poker buddies. Yes, my mom plays poker, and she's quite good at it too.

I turn toward the hallway that leads to the bedrooms when I hear Savannah open the front door and exclaim in surprise, "Uh… hello."

Turning around, I see Hunter standing there with his fist raised to knock on the door. He's surprised to see Savannah, and then his eyes move past her and on to me. His gaze slowly slides down my body, and it's at this point that I realize I'm in my pajamas… which means I'm wearing a tight tank top that doesn't even cover my stomach fully and a pair of bikini underwear. Definitely not clothing I'm embarrassed to wear in my own home and in front of Savannah, but totally a different matter when Hunter is standing in my doorway.

He eyes me appreciatively, and a smile curves those lips upward. Dragging his gaze back up to mine, he says, "Nice outfit."

I could be embarrassed, flub out some type of apology, and then scamper to my room. But that would give him power over me, so instead, I push my shoulders back, tilt my head proudly, and walk up to him. His smile just gets wider as I approach.

"What do you want, Hunter?"

He does a quick rake of his eyes down me one more time now that I'm standing close, and then turns to look at Savannah. Sticking his hand out, he says, "I'm Hunter Markham."

Savannah looks at me in question briefly, and then turns back to Hunter to shake his hand. She's never met Hunter in the times that he's been back home to visit, but she's heard Casey and me talk about him, of course. "Savannah Shepherd. And I'm running late, so I'll catch you guys later."

With that, Savannah shoots out the door and leaves me standing there alone with six-foot-three of golden surfer dude, who is looking incredibly gorgeous in a pair of board shorts and a Ron Jon t-shirt. His hair is sticking up in a hundred different directions, and it's clear he just rolled out of bed.

"Again," I ask with not even the slightest bit of patience. "What are you doing here?"

Hunter crosses his arms over his broad chest and leans up against the doorjamb. Giving me an easy smile, he says, "I was just on my way to the beach to catch some waves, and thought I'd stop by."

"You thought you'd stop by?" I ask, confused,

because there is no reason he should be here.

"Yup. And I can't say I'm sorry to have you greet me this way. Maybe I'll come by in the morning more often." He punctuates the statement by letting his eyes fall to the top swells of my breasts, which are plumping up over the edge of my tank top. It's the same exact move that I cursed Kevin Zulekis for making last night, but for some reason, it doesn't gross me out when Hunter looks at me this way. In fact, it makes me a bit tingly, and my freakin' nipples tighten in response.

Just great.

Mentally kicking myself in the ass for even allowing those feelings to creep up, I put on my most ferocious glare. "Don't bother. You're not welcome here."

To make sure he clearly understands that sentiment, I grab the edge of the door and start to close it in his face. He sticks out a flip-flopped foot and stops it from shutting though.

"Not so fast," he says. "I have business to discuss with you."

My eyebrows rise up in skepticism. "Business?"

"Yes," he says, like he's talking to a five year old. "Your bid? The one you handed me less than twenty-four hours ago?"

I can't stop myself. I know I should just shut my mouth, but there's something about his smug confidence that just rubs me the wrong way.

"And I believe I told you what you could do with that bid," I point out.

Hunter just stares at me for a few moments, his face impassive, and I have no clue what he's thinking. His voice is soft when he says, "Come on, Gabs. Don't let your anger at me ruin the chance for you to get this project. I know it's important to you."

The chastening nature of his statement gets my hackles up, but I do heed what he's saying. I assumed any chance of me getting that bid was ruined the minute I told him to "Fuck off," but here he is implying that it might still be open for consideration.

So I bite my tongue, smooth out my features so he doesn't see the derision I feel, and push back from the door. "Come on in. Let me get dressed, and I'll make some coffee."

He walks in, looking around in interest at our living room. It's not much, but we have it decorated with some of Savannah's photographs she took of the wild horses on Corolla, which I framed in whitewashed driftwood.

"Don't feel like you have to get dressed," Hunter says with a grin as he flashes me another appreciative look. "I'm perfectly okay with conducting business as is."

I merely snort in response and turn my back on him, walking back to my bedroom while feeling his heated stare on my ass, which I know is barely covered by my panties.

Oh, well… let him look and suffer knowing what he missed out on.

I throw on a pair of sweatpants and a t-shirt over my tank, and by the time I make it back out into the kitchen, I see Hunter working the coffee pot. I take a seat at the table and when he gets the brew going, he turns around and leans back against the counter, resting his hands on the edge.

"So… you made a few suggested changes to the design plans. I've been thinking about them and wanted to hear more about your ideas."

I stare at him just a moment, trying to determine if he's just humoring me or really wants to know, but I can't figure him out… apparently never could… so I get up, grab my leather satchel briefcase that's laying in the living room, and take out the plans.

Spreading them out on the table, I point to the area that comes off the back of the restaurant. Hunter pushes away from the counter and comes up to stand beside me. His nearness is disconcerting, and I have to concentrate so that my words come out with assurance.

"The architect wants to build a completely enclosed area on your deck. This will require new sub-flooring, frame, and sheetrock, not to mention you're losing your deck. I mean… come on. We've lived our entire life on the beach. Everyone wants to sit out on the deck and enjoy the ocean view, right?"

"Agreed," Hunter says. "But I need more room. More tables means more customers, which means more money."

"I agree with that," I concur. "But I think you should build out your existing deck, and then just cover a portion of it with a roof. Leave the walls open with retractable walls that you can open up during the warm months, and close off during the cool. You can put out portable heaters rather than installing an HVAC system. Those changes will give you more space than originally planned, as well as cheaper building costs."

"Do you have those numbers broken down?"

I nod and grab my binder, flipping to the cost-comparison spreadsheet I worked up. I show him the figures of what it would cost to build out as proposed by the architect, and the savings doing it my way. Flipping to the next page, I show him my calculations for the increased capacity it will seat, so he can get an idea of the growth in potential revenue my design will bring him. Hunter bends over and starts reviewing the numbers, so I busy myself by pouring two cups of coffee, bringing them over to the table.

He studies the numbers thoughtfully, rubbing his finger across his chin in concentration. It draws my attention to the scruffy beard on his face. It's not quite a full-grown beard, but it's a bit more than a five o'clock shadow. For as long as I can remember, Hunter has always kept some sort of scruffy facial hair. It's a surfer thing for sure, and also a lazy thing. He once told Casey when she teased him about it that he hated to shave. I hate to admit, but it's part of what makes him incredibly sexy, that he looks just so windblown and raw all the time.

Hunter turns his gaze to me, and I have to quickly move my eyes to his so he doesn't know I was carefully studying his face. "This is really impressive, Gabby. Your dad would be really proud."

Oh, fuck, the man knows how to hit me below the belt. He gave me a one-two punch, first by calling me Gabby and not Gabs, which told me he was not joking. Second, he used my kryptonite against me… my love for my dad and the sincere need to make the business he started successful.

I swallow hard to get past the lump of emotion sitting in my throat, but my voice is still raspy when I say, "Thanks. That means a lot."

Hunter just stares at me. I return it, and for a second... we're having a *moment*. It's personal, electric, and for one crazy, fleeting second, I feel like we are back five years ago in that time just before we kissed. If Hunter even leans toward me slightly, I'm afraid I might just accidentally topple onto his lips.

Instead, Hunter pulls me back to reality when he says, "The job is yours if you want it. And I want to implement your changes."

Shaking my head slightly from the shock, I ask with disbelief, "It's mine?"

His smile is warm. "Yup. If you want it."

I can't even think of words to say at first, but then I snap out of it. "I do... I want it, of course. Thank you."

"Good. Let's plan on meeting tomorrow to talk about when you can start, and the timetable for the project. Now... I'm off to hit the surf."

Hunter picks up the cup of coffee I had brought him and gives me a last, long look before heading toward the door, taking my cup with him. When he turns the knob, he glances back at me and his voice is husky. "Oh, and Gabs... I really, really enjoyed seeing you in your pajamas this morning."

My mouth sort of just falls open, stunned that he would jump from professional business talk to some steamy flirting. It takes me a moment to compose myself.

Narrowing my eyes, I ask, "So... I really have the job? That's set in stone, right?"

He looks at me curiously. "Right."

"Good. Then let me tell you... stop the flirting, jackass. I'm not interested."

Surprise spreads wide over Hunter's face, and then he throws his head back and starts laughing. When he tilts his eyes back on mine, he says, "Good one, Gabs. You keep saying that if it makes you feel better."

Before I can even respond, he's out the door and shutting it softly behind him.

FOUR

Hunter

"I just opened up the last case of Jack Daniels, and you're running low on Grey Goose," Brody says as I push the pitcher of draft beer I just poured across the bar to a customer. He hands me a ten-dollar bill and tells me to keep the change.

Thanks, asshole... the pitcher is ten bucks!

I turn around to the cash register and ring up the sale, sliding the money in the drawer. Turning to Brody, I nod. "I've got it ordered. Should be delivered on Monday."

"Hopefully what we have will last through the weekend. It's been busy the last few nights."

I smile, because yeah… business is better than I thought it would be and I'm starting to feel more comfortable about the expansions, particularly with the summer season just around the corner. It's been a learning curve to say the least, trying to figure out how long my stock will last and ordering appropriately from the distributors, who only do deliveries in our area once a week.

"If we get too low, I can run over to the ABC store and buy a couple of bottles."

Brody doesn't even bother to respond and moves to the other end of the bar to take the orders from two girls that approach. They look young… maybe too young to be served, but I watch as Brody cards them. They flirt and giggle, but he doesn't even spare them a glance as he hands the IDs back and turns to make their drinks.

Sighing, I reach over to the flat of pint glasses that were just washed in the kitchen and start stacking them in the cooler to chill. Brody is still just as withdrawn as he was the day he walked out of prison, but he seems to be handling himself okay. I mean, he's not exactly effervescent with the customers, but he doesn't seem to piss them off, and he does his job well. He's just so damn quiet that I want to shake him sometimes and tell him, "Get over it. You're back in the real world. Enjoy it."

But I immediately feel like shit for even thinking such things, because I can't even begin to imagine how tough it has been for him. I had a nightmare the other night about Brody in jail, getting beaten up by a gang. They held him down, kicking and punching him. I woke up, thankful the nightmare had been interrupted, and terrified of what else I might have seen had I let the dream go on. Brody has never talked about what life was like behind bars, and I haven't asked him. I'm not sure I really want to know.

I look up and down the bar. Everyone seems to have full drinks, so I take a moment and lean back against the counter, pulling my iPhone out. I check my emails, but there is nothing new since I last checked only about an hour ago.

It's pathetic of me, but I'm hoping to get an email from Gabby. She was supposed to meet with me the day after I went to her apartment to give her the job, but I woke up that morning to find an email from her. It basically said there was no need to meet, that if I would just tell her what day I wanted her to start, and what hours she could have access to the building, then she would handle getting everything coordinated. This started an email exchange between us, ironing out the details and setting the start date for next Monday. My last email to her yesterday had asked when she could come by and get a key to the building, but I haven't heard back from her.

Yes, I want to see her badly after that morning in her apartment, but she's effectively cut me off at the knees. The image of her standing there in that tight tank with her nipples poking through and her barely there panties was burned solidly into my brain. I can hardly close my eyes without seeing her like that, and I'm having a hard time shaking it.

Over the years, I had seen Gabby in her bathing suit more times than I can remember, and while, as she got older, I had a vague appreciation for the beauty of her body, I never obsessed about it like this.

And now?

I really want to see what's underneath, which has me groaning at myself over the absurdity of it.

It can't happen, and let me tell you why.

First, there's the fact that she's Casey's childhood friend and someone who I viewed as a little sister for many years.

But you don't view her like that now, my subconscious pipes up.

Shut the fuck up, I tell my subconscious.

Second, Gabby is clearly so angry with me that she'd never entertain the thought of… of…

Well, hell… I'm not even sure what I'm entertaining. Do I just want to sleep with her, or do I want something more? Because if it's something more, am I even ready for that?

It's all moot anyway. I can't seem to make it past my first concern, so there… no need to even to think about it further. She's like a little sister, so she's off limits. It's done. I'm putting her out of my mind, and I vow to myself that I won't even think about her the rest of the night.

"Hey, Hunter. Thought I'd come by and pick up the key from you."

I close my eyes briefly and mutter a curse, because just like that… I'm thinking of Gabby. Hard not to… what with her sexy-as-fuck voice coming from just off to my left somewhere. Opening my eyes slowly, I wipe any expression from my face and turn to face her.

Son of a bitch!

She looks like a wet dream. Her body is poured into a tight, black minidress, and she's rocking some ass-kicking stilettos. Her hair is loose and wavy around her face, pouring over her tanned shoulders and spilling down her back. I want to wrap my hand in it and pull her toward me, which causes me to internally curse myself for those thoughts.

It's then that I notice her roommate, Savannah, standing behind her, along with Alyssa Myers. I smile and nod at them, then turn my attention back to Gabby.

"You're awful dressed up to pick up a key," I tell her.

She gives me a cautious smile. "Well… it *is* Friday night… time to let loose. We're headed out to a nightclub over in Kitty Hawk but thought we'd come have a few drinks here to start out. Savannah's DD tonight."

"Well… you look really nice. Beautiful, actually."

Gabby looks at me like I sprouted an extra head, as if I've never paid her a true compliment before, but before she can respond, her attention goes to something behind me. Turning, I see Brody grabbing some orange juice out of the refrigerator.

"Hey, Brody," Gabby says. I notice him flinch slightly as he turns to look at her but she steps up closer to the bar. "How you been?"

"Good," he says as he makes a Screwdriver. "You?"

"Good, thanks. Hey, listen… I want you to meet

my roommate, Savannah Shepherd, and you remember Alyssa Myers, right? She was always around in the summers growing up, but she's moved here permanently."

I know the last thing Brody wants is to be introduced to people, but he politely nods at Savannah, his lips never even cracking from their grim line. Then his eyes slide over to Alyssa and something interesting happens. He sort of stares at her for a moment, his eyes flaring just a bit. I glance over at Alyssa, and she's giving him a soft smile.

"Hi Brody," she says warmly. "It's good to see you again."

Brody just stares for what could be considered an awkward moment, and then he mutters, "Same here," before turning away and walking to the other end of the bar.

I sigh once again, sad that my brother is having such a hard time even carrying on short conversations with people.

"He'll come around," Gabby says, and I turn to look at her. She's watching me with understanding. She knows… knows that it kills me to see him like this, and all I can do is just nod at her.

"Listen, why don't you girls go grab a table? Someone will be over to get your drink orders shortly.

Gabby… the key is in my office, and I need to show you how to work the alarm system."

I turn around and walk back toward my office, confident that Gabby will follow. When I reach the door, I open it and motion for her to walk in first. I step in behind her and pull the door closed, not quite understanding why I feel the need for privacy.

Turning around, Gabby studies me with perception and completely catches me off guard when she says, "I know you're worried about Brody. Casey is too. He just needs some time is all, and a whole lot of love and support."

I blink at her in surprise. It's the nicest thing she's said to me in well over five years. "Casey's worried, too?"

"Yeah… she's having a hard time. Not sure how to talk to him."

I'm silent for a moment, not quite sure what to share with her. But then I venture forward. "I just miss the guy he used to be."

"Me too," she says quietly. "But we all change. This may be the Brody we have to accept."

"I don't want to accept it."

"No, I don't suppose you do. You've always been stubborn that way."

I snort over that comment, walking over to my

desk to grab the extra key I had made a few days ago. Turning to her with a grin, I ask, "So… are we like having a normal conversation?"

She flinches in astonishment, and then her gaze narrows at me. "What? No. I don't even like you. Of course not."

"Of course not," I muse, my grin growing bigger as I hand the key to her. When she takes it from me, I let my finger slide along the back of her hand and I don't miss her sudden intake of breath. Her eyes snap up to meet mine, and they are glaring at me ferociously.

I decide to put a stop to her anger once and for all. It's time to man up.

"I'm sorry," I tell her simply.

Taking a step back, she asks suspiciously. "For what?"

"For the way I treated you that night."

"That night?" she mumbles.

"That night," I tell her with conviction. "That night we kissed."

Her gaze drops to the floor, and her hands grasp tightly onto the key I gave her. I wait but when she finally looks back up at me, her face is tight and unyielding. "Nothing to apologize for. I've forgotten about it. You should do the same."

No, that won't do at all.

Taking a step toward her, I come in close so she has to tilt her head up to look at me. "You haven't forgotten it, Gabs. It's why you're so angry with me. And I'm telling you I'm sorry because I truly am. If I could go back and change it, I would."

My nearness affects her, just as it affects me, so she moves back a step. I viscerally feel the loss of warmth within the distance she's put between us. She pulls her lower lip in between her teeth and casts her gaze sideways, as if she's pondering the merit of my last statement.

When she turns back to look at me, she asks, "What would you have changed?"

She's curious... too curious for her own good, and I can see that this has indeed plagued her for quite a long time.

Sighing, I move back toward my desk and sit down on the edge, tucking my hands in my pockets. "I handled it badly. I mean, you shocked the shit out of me, and then I shocked myself when I kissed you back. I guess the thing I want you to know, is that I was never mad at you, even though I acted like an ass. I was mad at myself, and I took it out on you."

Gabby tilts her head to the side in interest. "Mad at yourself? Why?"

"I guess because on one level, I was telling myself that it was wrong... the attraction I was feeling. But then I had no control over myself. I wanted to kiss you. I wanted more from you that night, but I told myself it was wrong. I was pissed because I was denying myself. Denying myself something I very much wanted."

I can see that she's shocked over my admission because her mouth hangs slightly open. "You wanted me?"

"Of course I did. Didn't you feel it when we kissed?"

I know damn well she felt my hard-on, but that's not what I'm talking about. I'm talking about the yearning that was inherent in that kiss. She merely nods at me, casting her gaze back down to the floor.

"But I thought I disgusted you. At least... that was the expression on your face."

Okay, that kills me... hearing her say that, knowing that she's been thinking that for the last five years. I can't help my reaction when I push away from the desk and walk up to her, taking her face in my hands so she looks at me.

"Gabby... trust me when I say, disgust is not something I've ever felt toward you, then or now. I'm really sorry if you've been thinking that, and I really hope you can forgive me."

She just stares at me... pulling me into those hazel eyes. I can see her thinking back over all the misconceptions she's been laboring under for several years, and trying to reconcile the fact that I'm telling her she was wrong.

I'm not letting her go though, until she tells me she believes me. Until she knows, without a doubt, that disgust has never been on my list of feelings for Gabby Ward.

"Are we okay?" I ask her, practically holding my breath for her answer.

She doesn't make me wait. Giving me a tentative smile, she says, "Yeah... we're okay."

I'm so grateful that I pull her into a hug, wrapping my arms around her tight and resting my chin on top of her head. She's stiff at first, but then her arms wrap around my waist and I feel her sigh into my chest.

We hold each other for just a minute, and then she pulls back. "How about showing me that alarm system? I probably need to get back out there."

"Sure thing."

I take her out to the front area and go over the features on the security panel with her, explaining how it works and giving her the code. We talk for a few more minutes, going over the hours she'll be working. I had decided to close the bar for the lunch hour until she could get the inside portions done, which would give her several good daylight hours of work. Once she was ready to start on the outside, we would just close the deck area to customers. It would be difficult to work around, but it was something we'd be able to accomplish.

When I'm done, Gabby gives me another smile before she heads off to her friends, promising to see me on Monday when she starts. This time it's bright and unforced, and I feel it slam into me like I've been hit by a truck. And just because I'm a guy, and there is no way that I'm not noticing, I watch her ass as she makes her way over to her table. When she takes a seat, I head behind the bar to help Brody.

Over the next hour, I can't help myself. I keep glancing over at Gabby… avidly curious about her. I notice details that I never noticed before. Like how she always tucks her hair back behind her right ear, but never her left. Or she how she has a habit of twisting the ring on her right hand while she talks. While ogling her legs, I even notice that she has a tiny tattoo on the outside of her left ankle, although I'm not close enough to see what it is.

A few times, she lifts her head and turns it my

way. I think I'm able to avert my eyes every time, and she has no clue I've been checking her out. I feel like a fucking thirteen-year-old kid crushing on the popular girl in high school, and that actually amuses me.

Gabby Ward is under my skin. I've repaired my friendship with her, but I'm certainly not looking at her as a friend anymore. And it's clear to me as well... I'm sure as hell not looking at her like a little sister either.

I just don't know what to do about it.

FIVE

Gabby

I can't believe I let Casey talk me into hanging out at the beach today. It's not that I'm opposed to it. Hello, beach girl here. But this morning when she showed up at my apartment, begging me to go out to Cape Hatteras with her, I so didn't want to oblige. Not because I abhor a day at the beach with my bestie, but mainly because she told me that Hunter and Brody would be there.

Not that I'm opposed to Brody. I'd like to hang

out with him some… help him get back into the swing of things. But the thought of spending the day on the beach with Hunter in close proximity has me wigged out for some reason.

The nature of our relationship changed the other night when he apologized for the way he treated me after our kiss. I accept that he was sincerely sorry, and I've moved past the hurt because of it. For that, I'm extremely grateful. But, when he hugged me afterward… there was something within the emotions surrounding us that didn't take us just back to our pre-kiss friendship. It went somewhere different, and I'm not sure what to make of it.

I mean… it could be nothing. Maybe I'm imagining it, but I don't think so. When I add it all up… the way he admitted he wanted me, the way he looked at me when I was standing half naked in front of him in my apartment, the way he pointed out that there was something in that kiss that both of us felt… well, it has a lot of the old feelings I use to harbor for Hunter starting to resurface.

And I so don't want to go there. I'm not ready to lay myself out on the line like that. I'm not ready, nor am I willing, to get hurt again.

Hunter Markham has the ability not just to hurt me. He's a man that could destroy me.

And that makes me cranky.

So my plan is simple. At least, the plan I devised when I came home that night. I decided I was going to stay as far away from Hunter as possible. I knew I'd have to deal with him on probably a daily basis while I worked on the remodel, but I could keep that professional. I certainly don't want to get into any social situations with him. He's too charming, too vivacious. He'll suck me in like a pit of quicksand, and I'll be helpless to claw my way out.

I tried my damnedest to decline Casey's invitation, but she pulled out the big guns. She looked at me with her big eyes moistened with tears and told me she was nervous about spending the day with Brody. She's been having a hard time connecting with him, and she felt that with me by her side, she would be more comfortable.

It was a load of horseshit, in my opinion, because Casey has confidence in spades. She's so damned bubbly that you can't help but be happy around her. If anyone can wear Brody down and break him out of his shell, it's her. Regardless, when she flashed those glistening baby blues at me, I hung my head low in defeat and went to change into my bathing suit.

We make it to the cape in good time. She immediately recognizes Hunter's jeep, pulling in

behind it. We unload our bags, cooler, and beach chairs, hauling them out across the dunes. There are several surfers in the water—no telling which ones are Hunter and Brody—so we just find an empty spot and make camp.

The beach is getting crowded, this part of the North Carolina coast being one of the best surf spots in the east. This is because the continental shelf ends in a steep drop-off, creating powerful sets with wide beach breaks. I never quite understood what that really meant but I remember Hunter telling me that once when we were younger. It's where we always hung out growing up, coming out to cheer on Hunter and Brody when they surfed in amateur competitions. Yes, Brody surfed as well, but he never had the competitive spirit that Hunter did. Brody was the brainiac in the Markham family, and was getting ready to start his second year of medical school at Duke when he was arrested. The thought of everything Brody lost because of one stupid and tragic mistake makes me so sad. I wonder how you ever recover a broken spirit from a fall that high?

I slather on some high SPF oil and slip my sunglasses on. Casey reaches into the cooler and hands me a beer that, even though it's only 10:30 AM, I gladly accept. It's just a thing… beach and beer.

Scanning the water more closely, I finally recognize Hunter. It's not that I can necessarily make out the details, but I recognize his talent as clear as day. There are plenty of great surfers along the Hatteras coast, but Hunter Markham is in a different league. He was the number two-ranked surfer in the world just months ago, and he stands out. In fact, a lot of people walking up and down the beach stop to watch him and, before long, he's drawn quite a crowd.

I even hear a pair of girls talk about him when they walk by us.

"I heard that was Hunter Markham out there," one of them remarks

The other squeals with excitement and says, "Oh. My. God. I want to give him my phone number."

The other girl jumps up and down, also squealing with equal delight. "Screw that. I want to give him my babies."

Casey apparently hears that conversation too and snorts out loud. I turn to look at her and start giggling. As the girls make their way closer to the water to watch Hunter, I say, "Your brother is a real stud."

She rolls her eyes at me. "Don't I know it? He's left a trail of broken hearts all over the world, I'm

betting."

I have to, no doubt, agree with that, thinking, *Yeah, starting right here in the Outer Banks with me.*

I watch Hunter for a bit more, even recognizing Brody out there. He and Hunter sit side by side on their boards, bobbing in the water while they wait for the next set to roll in. Sometimes they turn their heads toward each other, clearly talking about something. I hope that they're having a good time together. As identical twins, they shared an unbelievably close bond before Brody was sent away. I know it's taken quite a hit over the last few years.

Finally, the heat from the sun and the beer I drank starts to make me drowsy, so I lay my chair down flat, close my eyes, and let the warmth and sounds of the waves lull me to sleep.

I have no clue how long I was out but cold drops of water pelting down on me brings me out of my slumber, and I have to shield my eyes as I look up above me. A large body is silhouetted by the sun, but I can tell by the length of his wet hair and his build that it's Hunter. He stands there with his surfboard wedged into the sand, his arm casually resting on the tip of it.

"What are you doing out here, Gabs?" he asks.

I sit up in my chair, raising the back up to

support me, and glance over at Casey. She's out cold. Looking behind Hunter, I see his fan club hasn't dispersed. There are several girls huddled together about thirty feet away, looking at him hungrily.

Glancing back at Hunter, I shrug my shoulders. "Casey begged me to hang out with her today."

Hunter glances back at the water, and I follow his gaze. Brody is still out there, just sitting astride his board and looking out at the horizon.

"How's he doing today?" I ask.

Leaving his board, Hunter walks to the other side of my chair and plops down on the sand beside me, resting his forearms on his knees. He keeps his gaze on Brody but addresses my question. "I think he's having a good time out there. First time he's been in the water in over five years. I think he even cracked a smile when he caught his first wave. Of course, it could have been a grimace, but at least it wasn't that somber look he seems to constantly wear around."

"That's good. You just need to keep him busy... get him back into the swing of things."

"Yeah," Hunter muses as he watches his twin. "He needs to figure out what to do for his community service. It's part of his parole requirements, so we were talking about it some out there."

"Why doesn't he volunteer at The Haven? God knows, Alyssa can use the help. She's trying to do everything herself and practically killing herself in the process."

"That's a great idea, Gabs. Thanks. I'll talk to him about that. He loves dogs, so that is right up his alley."

We lapse into a comfortable silence for a while, gazing out at the ocean and watching some of the other surfers. Casey eventually wakes up and passes out beers to Hunter and me. We chat about inane stuff, and I question Hunter relentlessly about his time on the ASP World Tour. I purposefully never asked Casey about it, preferring to keep myself distant from all things related to Hunter Markham over the last five years.

He obliges me and tells me about all of his favorite places he's surfed. He's been everywhere... Australia, The Maldives, China, Micronesia; the list went on and on. But then he looks back out wistfully at the waves as they break against the shoreline and says, "But my heart will always be here... where I started."

There's something about his tone of voice, or maybe it's the way he watches the water and keeps his eye on Brody, that makes my heart turn over and swear fealty to Hunter. Which again, makes me cranky, because I don't want to have those feelings.

Casey stands up and heads toward the water, walking in up to her knees and scooping up the salty liquid to cool herself. It doesn't escape my notice that practically every surfer turns their attention to watch her rather than the set of waves coming in.

I use the opportunity while Casey is gone to ask Hunter a question that I've been insanely curious about. "Why did you retire from surfing? You were at the top of your game."

He doesn't respond at first, just watching his sister and brother. Then he turns to me and smiles. "You know the answer to that."

I think I do, so I go ahead and lay it out there. "You came back for Brody."

"That I did," he says and then stands up from the sand, brushing the back of his shorts off. "Want to go out in the water?"

Shaking my head, I smile. "No way. It's not nearly warm enough yet. Hit me up in July, and I'll think about it."

"Sissy," he says with a smile, as he grabs his board. He heads off toward the surf, and then turns back suddenly. "By the way, Gabs... that bikini on you is slammin'."

He lets his gaze roam over me in a leisurely way, and then drifts back to my eyes, which I'm sure are wide with shock. He gives me a wink and then trots off to the water with his board under his arm.

My gaze narrows at him because I just don't know how to handle this new friendship with Hunter. It's what we had before... an easygoing, laid-back relationship. Not too deep, not too frilly. But now... Hunter laces his looks and words with sexual innuendo, promise, and longing. It's exactly what I always wanted from him, but now it's just sort of freaking me out. While I accepted his apology and I truly believe he's sorry for how that unfortunate incident played out, I really can't accept that he wants me in any way. I mean, I want to accept that, but I can't. It's too risky.

The sun rose and set on Hunter Markham as far as I was concerned five years ago. When he disabused me of my fantasies, I buried that love and longing very deep. While I can let go of my anger, I'm not sure I can let go of the lock that I put firmly around my heart.

I know Hunter isn't looking at me and wanting a serious relationship. This is about sex, no doubt. He appreciates me as a grown woman now, and there is chemistry between us. If he's flirting with me... if he's making a pass… it is solely from the fact that he's a man and thinking with his dick.

Not that there's anything wrong with that. I'm a healthy, sexually aware woman myself. I've had my share of casual relationships, which focused around an easy friendship coupled with some smokin' hot sex. In fact, I have never once felt a strong, emotional pull toward any of the men that I've had relationships with since I lost my virginity my freshman year in college. I think… deep down, knowing that I'd never have Hunter Markham's heart ruined me from having anyone else's.

And like I said before, all of this knowledge and confusing array of emotions that Hunter has evoked in me the last few days makes me grumpy as shit. I'm seriously not liking what this man does to me. I need to harden up a bit where he's concerned.

"Those look like some deep thoughts you have going on in that head of yours."

Glancing over to my left, I see Brody taking a seat on Casey's chair. It's the most words he's said to me since returning home.

"There's some beer in that cooler," I tell him, pointing to where it sits behind our chairs.

"Nah. I don't drink," he says, and I cringe internally… because, of course, he wouldn't drink anymore. Not after that night.

I take a moment to really look at Brody. His face is identical to Hunter's. Same straight nose, square jaw with a slight dimple in the middle of his chin, and full lips. His hair color is darker because he's spent the last five years locked away, while Hunter's has been streaked pale by the hot sun. He wears his hair much longer than Hunter does, coming down to his shoulders with the top half pulled back into a ponytail. He has a full beard compared to Hunter's scruffy look, but he keeps it trimmed close. The biggest difference that I see though, is the lack of light in Brody's eyes. They are dim and shaded, while Hunter's are bright and accented by laugh lines in the corners. The men could have identical haircuts and coloring, but stand them side by side and you'd know the difference based on their eyes.

Turning toward the ocean, I see that Casey's in the water using Brody's board. She and Hunter are just bobbing on the water, apparently not really caring if they catch a wave. Hunter says something to her and she smacks at the water to hit him in the face, laughing at whatever he just said. Casey can surf... her brother's made sure she knew how from when she was little, and they taught me as well. I mean, I pretty much suck, but I know the fundamentals. But right now, brother and sister are just content to sit out on the ocean and hang together.

Peeking over at Brody, I see he watches them intently and his lips are curled slightly upward. No matter what horrors Brody has suffered, it didn't kill the love he has for his family. It's written all over his face. I suppose that's just not an emotion you can suppress, no matter what dark demons you have boiling inside.

"So how was the surfing? Was it like riding a bike?"

Brody turns those sad eyes to me, and I see the briefest flicker of interest in what I just asked. "Yeah… it was good. I'm really rusty, but it felt good."

"You looked good out there," I tell him. "Gave Hunter a run for his money."

Then the most joyous sound erupts from Brody. He gives a short bark of laughter. "I don't think so. Hunter was just out there playing. Letting me look good."

I shoot him a bright grin and he responds, letting his smile widen so I see a flash of teeth. "I like seeing you laugh, Brody. It's a good look on you. You should do it more often."

I expect him to withdraw, because my statement

is meant in jest, but it's also a pointed reminder that we are all aware of how unhappy he is. Instead, he keeps the smile in place, even as his eyes hold a touch of wistfulness. "I'm trying, Gabby. I'm really trying."

I reach out and touch his arm lightly with my fingertips. "You can do anything you set your mind to, Brode."

He glances down at my hand laying against his warm skin and then reaches his other hand over to cover mine, giving it a slight pat. "Thanks, kiddo."

Then he pulls away and leans back in Casey's chair, closing his eyes and lifting his face to the sun. I watch him for a few more minutes, and I take joy in the peaceful look on his face right at this very moment. I think Brody will be okay.

I hope he will.

SIX

Hunter

I'm not sure what in the hell happened between our day at the beach Saturday and Monday morning, but Gabby reverted back into the shrew that I had come to know and loathe over the last five years. I thought we made it past all that shit, but when I came into the bar on Monday morning, I was met with coolness from her.

I tried to make some light conversation while I sipped on a cup of coffee, watching her take measurements of the existing front bar, and she snapped my head off.

"I'm busy, Hunter," she grouched. "If you want me to make my deadline, you need to let me work."

Raising my eyebrows at her, I just nodded and walked away.

On Tuesday, I brought over some bottled water for her and her crew, and she didn't even spare me a glance. And just before she was ready to leave for the day, and before I opened the doors for the evening crowd, she cornered me, demanding to know if I was going to hover over her every day.

"Gabs… I'm not hovering. I have work to do, and it just happens to be in the same building that you're working in."

She stared at me fiercely for a moment and just nodded before turning around to leave. She threw back over her shoulder, "And don't call me 'Gabs'. I'm not fucking ten years old anymore."

I heard Brody snort as he was opening up the register to stock it with cash. Turning to look at him, I gave him the stink eye and I swear I saw a smirk on his lips just before he turned his back on me.

"What the fuck is wrong with her?" I grumbled.

"You're clueless, dude," Brody said while he placed the twenties, tens, fives, and ones in their respective drawers. He opened up the rolls of coins and emptied them in their slots. "Absolutely clueless."

Walking up to the bar, I pulled a stool out and leaned one ass cheek on it, laying my forearms on the bar. "Want to enlighten me?"

Shutting the register drawer, Brody turned to look at me. "You two remind me of two kids who like each other but don't understand it. So rather than confronting it, you pick at each other, letting your confused emotions come out as anger and stupid words."

"I'm not the one picking at her," I pointed out.

"True, but I expect Gabby's feelings run in a different direction than yours. You're running around with your tongue hanging out, panting after her, and she's got her heart tied up. It's the classic difference between men and women."

I stood there with my jaw hanging open, staring in wonder at Brody. He just fucking 'Dr. Phil-ed' me, and I was in awe.

"How in the fuck do you know that?" I asked.

He shrugged his shoulders and walked out from behind the bar, heading toward the stockroom. "One thing in prison you have a lot of… is time. Three things came out of it. I devoured a lot of books, I had plenty of time to think, and I sharpened my observation skills. I see plenty of what goes on, even if you and Gabby don't."

I was struck dumb. My brother... the felon... the philosopher. I was beyond grateful that he was actually having a conversation with me. I was blown away at the nature of said conversation. My respect for my brother increased tenfold, because I realized that prison might have actually made him smarter... keener... even potentially more well-rounded.

"You amaze me," is all I could think to say.

Brody just snorted at my comment and walked into the storeroom, while I stared after him. Maybe that was a turning point for Brody, actually doling out advice to his dumbass brother.

Now it's Wednesday morning and, as I pull into the parking lot of Last Call, I see Gabby's work truck. None of the other crew members have arrived, but it's only 7:30 AM and they don't usually clock in until around eight. I have no clue what time Gabby shows up each morning, but I'm guessing it's way earlier than seven thirty.

Unlocking the door, I let myself in and relock it behind me. I'll open it back up at eight.

I hear sounds coming from the back room, which leads out onto the existing deck. Gabby said they'd be starting the deck expansion today, so I expect to find her out there.

When I walk back there though, I find her still inside, bent over one of the pool tables, reviewing the design plans she has spread out before her. She's wearing her classic work clothes... jeans, a t-shirt, and work boots. She has her tool belt riding low on her slim hips, and she's chewing on the end of a pencil while she peruses the documents in front of her. With her hair pulled up in a ponytail, she looks young and fresh... and it makes me want to kiss the fuck out of her.

"Good morning," I say, and her head snaps up.

For a brief moment, her face is placid and relaxed. But the moment she realizes it's me walking in, her lips set in a grim line and she turns her attention back down to the plans before her.

And that just pisses me off. Fuck what Brody said about her liking me, and that's why she's so cranky. It doesn't make any sense, and I'm getting tired of her bratty behavior. It makes me want to be a brat in return, so what do I do?

I walk up beside her, getting up close and invading her personal space, and lean over the plans. "Whatcha doin'?" I ask in a friendly voice.

I swear I can hear her teeth gritting from my nearness, and she takes a step to the side. "Just going over the specs on the back deck extension, so I can get the crew started when they get here."

I slide a step closer to her, bending over the drawings. "Explain what you'll be doing today."

She curses under her breath, and I have to suppress a chuckle. I'm enjoying what my bratty side is doing to her.

"I don't have time for this, Hunter. You either trust my work, or you don't."

I turn to look at her, and she's glaring at me. "You're cute when you're angry. I particularly like the way you pout. It's sexy."

Flames leap out of her eyes, I kid you not, and she takes a step in closer, while jabbing me in the chest with her finger. "Just cut it out, Hunter. I know you think this banter is funny but it's not. It's really pissing me off. I'm trying to do a job here, and you're not making it—"

I've had enough—enough of her rancor and PMSing or whatever the fuck her problem is. Brody said she likes me, and I'm going to see if he's as smart as I think he might be.

Grabbing her shoulders, I pull her in hard to me so her breasts mash into my chest. She lets out a tiny gasp, her hazel eyes going wide, and her lips full and slightly open. It's the only invitation I need before I bring mouth down on hers… fast and hard.

I unleash all the pent-up frustration I have toward her cranky behavior into her mouth, slamming my tongue up against hers, scraping my own bottom lip against her teeth. The pleasure-pain is exquisite, and I groan at the first contact.

She's stiff… just for a second, her hands hanging loosely at her side. I let it cross my mind briefly that I could be making a very big mistake, that this could be bordering on assault, but then her arms come up and she clutches my hips with her fingertips.

That spurs me on, and I tilt my head, angling for a deeper contact. She responds tenfold, sliding a sexy whimper into my mouth, and I feel myself starting to grow painfully hard.

All from a fucking kiss.

A kiss that is just like five years ago, yet so very different. Then she was forbidden, young, innocent. It was shocking and altering, two things that fueled my lust.

Now, it's a desire that's fueled by years of wondering, fantasizing, and maybe even a bit of regret. It's also a flame that has recently been fanned by anger, and let's face it… there's nothing hotter than being in the middle of an argument and releasing that emotion through the sexual channels.

My heart is slamming inside my chest, and my dick is aching. I want to do nothing more than take Gabby, lay her across the pool table, and fuck the meanness out of her. I want to sink myself in her warmth, make her body mine, and when it's done, have her look at me with something other than disdain.

But now is not the time, and it's certainly not the place. When I take her—and I will—it's going to be somewhere private so I can do things that might border on depraved... but will certainly wipe that smug look off her face. Just the thought has me smiling against her lips.

I bring one hand up and cup the back of her head, pushing her mouth harder against mine for just a second, taking a last swipe at her with my tongue. Then I pull back, gripping onto her hair to hold her in place.

I stare at her intently, watching her eyes, which are clouded with lust and longing. Without the power of the kiss driving us, her gaze starts to clear, and I enjoy the myriad of emotion that filters through. Desire is replaced by confusion, which is then replaced by anger.

She pushes back against my body, her hands still at my hips, but I hold tight to her hair and I don't budge an inch.

"What the hell was that for?" she seethes.

I give her a calculated smirk, running my eyes over her face and leaning down to nip at her lower lip with my teeth. She shivers in my arms and I internally gloat, because while she acts like she's mad, she wants me. There's no denying it.

Pulling back slightly, I rub my nose against hers, and then say, "It was the only way to get you to shut up."

She looks at me blankly for a moment, and then it sinks in what I just said to her. She practically screeches as she rips away from my embrace, and I quickly release my hold on her hair so she doesn't tear a chunk of it out. Stepping back a foot, her eyes do a slow burn and her hand comes up to wipe it across her lips. It's a calculated move… to show me that the kiss disgusted her, but she's not fooling me. I invented that move, used it on her five years ago in fact. I know all about masking my true feelings.

Leaning against the pool table with one hip, I cross my arms across my chest and give her a lazy smile. "Don't act affronted, Gabs. You enjoyed that just as much as I did."

"Oooohhh," she screeches again, and I wince at the sound. "You're an asshole. If you touch me again,

I swear I'll… I'll…"

"What?" I taunt her. "Kiss the fuck out of me again? You wanted it… you enjoyed it. Accept it."

"I did not," she insists, stomping her foot. "You caught me off guard."

Laughing at her silliness, I take a step forward, even as she takes a step back to keep distance between us. "You may not know what's going on here, but I do. Brody enlightened me the other day."

That gets her attention because she can't help but ask, "What do you mean?"

I decide I'm done playing for the day. I can see she's going to need time to process this, and I'm fully expecting to deal with a she-devil tomorrow. So I just turn around and head back out to the front of the bar, telling her over my shoulder. "Ask Brody. He'll fill you in."

I hear her curse behind me, dropping a few F-bombs in the process. I just laugh, and I know she can hear me because a few more choice words follow me out the door.

I don't see Gabby the rest of the day. Shortly after our exchange, she slammed out of the bar and I heard her truck spin out of the parking lot. I asked her foreman later in the morning where she was and he said she was working at her shop, building the custom bar that would go on the outdoor deck.

There's a small part of me that wonders if maybe I went too far, but then I remember her reaction to my kiss. She was fully in. Her tongue battled with mine, she moaned hot into my mouth, and her hips pressed in against me. She may be a master at denying her feelings, but her body has a mind of its own, and it was speaking the utter truth to me.

Something's holding her back though. Clearly, my apology didn't work the charms I thought it would, and I could do one of two things. I could sit her down and have a talk with her, find out what has her panties in a twist again, or I could just keep wearing her down. The thought of wearing her down seems to be the logical choice, because talking to Gabby has done nothing more than resemble the biggest of wipeouts I had while surfing the Pipeline in Oahu. Having my body dragged over sharp coral reef seems less painful than having an actual conversation with her at this point.

While I ponder my Gabby dilemma, my phone starts ringing and a huge grin pops onto my face as I see who's calling.

On the ROCKS

My best surfing buddy, John Hammer.

I answer with a, "What's up, Shredder? Still learning how to boogie board?" This, of course, is only funny to someone in the surfing world. John is a legend on the Tour and has been my mentor for many years. He's five years older than I am, and although he's reaching his prime, he's still killing it on the pro circuit.

"Hey, my man… long time, no talk to. How's life treating you?"

"It's good," I tell him, even though a sudden pang of regret courses through me over retiring. All of my friends told me I was crazy. They told me the number-one rank was mine the next year, that I was committing surfing suicide by walking away.

Only John understood what drove me, and he supported my decision. We were sitting in a bar in Huntington Beach, drinking ice-cold microbrews and chowing on some chips and salsa. When I told him my plans, he just nodded and said, "I understand, dude. Family is what's important. You do some crazy shit for love."

His words were comforting and slicing at the same time. There wasn't anything I couldn't talk to John about, and he always had my back. I knew he'd understand my need to return home, and I knew he'd never try to talk me out of it or make me feel bad.

But his words also settled like a pit in my stomach. He knew all about the ways in which I struggled the few years prior with the concept of love and the crazy things you might or might not do for it.

You see, there was a time I fashioned myself in love with his younger sister, Sasha. After John and I had become friends, he introduced me to her at a competition one day, and I fell hard. She was beautiful, smart, and she surfed. Sasha was amazingly good, competing in the junior pros and finally the women's pro tour. She traveled the world with John and me to the various competitions, at first being a good friend and supporter to me, and then she became my lover.

I thought that my life was perfect, and I couldn't imagine wanting anything different. Sasha and I seemed perfect for each other. We had the same career paths, we loved traveling the world together, and we burned it up between the sheets. But then Sasha took a bad spill during a practice session and dislocated her knee. It was a career-ending injury, as she was never able to make it back onto the tour.

While having something like that happen may have devastated me... having my dreams and goals crushed beyond my control, Sasha didn't seem to mind giving up the competition. Instead, she happily followed John and me around, always being the loudest to cheer me on, and warming my bed by night. To me... life was still perfect.

Then things started to change. Sasha got tired of life on the road, and of sleeping in a different hotel every week. She started wanting to spend more time back home in Southern California and would get angry at me for needing to be on the road so much. Her travels with John and me became less and less, and the times I spent with her in California became filled with fights and tension.

I'm not sure exactly what happened, but things between us started to fall apart. It all came to a head a year ago when Sasha told me she was unhappy, and she wanted me to quit surfing. She wanted me to move to California, marry her, and give her children.

We had talked about marriage some, and it had been more or less understood that we would, indeed, get married one day. But I sure as hell wasn't ready for it when she demanded it, and there was no way in hell I was ready to give up my career.

My refusal to meet her demands was our demise, and we had a bitter split. John walked the fence between us, understanding both of our positions. He did the best he could to be a loyal older brother and continue to be my friend. He never once let Sasha's bitterness or my hurt mar the friendship. John was just golden that way.

When I told John that I was giving it all up to move home for my brother, I remember him whistling low through his teeth. "Sasha's going to go apeshit when she hears that, dude."

I nodded, because I figured as much. Here I was… walking away at the height of my career because my felon twin was getting out of prison, but I wouldn't give it up for her. I knew she wouldn't be happy about that. I never did ask how she took the news when John told her. I figured I was better off not knowing.

"So," John leads in, breaking into my thoughts. "I'm skipping the Billabong Rio Pro this month. My fucking back is acting up again. Thought I'd come visit you and check out this bar of yours."

Laughing, I tell him, "That would be awesome, man. I'd love to see you. When you coming in?"

"I'm going to go home and visit the 'rents for a bit. I was thinking the week after next?"

"That would be great, John. I'm really glad."

We talk on the phone for a bit longer, although he carefully stays away from the subject of Sasha. Which is fine by me… my thoughts are too preoccupied with Gabby and her wily ways. I'm trying to figure out my battle plan with her, because this is a war I intend to win.

And Gabby's the grand prize.

SEVEN

Gabby

I'm a moron… and a brat.

I know this. And yet, I can't help myself.

Hunter Markham is stuck on the yo-yo of Gabby Ward's life. I went from treating him with disdain for the past five years, to accepting his apology and trying a bit of a truce, to hopping right back on the bitch-train with him. I know it's not fair, yet I don't know any other way to keep myself emotionally distanced from Hunter.

On the ROCKS

I'm not angry with him anymore. I swear it. His apology gave me peace, and the fact that he regretted the way he treated me truly soothed the hurt away. But when we were sitting on the beach, side by side, and he confessed the reason he returned was to help Brody, I knew, without a doubt, that I was only minutes away from falling helplessly back in love with the man.

He is dangerous, and I am like an adrenaline junkie.

I know myself. I know that I would seek his danger, that my heart would open up wide for him, and then at some point, I would get hurt. I would get hurt ten times worse than what I ever felt at the tender age of eighteen, when all of my young and innocent fantasies were crushed. It would hurt more now because I had a greater appreciation of what I stood to lose.

As I sat on the beach the rest of the day, watching Hunter interact with Casey and Brody, I felt my heart thumping in yearning to have him look at me that way, to treat me as if I were treasured. It would be so easy for me to fall there again.

Except… I vowed to myself I wasn't going to let it happen. I was going to distance myself from Hunter, and I was going to move on with my life. The only way I knew how to do that, with even any hope for success, was to go back to the tried-and-true method of showing Hunter my inner-bitch. It had worked well for me for five years—it would work well for me again.

It was nothing for me to lapse back into my role. Sure, for every snide word or catty remark, I would have to school my features so he'd never guess that I really wanted to throw my arms around him.

And it was working fine, too.

Until that jackass had to go and kiss me.

And gosh, just the memory of that kiss is succeeding in chasing away the bone-cracking coldness that has overtaken my body with shivers.

Because I'm stuck on the side of the road in a driving rainstorm that's plummeted the temperature down twenty degrees in the last ten minutes. When my old Ford conked out while I was running errands Thursday morning, I popped the hood and stood up on the front bumper, fiddling around with the various wires and gadgets on the engine. I didn't have a freakin' clue what I was doing. I might be able to build an armoire out of a few scraps of lumber, but I knew shit about engines and what made them work. I was hoping something had just rattled loose, and I'd be able to tighten it back up again.

On the ROCKS

It wasn't five minutes after I started messing around with the engine that the sky decided to open up and pour freezing rain down upon me. I was soaked in less than twenty seconds, and my resolve to figure out the problem increased out of desperation. I doubled my efforts to rattle around different parts of the engine, intermittently jumping back in the truck to turn the ignition.

I got nothing.

On my third such attempt to climb back up on the bumper to work my magic, I heard, "What in the hell are you doing, Gabby?"

Spinning around, I lose my balance and hop off the bumper, straight into a huge puddle, which now coats the bottoms of my soaked jeans with mud. Wiping a wet lock of hair out of my eyes, I peer through the driving rain and see Hunter stalking up toward me, his Jeep parked just ahead of my truck.

"What does it look like?" I grumble, lifting my leg up to climb back on the bumper.

Hunter's arms wrap around my waist and he pulls me off, setting me carefully beside the puddle. "Let me look," he says, and I let him… because I clearly know shit about engines.

After he pokes around a minute, he climbs into my truck and tries to start it. I hear the faint clicking noise that I had heard before, but nothing else.

When he gets back out, he grabs my elbow and starts leading me back to his Jeep. "Your battery's dead."

Pulling my arm away, I stop, and he turns to look at me. "Thanks. But I'll just call a tow truck."

"Don't be stupid," he says, and grabs my elbow again, pushing me once more toward his Jeep. "I can take you to buy a battery and install it faster than you can even get a tow truck out here."

I start to argue but the minute my mouth opens, my teeth start chattering so hard I'm afraid I might end up making an emergency visit to Dr. Kevin Zulekis to fix the cracks in my molars. I capitulate and gratefully step up into the passenger seat while he holds the door open for me.

When Hunter gets in the driver's seat, he turns the ignition and immediately cranks up the heat. "You're going to be lucky you don't get pneumonia," he admonishes.

I want to answer him with a smart-ass response, just so he knows that I'm still in uber-bitch mode, but my teeth are clacking violently and I can't even get words out of my mouth.

Hunter pulls out onto the roadway, but it's slow driving. He's silent, but that's fine by me. I lean forward and try to catch as much of the hot air that's blowing out of his vents as possible. I figure about some time mid-summer, I'll finally get warm again.

When Hunter turns off the main road, I glance over to ask him where he's going. He anticipates my question though and says, "I'm taking you to my house to get you dried off. It's closer than yours, and I don't want you getting sick and dying on me before you finish the remodel."

I start to argue with him but another round of shivers racks my body, and it would just take too much effort. Within minutes, we've arrived at his oceanfront cottage and I look up at it in surprise. It's a classic stilt home with light gray shingles and a wraparound porch. I'm surprised because it's actually quite small. I just assumed Hunter would buy something big and ostentatious, because I know he has money practically seeping out of his pores. Yeah, being a professional surfer might seem like a lot of fun and games, but with the hard work and dedication came big rewards. Between his professional sponsorships and prize monies of upward of four-hundred thousand per first place finish, Hunter had the cash to throw around. At least, that's what Casey told me.

He helps me out of the Jeep and leads me in

through the front door, where I bend over and kick off my muddy boots. Hunter does the same, although he does nothing more than step out of his flip-flops, and then he swings me up in his arms and carries me up a flight of stairs that are just off the foyer. I can't even think to protest before he's depositing me inside a bathroom and ordering me to get in the shower.

"Throw out your wet clothes, and I'll put them in the dryer. I'll bring you something to wear."

Then he turns around and heads back down the stairs.

I stand there just a few seconds, debating what to do. Between the heater in the car and the dryness of his house, I'm feeling marginally better and part of me just wants to flee. But the other part... the one that still has a tiny shiver running through me every now and then, glances longingly at the shower and before you know it, I'm stripped bare and hopping under the spray.

Several minutes of hot water pours down on me before my muscles start to loosen, and my brain seems to start functioning again. I formulate my game plan, which is to get back in my clothes, be damned if they're still wet, and hightail it out of here.

The door to the bathroom opens up, and I peek outside the shower curtain. Hunter is in the bathroom, bending over to pick up my clothes. When he stands, he sees me watching and gives me a smarmy grin. "I brought you my robe to wear until your clothes are dry. Come down when you're done. I'm making some hot tea."

And with that, he leaves, closing the door firmly behind him.

I stay under the hot water for several more minutes, finally climbing out after availing myself of his shampoo, conditioner, and soap. After I dry off, I use a brush I find under the sink to brush my hair out and slip the robe on. It's massive and swamps me completely, but it's soft and warm, and oh shit... it smells just like Hunter.

Walking into his kitchen, I see he's changed out of his wet clothes and has on just a pair of jeans that ride low on his hips, his bare feet poking out from below. His back is broad, muscular, and sun-kissed. It makes me want to run my hands along his skin just to feel the warmth of it. He turns to look at me and gives me a smile.

"Feel better?"

"Yes," I say quietly. "Thank you."

Picking up a steaming cup of tea from the counter, he hands it to me. "No problem. I like to help damsels in distress."

"I'm not a damsel in distress," I snap, because it seems natural to try to take his head off. I take a sip of the hot tea and almost groan over how good it tastes.

Hunter takes a sip of his own tea, leaning back against the counter. "Funny... you looked like you could use some help when I stopped."

Glaring at him, I say, "Whatever. All I had to do was call for someone. It's not like you saved me from the zombie apocalypse or anything."

Hunter laughs, his eyes alight with humor. "You crack me up, Gabs."

"I'm glad I amuse you," I grouch.

"You do a lot of things to me. Amuse is just one."

His voice is husky, his eyes serious as he says that, and my stomach flips end over end. I just stare at him, because his words... the way he's looking at me, it's completely hypnotic. For some strange reason, I want to drop my tea to the floor and just rub up against him.

Focus, Gabby, I tell myself. *You have a mission—to push Hunter Markham as far away from you as possible.*

I can do this. Chin up. Resolve in place.

Opening my mouth to ask where the dryer is, because I fully intend to leave, Hunter cuts me off.

"I'm going to let you in on a little secret, Gabriella Ward."

His words stun me, more so because he used my formal name and the only person that does that is my mother… and only when I'm in trouble.

I'm a glutton for punishment though, and I can't help but croak, "What's that?"

"I have this figured out."

He doesn't say anything more but takes a sip of his tea, watching me over the rim of his cup. He's baiting me… wanting to see how much I really want to know about his epiphany.

I don't make him wait long because my curiosity is killing me. "What do you have figured out?"

He smiles at me and it's carnally hot, invading every cell in my body. My skin warms… just from that smile, and my breath gets shallow. He notices my reaction to him, and it pleases him because his smile now turns triumphant. He never answers my question but sets his cup down and pushes away from the counter. As he walks toward me, I swear I get a little faint from the rush of blood that fires through my veins. His eyes are sparking with intensity and I'm powerless to look away.

Stopping just inches from me, he takes the tea from my hand and turns to set it on the kitchen table.

When he turns back, he stares down at me at me a brief moment before he raises one hand. It's as if he's in slow motion. I don't dare look away from his gaze, but I can see his hand rising up in a leisurely fashion from my peripheral vision.

My face. Yes, he must be bringing it up to touch my face.

But it rises no higher than my chest.

Placing his finger just at the base of my neck, he skims it south across my skin, ever so lightly. He pushes downward, right through the v-gap in his robe I have on, and my breath freezes in my lungs when the material starts to part.

Hunter's eyes are no longer holding mine, but he's watching his finger trail down the skin over my sternum until it glides right down between my breasts. Liquid fire swarms low in my belly. For a brief moment, my brain screams at me to go back into defensive bitch mode, but my body is also screaming for me to leave well enough alone and see where this goes.

Pushing further, Hunter continues dragging his finger down, now being slightly impeded by the flannel material, but it no way stopping his descent. He pushes right past my heart, below my breastbone, and over the top of my stomach. Only when his finger reaches the knot, which is tied firmly across my belly button, does he stop.

He raises his head, and I raise mine to meet his gaze. His blue eyes are almost the color of dark denim, and they sear into me. He holds me captive in his look for just a second, and then he looks back down again. I lower my head, fascinated, as I watch his other hand come up and work at the knot holding the robe together.

Whether it's a desperate act of self-preservation, or just an instinct born of fear that I'll get hurt, my own hands come up and cover his, attempting to stop his progress.

He stills for a moment, never taking his eyes off the knot.

"Don't," he rasps out. Then he looks up at me, and his eyes are almost pleading even though his voice is commanding to me. "Just don't."

And just like that, my hands fall away as I submit to his request. He regards me for a moment more, and then he looks back down to his end goal. His hands are deft and he manages to pull the belt apart quickly, dropping both ends. The robe however, stays in place, gapping slightly at my breasts.

Hunter's hands grab ahold of the edges, and I'm amazed to see they are slightly shaking as he pulls them apart. Cool air hits my belly and breasts, while Hunter's eyes roam over me. His breath comes out in a rush across his lips, hitting me in the face with a warm caress. It smells like peppermint tea, and I wonder if I'll be able to taste it on his tongue.

As he pulls the robe further apart, he whispers in awe, "Christ... you're perfect."

My knees almost buckle from the longing in his voice, and it dredges up memories of five years ago when I wanted to hear just those very words from him. For some reason, they sound sweeter at this very moment, because I understand how far both of us have come to reach this point.

Releasing the edges of the robe, Hunter brings his hands up and they lightly encircle my throat... just for a moment, before he smoothes them down the sides of my neck and across my shoulders, pushing the robe off.

"Tell me," I whisper.

His hands still against my skin, and his eyes leap toward mine. "Tell you what?"

"Tell me what you have figured out."

He smiles in understanding and leans forward to caress his lips over mine, digging his fingers slightly into the skin of my shoulders. When he pulls back, he says, "I figured out that you and I... that we're going to happen no matter what."

The minute he utters those words, I know they're true. As much as I wanted to keep him at bay, as much as I feared what this would mean for my sanity and the sanctity of my heart, I too knew this was going to happen.

I give him a small nod of understanding and he rewards me with a brilliant smile, his eyes lighting up from within.

"Good," he says. "We're in agreement?"

I nod again and whisper, "Yes."

"Gabby?" he says just before he leans down and kisses me on my neck. Goose bumps break out all over my body.

"Hmmmm?"

"This is going to feel so fucking good," he promises, his voice deep and laced with so much sensuality, liquid heat floods between my legs.

Then his lips come to mine, and yes… he tastes just like peppermint tea. My head swirls as his tongue mates with mine and just as my eyes flutter closed in rapture, I think… *Yes, this is going to feel so fucking good.*

EIGHT

Hunter

When I was seventeen and on the Junior Pro tour, I surfed Pipeline at Oahu's North Shore for the first time and the exhilaration of the moment almost killed me. I literally thought my heart would jump out of my chest it was beating so hard when I caught the first wave in my heat. It was the biggest water I had surfed in my young career and, in my entire life to date, it was the most thrilling moment.

Until now.

On the ROCKS

Now I'd have to say the moment Gabby nodded at me... giving me the go ahead to have her... it knocked the Pipe clear out of my memory. Because now my heart is hammering with nuclear thunder at the mere prospect that I'll be sunk deep inside of her before too long, and I'm almost drunk with pleasure just knowing that.

She looks at me, right this very moment, with heat and desire, and I have never wanted another woman the way I want her now. If I could freeze this moment in time, bottle this feeling, and sell it, I'd be a fucking millionaire ten times over.

I contemplate exactly what I'm going to do to her... what will make her writhe against me or what will make her scream the loudest. I'm just about set on throwing her over my shoulder to carry her into my bedroom when she reaches out and grabs ahold of the waistband of my jeans, sinking her fingers inside. My gaze snaps up to hers and I see a bit of a challenge in those green-gold eyes, just before she lowers her gaze and unsnaps the button.

She doesn't have an ounce of hesitation... dragging my zipper down assuredly and peeling the fly apart. I was hard just from the first touch of my finger at the base of her throat, but when she pulls her lower lip in between her teeth, gazing at her hands as they grip onto the denim, I swell to almost painful proportions.

Gabby slips her fingers under the edge of my underwear and I suck the air between my teeth when she burrows down and takes my dick in her hand, squeezing me gently.

Tilting my head back, I close my eyes and mutter, "Fuck, that feels good."

"Yes, it does," she murmurs, and then releases me, only to grab my jeans and underwear and push them down past my hips, all the way to my ankles. She drops to her knees before me, pulling my clothes off and tossing them aside. She looks back up at me, her mouth hovering just in front of my cock, and I watch, spellbound, as she takes me in her hands again. Peeking up at me briefly, she leans in to lick the tip.

Electric fire courses through me and I jerk forward, right into her open mouth. I feel like I'm falling down the rabbit hole as she takes me all the way in and sucks hard against me, causing my knees to practically buckle from the intense feeling of pleasure.

My eyes fly open and I grab her shoulders, pulling her off and into a standing position. Her eyes are fevered and glazed, as she looks at me in confusion.

"Can't have you doing that just right now, Gabs. I'm barely maintaining my control as it is."

I pull her in hard, crushing her body into mine, and kiss her with an almost violent passion. She responds with equal zeal, and our teeth clash while our tongues duel. Her hands reach out to find my cock and, once her fingers circle around me, I'm almost driven to my knees again. Her touch is just that catastrophic to my senses.

Quickly grabbing at her, I encircle her wrists and pull her hands away, taking her bottom lip in between my teeth and biting down. She jerks forward, and her skin practically burns mine, even as she tries to evade my grasp so she can touch me again. If she keeps it up, I'll spill in her hand like a fucking kid in junior high, jacking off to his dad's Playboys.

"Am I going to have to restrain you?" I growl at her, leaning down to suck at her neck.

She laughs at me, her voice husky and dripping sex. "Maybe," she taunts.

I sort of knew that Gabby would be a hellion in the bedroom. She had too much fire not to be, and I'm pretty sure I have my hands full.

Which gives me a brilliant idea.

Leaning down, I kiss her again. Kiss her to distraction so she doesn't think twice as I peel my

121

robe off her shoulders and push it down her arms. Reaching down quickly, I grab the ends of the belt on each side of her, looping it around each wrist twice, then pulling them behind her back. Before she can even register a complaint, I deftly tie a knot between the two ends, effectively binding her hands behind her.

Then I step back to admire my work.

Gabby is standing there, her skin flushed, her nipples hard as little pebbles, and her chest heaving. She's glaring at me, but not in an, 'I'm going to kick your balls in for doing that to me,' kind of way. No, she's pissed because she can't touch me, and the knowledge that she wants it so much makes my dick go even more impossibly hard, especially when she looks down at it in longing.

"Bad girl," I tease her, and then take her face in my hands to kiss her again. This time it's slower, not as frantic, and I relish the warmth of her mouth against mine.

Pushing Gabby backward, I step into her, causing her to move across the kitchen. I walk her right back into the wall and when it halts her progress, I press my body against hers, my dick twitching when it touches the smooth skin on her stomach.

Dropping my hands to her breasts, I take one in each palm, testing their weight and then squeezing them. Gabby lets her head fall back and it hits against the wall, but she's not feeling any pain.

"You're so beautiful," I tell her before I bend down and take a nipple in my mouth. I tongue at it gently, listening to her tiny gasps of pleasure. Then I suck on it hard, causing her to groan and buck against me.

Slipping a hand down in between her legs, I slide a finger inside of her, practically burned by the heat she's unleashing. A new bolt of lust shoots through me and I suck at her nipple harder, and then give it a small bite, causing her to cry out, "It's too much."

Releasing her from my mouth, I turn my cheek and rub the scruff of my beard against her breasts. "Not even close."

"Untie my hands," she demands.

"Not gonna happen," I tell her simply, as I pull away and look into her eyes. She's challenging me, seeing how much quarter I'll give her.

She's getting none.

I drop to my knees, just the way she did moments ago, and I feel like I'm getting ready to worship at the Temple of Gabriella. I'd gladly sacrifice all I have just to kneel down here again and again.

Running my hands up the length of her smooth legs, I look up at her. She's gazing down at me with such fever that I have a moment of nervousness, wondering if I can ever possibly do right by her. But then I draw on my spirit of competition… of determination, and know exactly what I'm going to do to her.

I gently lift one of her legs up and drape it over my shoulder. She has an idea of what I'm getting ready to do, but she really has no clue. Bringing a hand up, I stroke softly between her legs, causing a gurgling sound to well up in her throat. I smile, because this is getting ready to get crazy.

Bending and angling my opposite shoulder in between her legs, I nudge my way in and bring her other leg up and over. Now she's straddling me, suspended helplessly from the floor, with nothing but the strength of my shoulders and the wall against her back to support her.

She's staring at me with eyes wild in confusion and lust. I've shocked her, and it feels fucking awesome for some reason.

Leaning my head forward, I place a kiss just below her navel, and then stick my tongue out to give her a lick. Turning my face, I rub up against her again and murmur, "I like you like this… trussed up, suspended, and helpless. Not a damn thing you can do to stop me."

I look up at her to gauge her reaction. Rather than apprehension, I see challenge as her lips curl upward at me. "Do your worst," she whispers, and I can't help but grin back at her.

"Oh, I will," I tell her as I bring my hands up over the tops of her thighs and spread her apart for my pleasure… and hers.

The next lick I have against her… I'll never forget. She jerks so violently that I have to grip onto her legs hard to keep her from falling.

"Stop moving," I warn her as I nuzzle my lips in between her legs. "Or I won't be able to finish you off."

"Asshole," she mutters and I chuckle against her, causing her to thrust her hips forward from the vibrations emanating from my mouth onto her tender flesh.

"You won't be calling me that when I'm done," I assure her, and then I let her have it.

It's the best fucking head I've ever given in my life, if I don't say so myself, but then again… it's Gabby. I want to give her the best of everything. And she tastes better than anything I've ever had in my mouth before.

The effort I have to exert to keep her still and pushed against the wall is a constant battle because she won't stop moving, but it makes me even more determined.

My efforts pay off because it doesn't take long before she stiffens, clamping her legs against my head and screaming out.

"Fuck yeah," I murmur against her, licking and sucking gently as she comes down off what I'm betting is the mother lode of all orgasms.

She's still shuddering when I release my hold on her and bring her legs off my shoulders, causing her to sag like a bowl of Jell-O to the floor. But I don't have time for weak limbs. I stand up, lifting her along with me, and quickly untie the belt from around her wrists, shoving the robe off her.

I'm so fucking hard and horny right now, I'm not sure I'll make the short trek down the hall to my bedroom. Lifting her quickly up in my arms, I make my way back there.

She's limp and sated, barely able to cling onto me. I like her like this… at my mercy. Laying her on the bed, I make a mad grab for the condoms in my nightstand, fumbling to open the packet. My hands are shaking as I roll it on and when I turn to look at her, she's staring at me with longing.

"Hurry," she whispers, and I think I might just perish right there from the emotion that courses through me. She's completely wrecked and yet still wanting. What does that say about the level of desire that she feels for me? It makes me humble and thankful, and makes me want to prostrate myself at her temple again.

Shaking my head slightly, I kneel on the bed and crawl in between her legs, which open wider for me as I pull my way up her body.

I press myself against her, my dick coming right up against the heat that is begging me to come inside. I lay a soft kiss on her lips, and she gives me a sigh that warms me through and through.

"Hi," I tell her.

She gives me a slight smile and says, "Hi."

"Are you okay?"

"I've been better," she says softly, and my protective instincts rear up violently.

"What's wrong?" I ask urgently, moving my hands up to frame her face.

"I felt better about two minutes ago. I want to feel like that again," she says with a tart smile.

Relief courses through me, and I give her a resounding kiss. "You're rotten, but I think I can remedy that."

Before I can give her a chance to respond, I push into her without much effort because she is so wet and ready for me. We both give out identical groans from the exquisiteness of the feeling, and I drop my forehead against hers to get my bearings.

"That feels good," she says. I pull back and sink back in, causing her to groan again.

"Feels amazing," I concur.

I start to move against her, in her. The feeling is so intense as I fuck her slowly... softly. Pulling her hands up above her head, I lace my fingers among hers and prop some of my weight on my elbows so I don't crush her. Her legs raise up, her knees gripping along my ribcage, pulling me in deeper. We stare at each other the entire time, and it strikes me with wonder that Gabby is laying underneath my body and we are sharing in the height of intimacy between two people.

Things are never going to be the same between us.

I'm not sure if it's the way our hearts beat against each other as my chest lays flush against hers, but we are in sync... our bodies marching to the beat of the same drummer. Just as I feel her start to stiffen up, just as her head tilts back and her eyes close, I feel my orgasm start to prickle deep within me. It doesn't rush at me but rather builds like a symphony orchestra striving for their crescendo, then it crashes through me just as Gabby issues a soft cry of pleasure and starts to shudder below me.

I go absolutely still inside of her as my orgasm shoots hot out of me, squeezing my eyes shut. I don't make a sound or another movement, choosing instead to put all of my attention on what must be the most amazing feeling of my entire life. It seems to go on and on, and that's fine by me. I don't ever want it to stop, as wave after wave of bliss washes through me.

When I'm empty... completely devoid, I roll to my side and pull her into my arms. I listen as her breathing quiets, rubbing her back in soft strokes.

We lay like that for a while, listening to the rain beat down on the roof, both alone with our thoughts. I want to say something... but I'm not sure what. Things changed the minute I touched my finger to her neck, and there's no going back. I'm just not sure how to move forward, particularly in light of Gabby's apparent disdain for all things Hunter Markham.

I can honestly say, though, that I'm not surprised when Gabby pulls out of my grasp and rolls to the edge of the bed.

"I need to get going," she says brusquely as she stands and heads into the kitchen.

I roll out of bed on my side, taking the used condom off and tossing it in the trashcan. I follow her, finding her shrugging into my robe and looking around.

"Gabby… don't run off," I say as I pull my jeans on.

She turns to me, and her face is closed off. "Where's your dryer, so I can get my clothes?"

I step up to her and put my hands on her shoulders. Her gaze is averted, so I wait patiently until she looks up at me. My heart constricts when I see fear swimming in her eyes. "This was a mistake, Hunter. A huge mistake."

"No way," I disagree adamantly. "That was the best fucking thing that could have happened between us."

She pulls away and steps back. "It was sex, Hunter. There are better things in life than that."

Ouch… that hurt, but I really don't think she meant that. "It was more than just sex, and you know it. We have a history together."

She laughs then, and it's bitter. "History? Yeah, we have history, but it's not really that great of a history."

"We can make it better," I insist. "What just happened isn't ordinary. That was special."

Anger masks her face, and she goes right for putting my nuts in a vice-grip. "Oh, God, Hunter. Could you be any more of a girl? That was fucking, pure and simple. We both got off, and it was good. But don't go getting on bended knee and turn this into a fairytale."

What. The. Fuck?

I feel like I'm in the Twilight Zone. Am I being a girl? Was that not as special as I had built it up in my mind?

I open my mouth to say something... to deny what she's saying, but I can't think of a fucking thing to say. Maybe she's right. Maybe this was just a fuck. An amazingly great fuck, but just a fuck.

I harden my gaze at her and for a second, I see regret in her eyes, but then it's gone.

"I'll go get your clothes," I tell her. "Then we can go get your truck fixed."

She stares at me, emotions warring across her face. But then she nods and quietly says, "Thank you."

As I turn away, I realize I'm not really sure what she's thanking me for. The two incredible orgasms I gave her, the fact I'm helping her fix her truck, or maybe it's because I'm choosing not to press the issue with her?

Regardless, it's clear that this subject is closed.

NINE

Gabby

I'm so tired.

Utterly, bone-crushing tired.

I doubt I've had a total of sixteen hours sleep in the last four days since… since… well, since Hunter.

Without a doubt, I was completely shattered by him. The things he did to me, the words he said… the way he looked at me.

My heart painfully constricts when I remember him saying that what we shared was special. God… it was *so* special. It was beyond description. I have never felt closer to another human being in my life as he moved inside of me. This was the man I loved my entire life, buried deep inside of my body, and wedging himself tight inside my heart.

I reacted badly… I know it. But when my body cooled and I laid there in his arms, I got scared. So fucking scared. So I pushed him away, because I'm too much of a pansy ass to even try to filter through all the emotions coursing through me.

Hunter didn't try to talk to me as I got dressed, and he took me to the auto supply store. It had stopped raining by the time we made it back to my truck and I leaned up against the side of it, nibbling on my fingernails as he took out the old battery and installed the new.

His shoulders were tense the entire time but he worked efficiently, a look of relief crossing his face when he got in the cab and started it up. He got out then and didn't spare me a glance. He walked right by me and just said, "I'll catch you later."

My heart was crushed. I wanted to run after him and tell him I was sorry for what I said, but deep down inside… I felt this was probably for the best. I mean—what could happen between us? It was just totally awkward. We had amazing sex. I mean…

freakin' phenomenal, and I'm sure I'm ruined for any other man.

But Hunter is Hunter. He's an island. Sure, he's back home now, to help Brody get acclimated, but if anyone believes he won't get back on the ASP Tour, they are fooling themselves. He's too good, and he has too much of a career left in front of him. Besides, surfing is in his blood. He may call what he did "retirement," but it's really more of a sabbatical. Hunter won't be sticking around forever.

Hunter is fleeting.

If I'm honest with myself, though, that's not really the reason I think this is a bad idea. I'm really too much of a coward to put forth the effort into making this work. Hunter was the one who told me that what happened was special. That means he thinks there's something there to build on.

I, on the other hand, see only the potential failure. I recall how battered my heart was five years ago, and that was just from having a childhood crush squashed like a grape. I don't have it in me to suffer the type of disappointment and hurt that would come now that I've felt what it's like to have Hunter Markham make love to me. It's like handing a drowning man a life jacket, only to pull it away once he feels the safety and security of it in his grasp.

So, for the last four days I've avoided Last Call... and thus avoided Hunter. I've given instructions to my foreman on the work schedule, and he's handling things just fine. I've gone by to check on the work after the bar has closed down for the night, and spent the weekend working out of my dad's old shop, finishing the outdoor bar unit I built.

But that's done now, and I finished the last coat of sealant on the walnut last night. It turned out beautifully. My crew picked it up this morning to bring it over and install, and I need to get over there to oversee the process.

I stand from my kitchen table, where I was moping, and head back to the bathroom. Brushing my teeth, I pull my hair back into a ponytail. I look in the mirror and try out a tentative smile, just to see if I can get it to bring a measure of happiness to my sad heart.

Nope. I still feel miserable.

Sighing, I head out to Last Call, knowing that I'll be seeing Hunter within a few minutes, and I don't even know how to behave around him.

"Push it forward about two inches to the right," I

tell my foreman, Lee Reed. He came to work for my dad about five years before he died and gladly stayed on with me. Not out of any major sense of loyalty, I don't believe, but because work was scarce and I was able to keep paying him. He was good at his job though, and I had trust in his abilities.

Lee and another crew member lift up the edge of the massive unit and push it slightly, bringing it into alignment with the measured marks I had laid on the floor.

"Perfect," I say as I haul myself up and dust my knees off. "Go ahead and anchor it, and then cover it with the tarp."

Lee nods, and they get to work securing the unit to the floor. I watch them for a few minutes as they use the Ramset to shoot nails through the shoe board and into the concrete below. When I'm satisfied that they are on task, I head to the rear of the new decking that was installed, checking on the progress of the staircase the rest of the crew is building down to the beach. That should be finished by the end of the day, and we can start on the covered roof portion tomorrow. We'll hold off the staining until the roof is finished.

I added on one other project that I had talked to Hunter about last week, but it was something I planned to do in the off hours. I thought it would be neat to build a hanging wall from the edges of the floating roof, so that Hunter could hang his trophies from his competitions. On the ASP, your trophy was an actual surfboard and he currently had them stacked up in the rear of the storeroom, gathering dust.

Making my way back inside, I use the restroom and then walk to the front bar to grab a bottle of water, which Hunter had stocked for my crew and me. As I turn the corner, I'm brought up short by Hunter and Brody standing behind the bar, going over ledgers.

He was not here when I arrived this morning, and I had been out back all day. I knew I would run into him at some point, but I still wasn't prepared for the visceral reaction I got just from seeing him there. He and Brody had their heads bent close together, going over the documents in front of them, talking quietly. I thought about just walking away before I was noticed, but then I decided to just rip the Band-Aid off and get it over with.

"Hey," I say as I step behind the bar and open the refrigerator under the counter. Taking a bottle of the water, I start to turn away, but not before I see Hunter raise his head, his face bland and unreadable.

"Hey," Brody says, giving me a small smile.

Hunter says nothing, just watches me. It's unnerving, wondering what is going on in that handsome head of his, but it's an effort in futility. I want to say something... anything, so that I can get a reaction from him, so I can gauge what he's thinking, but my mind is blank.

I start to turn away, but his voice stops me. "Did you get the bar installed out back?"

Turning back, I say, "Yeah... they're anchoring it right now."

He just nods and turns back to the documents. Brody just sort of frowns at me, I'm sure not understanding the frost in the air surrounding us. The urge to flee is great, but then something pushes through my reticence and, before I can stop myself, I say, "Hunter... if you have some time today, I need to talk to you."

Looking up at me in surprise, he stares blankly, pushing away from the bar. "No time like the present. Let's go to my office."

Oh shit. My heart starts hammering because I wasn't ready to talk right this very moment. These things take time to figure out. There's a certain bit of finesse I need to employ, and that takes preparation.

I have no choice though, and I follow Hunter back to his office like I'm marching off to face a death squad. My mind is spinning, trying desperately to think of what I'm going to say. Should I apologize? Should I explain my fears? Should I treat this as a joke?

I have no fucking clue.

Hunter precedes me into his office and I follow behind, turning to close the door behind me. When I turn back around, Hunter is there in front of me. I'm completely startled when his hands come up to my face to hold me tight, and he kisses me.

I stiffen for just a moment, more from the shock, but then my senses give in to the feeling of his mouth moving over mine… and I give in. My arms snake around his neck and his drop to my waist, as we both pull each other in as close as possible.

The kiss is warm and languid. There's no frenzy… no urgency. It's as if we do this a hundred times a day, although the feeling is beyond extraordinary. His tongue is warm and commanding, his body hard against mine. It's a feeling I could get used to. It's a feeling I could become dependent on.

Before I can make another observation on the rush of thoughts that are circulating through my mind, Hunter pulls his lips from mine.

"What was that for?" I ask, my breathing coming out in sharp bursts.

His hands fall away, and he steps back from me. Frustration washes over his face, and he slides his fingers through his hair to punctuate it.

"Hell if I know," he says with a tinge of anger. "I couldn't fucking help myself."

My hands come together in nervousness, ringing against one another. I open my mouth to say something, but nothing comes out. I have no clue how to even begin a conversation with him. All seemed right in my world just moments ago when we were kissing, but now everything seems wrong.

Hunter watches me warily, waiting.

When nothing seems to be forthcoming, he sighs. "What is it you wanted, Gabby?"

"I—I—" I have no idea what to say. The only thing that is coming to mind is, "Please kiss me again," but that just doesn't seem appropriate.

When it's apparent that nothing intelligent seems to want to make an appearance from my lips, Hunter shrugs his shoulders and starts for the door. "When you figure it out, let me know."

When he walks by me, a sense of urgency hits and I reach out to grab his arm. "Wait."

He turns to look at me, his face unreadable and impatient. "What do you want?"

It's a simple question. At this very moment—

what is it I really want? There's only one answer, although I'm not sure exactly what it means.

"I want you," I tell him quietly.

He narrows his gaze at me, suspicious of my motivation. I can't say as I blame him. Stepping in toward me closer, he asks, "In what way?"

"I don't know," I practically whine. "I'm confused."

His features smooth out at my pathetic nature, and sympathy filters into his eyes. He reaches his hands out and frames my face again, leaning in closer. "Me too. So let's figure this out."

I take in a deep breath and let it out gratefully, some of the tension leaving my body. It helps to know he's confused as well. I don't feel quite so alone right now.

"I don't know what this is," I admit. "I don't know where this is going."

Giving me a small smile, Hunter leans in and gives me a kiss. When he pulls away, he says, "No one knows where anything is going... not for sure. Who's to say we need to know what waits for us? Maybe all we need to know is that we don't want to stay where we are."

He makes it sound so simple. It's so Que Sera Sera.

Great, now that song is freakin' stuck in my head.

"So… is this just sex?"

"No," he says quietly. "I told you the other night this was special. You know that, right?"

Shrugging my shoulders, I look down at the floor, not willing to let him look in my eyes, in case he sees that it was more than special to me. That would make me too vulnerable.

"At the risk of sounding too much like a girl," he continues, "I need to tell you that the other day… making love to you, fucking you… whatever you want to call it, was different for me. So that makes it special. So that makes it more than 'just sex'."

I look back up at him because his words are encouraging. "Yes. It was special."

He grins at me, complete relief awash in that smile. "So… that means we can keep doing it?"

"Sex?" I ask, not sure exactly what he wants to keep doing.

Hunter throws his head back and laughs, then pulls me into a hug. He rocks me back and forth, still chuckling. "Yes, Gabs. Sex, fucking, making love, getting you off, getting me off. I don't care what we call it, but I want to keep seeing you."

"Seeing me?" I ask again, I'm sure sounding like

an idiot.

He pulls back and looks at me suspiciously. "Are you drunk or something? You're usually not this slow."

I can't help the giggle that escapes, but then I make sure he understands me next when I say, "I don't want anyone to know."

He flinches slightly, and his eyebrows scrunch inward with confusion. "Why not?"

"It's just so awkward right now… trying to figure out what we have. I'd rather not have the glaring spotlight on us as we try to make sense of this. Just having to deal with the barrage of questions we'd get from our friends and family gives me the wiggins."

I punctuate my statement by shivering.

Hunter stares at me a moment, and then asks, "The wiggins?"

"Totally the wiggins," I affirm.

"Okay… while I don't relish the idea of keeping this a secret from our families, because fuck knows it's going to be hard to keep my hands off you, we'll take this slow and see where it leads before we go public."

My breath comes out in a massive rush. I didn't realize how important the secrecy was to me until he agreed. "Great. Thank you."

He nods, taking my hand and leading me over to a seat opposite his desk. He sits down in the other chair and turns it toward me. "We need to have a serious talk."

I blink in surprise, because I thought we just had our serious talk. "Okay."

"First... have dinner with me tonight at my house?"

"Um... sure?" I say as if it's a question, not a statement, because it's sort of weird the way he's asking as part of a 'serious' talk. I'm confused.

"Great. Second... are you on the pill?"

"What?" I ask loudly, totally not prepared for that question.

"Daft," Hunter mutters, and then he asks again. "The pill? Are you on it?"

"Yes. Why?"

"Because I want to fuck you right now, and I don't have a damn condom on me. Plus, I don't want anything between us. I want to feel you against me."

This conversation is strange, yet his words excite me because they are laced with urgency and need. I have to admit, the minute he asked me to come over for dinner tonight, I was already calculating the hours until he'd be inside me again. And now... it appears it may just be minutes.

"Okay, so here's where we need honesty," he barrels forward. "I trust what you tell me, and I hope you trust me. I'm clean. There's only been one person who I've ever been with without a condom. It was a long-term relationship and I've been tested since, and since that time... I've not been without one. So, I swear you have nothing to fear from me."

My jaw hangs open, and I can't even being to calculate how many things are unsettling about what he just said. First, we're talking about whether or not we have cooties, and the absurd nature of it makes me want to snort in amusement. I mean, I know this is an important conversation and any couple who is considering a monogamous relationship will have it. It just catches me off guard; particularly because I'm still focused on the fact that he says he wants to fuck me right now.

Secondly, I'm thrown off by the fact that he had a serious relationship in the past. Hunter just didn't seem the type, and now my curiosity is roused. Plus, I find myself oddly jealous that he's been with someone else "au naturel".

"Focus, Gabs," he says with amusement because of my slack-jawed lack of response.

"Um... I trust you, of course. And... I don't have anything. I mean... I've never been with anyone without a condom."

Relief washes over his face and he stands up from the chair, pulling me up with him. He draws me in tight and kisses me hard, but only briefly. When he pulls back, he takes his t-shirt off and starts unzipping his shorts.

"Get naked," he says seriously. "I really don't think I can wait another minute. Oh, and this is going to be kind of rough and fast, but I swear I'll make it up to you tonight."

Holy shit. My insides melt, and the space between my legs clenches involuntarily. I don't think twice before I start to kick off my boots. I'm apparently too slow because Hunter has all of his clothes shed and then he's kneeling down at my feet, taking them off for me. When he stands up, he peels the rest of my clothes off in record time.

Then, he's on me.

His hands are everywhere; his mouth is everywhere. His slides two fingers into me, made easy by the fact I went wet the minute he said he wanted to fuck me. Hunter kisses my mouth, my neck, my jaw… He nibbles on my ear and my bottom lip. He does all of this before I can even think to raise my hands to touch him, because he has me drowning in a rush of sensual pleasure.

"Can you take it hard and fast?" he whispers against my lips.

"Uh-huh," I say... well, actually I moan.

"That's my girl," he praises me. Turning me toward his desk, he bends me over, nudging my legs apart with his own.

Settling behind me, he positions himself squarely at my entrance and I hear him take a shuddering breath, just before he pushes his way in.

My head falls forward and knocks against the desk, so torturously good is the feeling of him inside of me. My fingers involuntarily curl around some documents they were resting against, crumpling them up tight in my grip.

"Fuck," Hunter gasps as he grips onto my hips. "Fuck, that feels good."

"Uh-huh," I mutter. He pulls out and slams back into me, causing me to cry out... really loud.

"Quiet, Gabs. Don't want Brody rushing in here to make sure I'm not murdering you," he teases, and then he starts pumping hard.

So hard that the desk starts sliding a little, and I have to clap my hand over my mouth to keep the screams inside.

It's just as Hunter said it would be... rough and fast, and this may now be forever my favorite pace.

He slips a hand around to my front, rubbing against me and causing me to buck backward.

"Come on, Gabby," he says urgently. "Come on."

Just the fact of knowing that he's about ready to blow, and he doesn't want to leave without me, causes my climax to start. I squeeze my eyes shut as it washes through me, a strangled cry lodging deep in my throat.

Hunter slams in hard one more time and goes still. I feel him shuddering as he comes in me hot and hard, his breath whistling through his teeth. He collapses onto my back and says, "I'm never going to get enough of you."

I smile, because I know exactly what he means.

Hunter

I wake up from a sound sleep and immediately roll over to see if Gabby has gone. The bed beside me is empty and cold, so I roll back over with a sigh as I stare into the darkness.

She's come over for the last three nights... since that amazing, incredible sex we had on my desk. We lapsed into an easy relationship the last few days, with her coming over to eat dinner. We'd talk about anything and everything, mostly catching up on each other's lives over the last five years. She's insatiably curious about my surfing career, even making me show her some DVDs one night of some of my competitions. She ooh'd and aah'd, gasping if I took a spill, which I'm proud to say didn't happen all that often. My chest and my head were swelling to epic proportions when she told me how proud she was of me, and even wistfully said she wished she could have seen me in action.

We laughed a lot, slipping back into the friendship we had enjoyed prior to that first kiss. It seemed so right, so natural, and it made me want to experience more with her.

Where we are truly compatible is in the bed though. And on the couch, the floor, the shower, and the kitchen counter. Gabby is an adventurous lover, and she now knows my body as well as I do. And let's just say I'm on a first-name basis with all the parts of hers.

But it bugs me that the past three nights I've woken up to find that she's slipped away. I'm not sure what she has against sleeping with me all night. It's intimate, sure, and it speaks to something more than just sex. But what she and I do to each other... the way that we have no-holds-barred with our lovemaking... there's nothing more intimate than that, so sleeping together shouldn't be an issue.

I vow that I'll talk to her about it tonight and, if I have to tie her to my bed, I'm getting her to stay.

But?

Fuck that... I'm going to haul her ass back here right now.

I jump out of bed, throw on my clothes, and grab my keys. Within minutes, I'm in my Jeep and headed to her apartment. I hope Savannah doesn't mind too much when I barge my way in.

As I drive down the highway, I let my mind drift. My agent called me today under the guise of checking in, but then he finally laid it on the line. My sponsors were clamoring to get me back on the Tour next year, and they wanted a commitment. They were offering ridiculous new money as an incentive, confident that I could take the World Championship.

I wasn't so sure, however.

True... I could probably be ready to get back in the game come next March. I could have the bar up and running, and Brody could run it probably better than I could. I had my doubts, though, about my own abilities. I was getting ready to turn twenty-nine and, while I was in the best shape of my life, there were always younger and better talent climbing the ranks. Self-doubt has never been a part of my make-up, yet here it was creeping in.

More than that, my first thought hadn't been about the bar or even my abilities—it had been confusion over how I felt about leaving Gabby. Everything was so new and exciting right now, and if asked to make my choice today, I'm fairly confident I wouldn't want to go. But I had no clue where this was going, and come this time next year, maybe we would be old news.

Unlikely, but maybe.

As I drive past Last Call, I give it a cursory glance. The parking lot is dark, but I make out a vehicle sitting in front of the building. I do a double-take and realize it's Gabby's truck.

With a curse, I put on my blinker and make a fast turn, thankful there's not a cop around to see my wild move.

What in the hell is she doing here?

I unlock the front door, immediately recognizing that the alarm is off. It's silent, so I make my way into the back bar area. I see Gabby standing behind two sawhorses, with a piece of wood laid between. She hears my footsteps, and her head immediately snaps up in fear.

When she sees me, she places her hand over her heart. "Geez, Hunter. You scared the shit out of me."

"What are you doing here?" I ask, completely bewildered that she's working at... glancing down at my watch... three AM.

"I'm working," she says, pulling her tape measure out and marking a line on the wood with a pencil, which she slips back behind her ear when she's done.

"It's fucking three in the morning. Are you crazy?"

She doesn't even look up at me. "No, I'm just hard working. What's got you in a snit?"

I ignore that question and ask another. "Is this where you've been each night?"

"Yeah," she says as she picks up the table saw that's lying on the floor. She flicks the switch on and starts cutting through the wood.

I'm pissed that she's ignoring me and pissed that she's working at three AM. I bend down to grab the extension cord that has the saw plugged into the wall and yank it out, watching her glare up at me as the saw winds down to a dead stop.

"What the hell?" she asks in exasperation.

"You cannot be sane enough to think that this is okay," I tell her. "You work all fucking day here, and now you come back and work in the early morning hours. No wonder you fall dead asleep as soon as I'm done fucking you."

Her eyes narrow at me, and she stomps over to the wall outlet to plug the cord back in. "You hired me to do this job, but you have no fucking say-so in how I do it, so just back off."

She walks back to her work area and, as she reaches for the saw, I grab the cord and yank it back out again.

Her head snaps up and flames shoot out of her eyes. God, she's fucking gorgeous when she's mad. She opens her mouth to lay into me, but I hold my hand up. Surprisingly, her lips snap together, although her glare is no less ferocious.

In a calm voice, I say, "Just tell me why you feel the need to work these hours?"

She takes a deep breath, closing her eyes. When she opens them, the heat has died down a little. "I need to stay on schedule to meet the deadlines we set. Since we added this project for the hanging wall for your trophies, I just need to put some extra hours in to stay on track. It's no biggie."

My heart flops over, and my pride and respect for her increases tenfold. I walk up to her and pull her into a hug, which she halfheartedly returns. Kissing her on the head, I tell her, "We can extend the deadline, Gabs. It's not that big of a deal. Besides... I miss you in bed at night."

I expect her to go all gooey and melt over my proclamation, so imagine my surprise when she pushes angrily out of my embrace. "Wrong! It is a big deal. It's my reputation."

I laugh, trying to ease the tension. "Seriously… no one is going to know if we extend the deadline by a few days."

"Wrong again, doofus," she says angrily. "When I make a bid for another project, they call you for a reference, and they ask if I stayed on schedule, are you going to lie for me?"

"Yes," I tell her simply, because I have no qualms about doing that.

"No," she says in frustration and stomps her foot. "This is important to me. A General Contractor staying on budget and on schedule is paramount to making it in this business."

Okay, I'm starting to have a newfound appreciation for the lengths that Gabby will go to make it in this world. My mind searches frantically for a solution, and then it comes to me.

"Let me make sure I got this right. You had a set schedule based on the original bid, right?"

"Yes," she says in a humoring tone.

"And we decided to do the additional wall after you started the project, right?"

"Right."

"Then we should have re-done the original contract. The fact that I added on additional work should have included an extension of the deadline."

"That's true, but—"

"But, nothing. It never crossed my mind the importance of a set deadline. I had no clue. So the easy solution is we redo the contract and budget in the extra time you'll need."

"Yeah, but in about another week, I could have it finished."

"At what price?" I ask gently. "You're killing yourself and for no good reason. It's an easy solution."

Gabby pulls that bottom lip in between her teeth and starts nibbling, a sure sign she's considering my solution.

"So we just redo the contract?" she asks skeptically.

"Duh," I tell her. "Isn't that what would happen on any other project?"

"Yes," she says, sounding defeated and a little embarrassed.

"Good. It's settled then. Now let's get you back to my place so you can get a few more hours of sleep."

She looks at me with a smile that's somewhat feral and a whole lot of hot. "I'm not tired."

My eyebrows raise at the husky tone to her voice. "You're not?" I tease. "Want to do something else when we get back home?"

She shakes her head and lowers her eyes shyly. "I want to do something here."

"Here?" I rasp out and, all of a sudden, a million dirty things I want to do to her come to mind. I eye the pool table, and I know that's exactly where we'll get started.

We step toward each other and her hands come up behind my head, pulling me down for a kiss. I engage her for just a moment and then pull away, grabbing her hand and leading her toward the pool table. She pulls back against me though, so I stop and turn to look at her in question.

"Thank you," she says.

"For what?"

"For looking out for me."

Then she stuns me by dropping to her knees in front of me, undoing my pants. She pulls them down past my hips and, since I went commando, my erection that had built quickly once I looked at the pool table pops free.

She takes me in her hands and starts stroking me,

eliciting a heavy groan from deep within my chest. I look down at her and drag my finger across her cheek. "Is this the way you thank me for looking out for you?"

Smiling, she looks up at me, never once missing a stroke against my dick. "No, this is just because I want you in my mouth."

Holy. Fuck.

Her words alone practically have my legs giving way, but then her mouth is on me and I have to lean my hand against the sawhorse to keep steady.

"Shit, Gabby. That feels good."

She hums against my dick as she moves her mouth up and down my length, reaching between my legs and gently squeezing my balls. It feels so fucking good, and I know exactly how it's going to feel shooting down her throat because she gave me the best damn blow job the other night.

But I find myself still thinking of the pool table, so I bend down to slide my hands under her arms and lift her from the ground. She makes a sound of dismay as I slip free from her mouth, and it takes all of my willpower not to put my hand on top of her head and push her back down.

Instead, I lift her up, wrap her legs around my waist, and walk over to the pool table, sitting her down on it. It takes me just moments to disrobe her, and when she's naked, I put my hand against her chest and push her back. She has to tilt her head to the side to avoid the pool light hanging low, but then she's laid out before me with her body lit up from the glow above her.

Smoothing my hands up her stomach and over her breasts, I tell her, "You are the sexiest woman I've ever seen."

She smiles at me, shy and soft, unable or unwilling to be able to handle a real compliment. That warms me to my soul and for a brief moment, I think about Sasha. If I had her spread out before me and laid the same sentiment on her doorstep, she would have smiled at me in triumph, her eyes clearly conveying, "Yes, I know I'm the sexiest woman, and you should be damn thankful for it."

I never realized that about her until just this very moment, but then I shake my head mentally. Sasha has no business being in my head at this moment, but I choose to believe that thought came unbidden to make me appreciate Gabby all the more.

"What do you want?" I ask her as I roll her nipples between my fingers.

She gasps and arches her hips off the table. "I want you inside of me."

"Are you ready?"

Her eyes challenge me. "See for yourself."

So I do.

I bring one hand down between her legs, running my fingers through her curls and down a little further. She's wet already and I sink a finger inside of her, fascinated to watch it disappear into her heat.

"Oh, baby," I murmur. "You're ready."

"For you... always."

My eyes snap up to hers and, for a moment, she seems embarrassed to have said that because her eyes slide to the side, hiding from me.

I bend over her, grasping her chin and bring my lips to hers, kissing her softly. When I pull back, I stare at her hard. "Don't. Don't ever hide what you feel from me. I love that you're ready for me... always."

She swallows hard and nods at me.

I push back from her and grab onto her legs, pulling her closer toward me so her butt slides over the lip and comes right to the edge. I step in between her legs, taking my dick in my hand and lining it up to her sweet core, having to bend my legs slightly to find the right angle.

Her eyes flutter closed in anticipation, so I choose not to make her wait. Flexing my hips forward, I start to sink into her slowly. Her lips part and a tiny puff of air comes out before she says, "Oh, Hunter."

My entire body shudders, not just from the contact of her warmth surrounding me, but from those two simple words she just uttered. My name… held with reverence and desire.

Nothing has ever sounded sweeter to me.

I straighten my legs, wrapping my hands under her ass and lifting her up from the table. It causes me to sink into her deeper, and it feels perfect.

With measured care, I start to move against her and, after just a few thrusts, I'm lost to her, picking up the pace with driving force.

It doesn't take either of us long, and the minute she starts to fall, I follow right along behind her.

ELEVEN

Gabby

Hunter has decided to throw a party this afternoon, and I'm petrified. Scared shitless. It's just a casual, Saturday afternoon get together with local friends, but I feel the spotlight glaring down on me.

I'm worried that people will know that we're fucking each other. He'll look at me a certain way, or I won't be able to take my eyes off him, and people will just know.

So far, it's not been that big of a deal... keeping our secret. We see each other at Last Call during the day, but he pretty much stays out of my way while I'm working. At night, I go to his house, where he does insanely wicked things to my body, and then I go home the next morning to shower and change for the next day of work. It's like shampooing my hair.

Lather, rinse, repeat.

The only person who knows that something is going on with Hunter is Savannah, and that's only because after the third night of not coming home, she asked me where I had been. And whether you consider it a fault or not, I'm not very good at lying when I'm confronted with a direct question.

So I answered her simply, "I've met someone, and I've been staying at his house."

Then she asked, "Who?"

And, of course, I couldn't lie, so I said, "Hunter Markham."

She didn't even bat an eyelash and said, "Not surprised. The way he looked at you when he came over here that morning... Whoa momma... it was hot."

I rolled my eyes at her but then promptly swore her to secrecy, which she gladly gave me. I mean, who would she tell anyway? She's friends with Casey and

Alyssa by mere virtue of the fact she's my roommate, but she's not super close friends with them. Besides, Savannah isn't a gossip. She'd never casually, or intentionally, drop that information.

Luckily, I've managed to avoid any questions from Casey or Alyssa. Oh, I talk to them frequently via phone, text, or email, but they've never come right out and asked, "Hey, Gabby... are you screwing anyone nowadays?" They've never seen me around Hunter since we started sleeping together, so there's been nothing to rouse their suspicions.

So all has been good and well... secret.

The only other person who may know is Brody. Hunter told me about the conversation he had with him the other day where he pointed out the reason we fought so much was because we had the hots for each other. I still shake my head in wonder thinking of the things that Brody sees, but he hasn't said a word to me.

I'm on Hunter's back deck, along with about twenty other people. Casey and Alyssa are here, as is Hunter's best friend, Wyatt. I invited Savannah, but she took on another gig with the douche photographer to earn some extra money. The only one of our core group that is conspicuously absent is Brody.

When I asked Casey where he is, she just shrugs her shoulders and says, "He tries to stay away from drinking."

"He works in a bar," I point out.

"I know… the irony is not lost on me, trust me."

Everyone is enjoying the warm weather today, the sun hanging low over the Atlantic, and the cold beer Hunter has supplied. I take a few quick peeks at him while he mans the grill, laughing at something Wyatt says to him.

He looks utterly gorgeous, his hair windblown and shining in the late afternoon glow. I know I'm not the only one affected, as evidenced by the three girls that also hang close to him while he flips the burgers. They're dressed no differently than any of the women here, wearing shorts and bikini tops as demanded by the unseasonable for late April, eighty degree weather, but the fact they are standing close to my man… flirting with him shamelessly, has me clenching my teeth together in anger.

"Geez… who peed in your Wheaties?" Casey asks from beside me.

I turn around to see her staring at me in interest. Shaking my head and giving her a smile, I say, "Nothing. Just thinking of some things I have to do Monday at Last Call."

Reaching into a nearby bowl of chips, she chews on one thoughtfully. "The project is going well?"

"Very well. On schedule, and it's coming together nicely."

"You've been busting your ass, girlie. I haven't even seen you all week. Are we still on for breakfast Monday?"

Even as I nod at her, I flush with a tiny bit of guilt that we haven't seen each other all week. Not that we would necessarily hang during the weekday. I mean, sometimes we would, but I feel a tad bit guilty because I know, without a doubt, that had Casey invited me to do something, I would have declined so I could spend my evenings with Hunter. I'm such a horrible friend, made even worse by the fact I'm screwing her brother and haven't told her about it.

I give her a wan smile and take another sip of my beer, sneaking another glance at Hunter. He's got the grill closed and is propped against the deck railing, leaning in close while one of the girls talks to him. His smile is carefree and he seems to be truly interested in what she's saying, which pisses me off.

Hunter's eyes slide briefly to mine, and they crinkle around the edges. He's amused with me, and I realize that the look on my face must reveal exactly how I'm feeling. I glare at him and turn toward the

167

house, intent on slamming the rest of my beer and getting another. Casey asks me to get her one too, and I just nod in response.

Oh God, this is torture. Being around Hunter, and yet not being with him. I know I'm the one that wanted to keep this secret, but it's killing me right now to not be able to talk to him. It's killing me right now not to be able to nudge my way in between him and the beach bimbo, so his eyes are only on me.

But this is my bed and I willingly crawled into it, so I have no choice but to put on my big girl panties and live with my choice.

As soon as I step into Hunter's house, I run straight into Steve Coursier. He's a few years old than I am and went to my high school. We occasionally see each other around town. He's always been friendly, in a goofy sort of way, and he's really cute on top of that. Steve's family owns a chain of novelty beach shops called The Shells along the Outer Banks, and he helps to manage them.

"Hey, Gabby," he says as he bends over to give me a quick hug. "How've you been doing?"

I give him a warm smile after he releases me. "I'm good. Busy. How about you?"

He shrugs his shoulders. "Same old. Gearing up for the tourist season."

"I bet," I tell him, walking by so I can head into the kitchen. "I'm on my way to get a beer—do you want one?"

He shakes his head, but then he says, "Hey… I'm glad I ran into you. I was wondering if, um… maybe you'd like to go out some time? Dinner— maybe catch a movie or something?"

My eyebrows raise in shock. I mean, I've known Steve for years and we've always been casual friends. He's never once indicated any interest in me that way, so I'm more than surprised about him asking me out on a date.

My mind goes blank. The unequivocal answer is no. Not because there's anything wrong with Steve, but because my heart is already being pulled in a million different directions by Hunter. The problem is, I can't say that—not out loud—and frankly, it's hard to admit it using my inside voice.

I open my mouth to start a gentle letdown when I hear, "She's not interested, Coursier."

Spinning around, I see Hunter standing just inside the doorway that leads out to his back deck. He has a bland smile on his face, but his eyes are hard as they bore into Steve.

After staring at Hunter for just a moment, Steve says, "If it's all the same, I'd rather hear it from

Gabby."

Hunter shrugs his shoulders in that "whatever dude" sort of way and steps past us. "Fair enough. Gabby, when you get done crushing his heart, do you mind if I talk to you in the kitchen... about the remodel?"

"Sure," I say, completely ill at ease that Hunter would take it upon himself to turn down a potential date for me. I mean, I was going to turn him down anyway, but his alpha tendencies are a little annoying.

Hunter walks into the kitchen, and I turn to Steve with an apologetic look on my face. "I'm sorry. But I'll have to decline."

He gives me an understanding smile. "No problem. Never hurts to ask, right?"

"Right," I tell him, relieved he took that gracefully.

I start to turn away when he asks, "When did you and Hunter start seeing each other?"

"What?" I say loudly as I spin back to look at him. I'm sure my eyes are wild with fright that he would say that out loud. "Why would you think that?"

Steve tilts his head to the side and smirks. "Seriously, Gabby? After he just practically lifted his leg up to pee on you, so he could mark his territory?"

My face goes beet red, and I start babbling.

"No… joking… just Hunter… not serious."

Steve just snorts at me and heads back out to the deck. Leaning back against the wall, I bang my head against it a few times, cursing inwardly that Hunter would do something so stupid.

Asshole.

Which I think I'll give said asshole a piece of my mind right now.

I stomp into the kitchen, and he's waiting for me as I turn the corner. I open my mouth to lay into him but he grasps the back of my head and pulls me in for a hot kiss, causing all of my thoughts to scatter.

My hands come up to his chest to push him away, but he feels so damn good in my mouth that my fingers curl into his t-shirt and pull him closer. He gives me a murmur of appreciation and kisses me harder.

When he pulls away, he places his forehead against mine. "God, I've been dying to do that all afternoon. This is killing me having you near but not being able to touch you."

I smile inwardly, because I know exactly what he means. "You looked like you weren't suffering out there."

"How so?" he asks quietly as he nuzzles against my neck.

"Your fan club," I say simply.

Pulling back slightly, he looks at me in confusion, and then understanding washes over his face. "You're jealous?"

"No way," I assure him. "It was just slightly nauseating to watch."

Hunter throws his head back and laughs, then brings his eyes, which are crinkled in amusement, back to me. "Who would have thought it? My girl's skin is tinged a little green."

I push away at him, angry that he'd throw that at me like it's a weakness. "I am not jealous. You can go screw all three of those girls hovering around you for all I care. In fact, I'm thinking that date with Steve is looking mighty fine right about now."

My efforts are futile because Hunter doesn't budge, managing only to pull me in closer. His other hand comes up and strokes my cheek. "Gabby, I don't want those other girls. I only want you, and I'll break Steve's legs if he so much as gets near you. And that, baby, is jealousy. At least I own up to it."

My lips curl up, so warmed am I by his admission. I even decide to throw him a little bone. "Okay, so maybe I was a little jealous, too."

Hunter gives me a satisfied smile and then leans down to kiss me again, wrapping his arms around my waist. His mouth is like heaven against mine, and I immediately submerse myself into the pleasure of it. His lips are so soft, as is the scruff of his beard when it rubs against me. It makes me want to shout out in joy, but yet I can't because then everyone would know that Hunter and I were seeing each other.

That actually makes me jerk away from him at the thought. He looks down at me in confusion.

"We need to stop," I tell him. "Someone could walk in and find us."

Understanding crosses his face, but he gives me a devilish grin and pulls me back in. "So what? Let's just tell everyone. Then we don't have to hide our feelings or let jealousy swamp us."

He bends down and runs his lips up my neck, giving a slight bite to the corner of my jaw, which has me melting against him. I push back against him again, only halfheartedly this time, and say, "No. I'm not ready. It's too soon."

There's no relenting and Hunter moves his mouth over mine again, murmuring against my lips. "It's silly, Gabs, keeping this a secret."

Then he slips his tongue in my mouth, deepening his kiss with burning need and causing me to moan in response. No longer am I thinking about getting caught, but just that easy, I'm wondering if we could

173

slip away to his bedroom without being seen. I'm just about to suggest the crazy notion, when I hear a gasp from the doorway.

As if zapped with an electrical current, I jump back from Hunter and turn toward the noise. Alyssa is standing there with her jaw hanging open, looking between the two of us. I sneak a peek up at Hunter and he has a satisfied smirk on his face, which makes me want to slap him.

I look back to Alyssa with urgency, even as I push Hunter's hand off my waist and take a step away from him. "I can explain."

"Explain what?" Casey says as she walks into the kitchen. She doesn't spare any of us a glance and heads to the refrigerator. "I got tired of waiting for you to bring me a beer."

I look to Alyssa and plead with my eyes for her to keep her mouth shut. Confusion overtakes her face but she gives me a slight nod, and I breathe a small sigh of relief.

I turn to Casey just as she pulls a beer out of the refrigerator. "About the new project I'm doing at Last Call. A wall to hang Hunter's trophies on."

"Cool," Casey says, smiling broadly and heading back out of the kitchen. "I'd stay and chat but Wyatt brought a friend of his to the party, and he's totally hot. I'm going to go see if I can corrupt him."

I roll my eyes as Casey saunters out and then turn to look at Hunter. "Do you mind giving Alyssa and me a moment?"

"Sure," he says with a small smile that seems a bit sad, and then he leaves. I watch his retreating back, wondering if I've hurt his feelings by perpetuating this secret of ours. He certainly didn't seem to mind when Alyssa walked in on us, but I freaked for sure.

"What the hell is going on, Gabby?"

Turning back toward Alyssa, I take her by the hand and pull her through Hunter's house. I push her out the front door, satisfied that the porch is empty and will give us a bit more privacy since the kitchen was a little too close to the rest of the party.

I close my eyes briefly and take a deep breath. When I open them, I look at Alyssa and tell her my story, starting five years ago.

When I finish, she asks, "I don't understand why you want to keep this secret. I think the idea of you and Hunter together is wonderful."

Sighing, I say with defeat, "I don't know, Alyssa. I guess I'm scared. Scared of what Casey will think, what our parents will think. I mean... we're practically family."

Alyssa snorts. "But you're not family. You're in

no way related, and there is nothing wrong with you two seeing each other."

I'm silent, chewing on my bottom lip as I look down at my feet.

"There's something else," Alyssa guesses.

Looking up at her, I tell her miserably. "I just don't think I can let this amount to anything. I think sex is all I'll let it be, and how well do you think that's going to go over with Casey?"

"How well do you think that's going to go over with Hunter?" Alyssa challenges me.

"What?" I ask confused. "Hunter is fine with this just being sex."

"I don't think so, Gabby. The way he looked at you, it just looked like a whole lot more to me."

"Well, it's not," I snap. "Trust me... this is just physical."

"Okay, put that issue aside for just a moment. I guess I don't understand why that's all you want."

I take a few steps over to the porch railing and lean my elbows down on it, gazing across the street at the next row of beach houses that stand proud on their stilts. Turning to look at Alyssa, I tell her, "Because... if I let it be any more, then I'll be crushed if this doesn't work out. It's safer this way."

Alyssa stares at me silently, her face sympathetic

and understanding. She takes a step closer to me, leaning her hip against the rail. "Gabby, I think you're looking at this the wrong way. I think you should open yourself up. Hunter cares for you a lot, and he could be the one."

I snort in condescending amusement. "See… that's just it, Alyssa. I know he's the one. He's been the one for me most of my life. I just don't think that I'm the one for him. I can't risk falling, knowing that he might not be there to catch me."

Opening her arms up, Alyssa pulls me in for a hug and whispers in my ear. "I never took you for a coward, girl. But I respect what you're saying."

When she releases me, I grab onto her hand. "Promise me you won't tell Casey."

"I promise. But I think you should tell her. She'd understand where you're coming from, and she's just going to be more pissed the longer you wait."

"I know," I say quietly. "I just need to wrap my head around this. I'll tell her… soon. Once I figure out what all of this with Hunter means."

TWELVE

Hunter

Yes, I could get used to waking up with Gabby in my arms each morning. She's so soft and warm, and she makes the cutest little sounds in her sleep.

Tightening my arms around her, I put my lips to her ear and whisper, "Gabs… wake up."

She groans and swats her hand back at me, so I grab onto it and bite the end of her finger. That causes her to groan again, but it's a different type of groan now.

"What time is it?" she asks groggily.

"About a quarter after six. I'm going to go surfing, but why don't you come out on the beach with me and watch the sunrise first?"

"Mmmmm," she says, still half asleep. "What's the temperature?"

I roll over and grab my iPhone to check the weather. Setting it back down, I roll back toward her, resting my chin on her shoulder. "It's fifty-seven."

Gabby reaches down, pulls the covers over her head, and mumbles. "No way, it's too cold out there right now."

Pulling the covers back off her, I grab her shoulder and roll her on her. Leaning down, I kiss her lips. "Come on, sleepyhead. Let's go watch the dolphins play and canoodle on the beach while the sun comes up."

Giggling, she pushes against my chest but it's a halfhearted attempt. She finally opens one bleary eye and looks at me. "You seriously want to go watch the sunrise?"

"Yup. Then you can watch your man shred some waves."

"My man?" she asks, giving a smiling yawn.

"Your man," I confirm.

She stretches her arms up, which brings my

attention to her bare breasts. I hear her yawn again, but I'm mesmerized by the round globes of soft flesh.

I start to bend down to lick one of her nipples, when her hand slaps against my chest and pushes me back.

"Coffee," she demands sternly. "Then we'll go out on the beach."

"I changed my mind. I don't want to watch the sunrise. I want to fuck you instead." I reach my hand out for her but she rolls away, nimbly jumping out of the bed with surprising dexterity, given that she was sound asleep thirty seconds ago.

"Coffee. Then beach," she says as she slips on her t-shirt and pulls on the underwear and shorts that she discarded the night before.

"Cock blocked by the sunrise," I mutter, but I roll out of my side of the bed and head toward my closet. It is chilly this morning, so I need to wear my wetsuit. I pull out one of the dozen or so I have hanging in there, all compliments of my sponsors, and worm my way in. I leave the top half hanging around my waist.

After we each drink a quick cup of coffee, I grab one of my surfboards from the spare bedroom. Gabby grabs two blankets, and we make our way down to the beach. The surf looks okay, breaking at only about three feet, but I'll be able to play around out there for a bit.

Gabby spreads one of the blankets out at the base of the dunes, while I stick my board in the soft sand. She takes a seat in the middle, pulling the other blanket up over her legs and, rather than sit down to her side, I plop down behind her, pulling her back into my arms.

We gaze out over the water, watching the sun make its appearance. Before too long, we see bottlenose dolphins break the surface of the water, making their way south down the coast.

"I never get tired of seeing that," Gabby murmurs.

"Me either," I agree.

We're quiet for a few more moments, but then I ask, "What are your plans the rest of the day?"

She shrugs her shoulders. "I don't know. What about you?"

"Well," I start out as I lean down to nuzzle my nose into her neck. "I thought I would surf for a bit, then I thought I'd bring you back inside and make wild love to you. Sound like a plan?"

She laughs softly, leaning her head back on my shoulder. "Yeah... sounds like a plan."

"Oh, I forgot to tell you... my buddy John is

coming in tomorrow to visit for a while. He's going to be staying here, so I need to head to the grocery store today and stock up."

"Oh," she says quietly, and I know exactly what she's thinking. She's just too unsure of herself and of us to come out and say it. So I let her off the hook quickly.

"I still want you to stay over here with me, Gabs. You'll love John… and he wouldn't say anything to anyone."

She's quiet, reflective, and this doesn't bode well.

Tightening my arms around her, I say, "Please say you'll stay. I really want you to meet John but, more than that, I want you here."

My heart sighs in relief when she quietly says, "Okay."

Leaning around to her left so I can see her face, she turns to look at me. "Okay? So you'll stay?"

She gives me a small smile and nods. "I'll stay."

I reach up with my right hand and slip my fingers in her hair, grabbing a fistful and turning her head toward me further. Leaning in, I run my lips over hers lightly, and then pull back to look at her. "Good. I don't think I can go a single night without you."

Her eyes grow warm over my sentiment and, for the first time, I think Gabby may let her walls down around me a bit. Oh, she's fully engaged with me when I'm lodged deep inside her body, but when sexual heat isn't swirling between us, she's remained a tiny bit guarded.

I lean back into my original position and pull her back against me again, wrapping my arms around her stomach to hold her tight. The wind has kicked up a little and she shivers, pulling the blanket further up her chest.

"Cold?" I ask.

"A little."

"Bet I can warm you up," I tease her, resting my chin on her shoulder.

"Oh yeah?" she asks. "How's that?"

Rather than answer, I show her instead. I take one of my hands and move it down her stomach until I reach the button on her shorts. I can feel her sharp intake of breath when I pop it open.

She stiffens slightly when I grab onto the zipper and lower it.

"What are you doing?" she gasps.

I push my lips against her ear and say, "I'm warming you up."

Her hand reaches down and covers mine, halting my progress. "Hunter, we're out in public. Someone could walk by at any moment."

"So," I tell her as I grab her hand and push it away. "Besides… you have a blanket covering you. No one can see what we're doing. Just don't go screaming my name or anything."

When I skim my fingers under the top band of her underwear, she holds her body stiff for a moment but then capitulates. I know this because her legs fall open, giving me access.

I push my hand down the front of her underwear but, unfortunately, her shorts are too tight and my access is restricted.

"Need to get rid of the shorts, baby," I breathe into her ear.

"No," she says, shaking her head.

"Yes," I tell her as I start pushing the material down her hips. "Just lift your butt up a little, and I can get them off."

I know she wants to argue, and I know she's nervous about being seen, but I know more than anything she wants my hand between her legs. She looks down the beach left and then right, apparently satisfied no one is coming at the moment.

She lifts her butt up, and I push the material down. She adds her own hands into the mix and, within a few seconds, both her shorts and panties are down around her knees, and she's kicking them off. If anyone had been walking by, I'm sure all the motion under the blanket would have been a dead giveaway that she was stripping.

Settling the blanket back over her and pulling it up to her chest, she leans back against my chest, her head resting on my shoulder.

"Warm me up, Hunter," she says softly, and I lean in to kiss her on her temple.

"Your wish is my command."

I don't waste any effort exploring the softness of the skin on her legs. I bring my hand down right to her center and run my finger up. She sucks in her breath and arches her hips.

"You like that?" I whisper.

"Mmmm. Hmmm."

Tilting my head, I can see that her eyes are closed, her tongue peeking out between those full lips.

I run my finger up and down her wet center, circling right where she needs me. Her hips starting gyrating in response and I go fucking hard as a rock within my wetsuit, which is slightly uncomfortable. Movement from the corner of my eye catches my attention and I see a middle-aged couple strolling down the beach, stopping every few feet to pick up seashells. They haven't noticed us yet, but within a few more paces, they will.

"You need to stop moving so much," I tell her gently. "Someone's coming."

Gabby's hand covers mine again, trying to stop my movements against her. "Stop for a second, Hunter," she demands.

"No fucking way," I say, sinking a finger deep inside of her.

She cries out softly and bucks her hips against my hand, causing me to laugh softly in her ear.

"Better be still," I warn her. "They'll know if they look up here."

I add another finger and she clamps her legs tight against me, trying to hold me still. It's at this moment that the couple sees us, shooting us a friendly wave.

I bring my unoccupied hand out from under the blanket and wave back, shouting good morning. At the same time, I'm pulling my fingers out and sinking them back in.

A low groan comes out of Gabby's mouth, but she holds her body perfectly still. I pump my fingers in and out, adding my thumb to rub up against her. Another couple comes from our left, glancing our way and then continuing on down the beach.

The entire time, I slowly, tortuously, fuck Gabby with my fingers, murmuring for her to hold still as

people continue to walk by.

My girl does me proud and never moves a muscle. She does plenty of moaning and gasping, but the strollers are too far away to hear her. Finally, I feel her body stiffen and then start to shake as an orgasm tears through her. She bends her head down into the blanket to muffle her soft cries as they rip through her body.

I hold on tight to her, keeping my fingers lodged within her heat. Every few seconds, I feel a tremor run through her and she squeezes reflexively against me.

When her body finally quiets, I gently remove my hand and wrap my arms around her tight. Sticking my nose in her neck, I tell her, "That was just beautiful. Watching the sunrise with you and having you come on my hand."

She turns her head toward me, leaning in to give me a kiss. "I want to do that more often," she says with a smile.

I grin at her. "I've turned my girl into an exhibitionist, huh?"

"That was just intense," she says in wonder. "Trying to keep still. I wonder if we could fuck out here and get away with it."

I groan at the thought, leaning down and biting

her shoulder. "You are so bad."

"You led me down this path of sin and corruption," she reminds me.

"That I did," I say with a soft laugh.

The sun has risen completely from the water's edge, yet I have no desire to go out there and surf. I'm completely content to just sit here with Gabby and watch the waves break without me riding them. It makes me wonder what that says about my desire to compete again.

"They want me back on the Tour next year… my sponsors… my agent," I tell her quietly.

She turns her head to look at me briefly before gazing back out at the ocean. "What did you tell them?"

"I haven't told them anything other than I'd think about it. I was kind of wondering what you thought?"

She's quiet for a moment, but then she gives a little chuckle. "Remember when you were surfing in that amateur competition up at Jeanette's Pier when you were like twelve… thirteen or something?"

I'm surprised by her changing the subject. "The one where I sliced my head open?"

"Yeah, I remember… rather than quit, you had your dad run you up to the urgent care clinic and stitch your head up. You made it back in time for your next heat."

It's my turn to chuckle now. "Thirty-two stitches. Dad thought I was nuts, and Mom was beside herself."

"Yeah… but I thought it was the most amazing thing ever. Your dedication. You loved surfing and the competition so much, and you did whatever it took to get back out there."

I'm silent for a moment, digesting what she's saying. "So you think I should do it?"

"I think if you still have that love for the sport, you have to go back. And I think if you do have that love for the sport, you'll do whatever it takes to go back."

"I don't know what I feel for it. That's the problem."

"Well, how often do you think about it? Does it plague your thoughts?"

I don't answer, because I'm not sure Gabby is ready to hear the answer to those questions. Yes, I do think about it. Quite a bit. But it doesn't plague my thoughts. No, Gabby plagues my thoughts, but surfing doesn't.

When I don't give her an answer, she presses on. "Look, there's no reason why you can't go back.

Brody can run Last Call. I know you think he needs you, but he can manage without you. There's not a damn thing holding you here."

There's you, I think to myself, but I would never voice that aloud. Gabby doesn't want to hear that, and frankly, that's what I'm feeling right *now*. But will I feel that way next week? Next month? Next year when the Tour starts back up?

I give Gabby a last squeeze. "I'm going to hit the surf. Think you can manage to get your shorts back on without me?"

"I think I can suffer through it," she says drily.

After a quick kiss on the temple, I jump up from the blanket. Thank God my hard-on has subsided.

I stand in front of her, pulling up the top half of my wetsuit while she shimmies slightly under the blanket to get her clothes back on.

"So, you'll stay the rest of the day with me? I don't have to go into the bar at all today."

"Sure. I'm going to stay out here and watch you a bit though."

I reflect upon her lovely face for a moment. The sun is still casting orange and pink, and it makes her hazel eyes sparkle. She's looking at me, her eyes wide and her head tilted slightly at an angle.

I wonder what she feels for me. Is she still

carrying around deep feelings, or did I crush them completely five years ago?

Is this just sex to her, or does she want something more? By the mere fact that she doesn't want anyone to know about us, I'm thinking this is just sex.

I'm a dude though, and that should be perfectly fine by me, right?

Right?

Hmmm. I wish I knew for sure.

THIRTEEN

Gabby

"So... have you given any more thought to telling Casey about you and Hunter?" Alyssa asks as we watch Casey get us another round of drinks at the bar.

Casey stands in all of her full vixen glory, wearing a pair of designer jeans, a baby doll camisole, and peep-toe pumps. She has her hair up in a high ponytail with large hoop earrings glistening from the backlighting behind the bar. Every guy in the place, regardless of whether they are single or sitting with their significant other, is checking her out in some way.

And she's not oblivious to it all. No, Casey is very much aware of the affect she has on the male persuasion, as evidenced by the way she stands on the railing at the bottom of the bar, her elbows resting on the glossy wood and her ass sticking out.

She says something to Brody as he makes our drinks, and he actually gives her a half smile. I can see him warming up more and more each day.

Turning my attention back to Alyssa, I shake my head. "No… but I will. I'm just trying to figure out how."

"Usually, opening your mouth and letting words come out works pretty well."

I give her a ferocious glare. "Smart-ass."

My eyes slide over to Hunter as he stands at the end of the bar, watching the crowd. He rarely works if he comes here at night, preferring to just be present and keep an eye on things. Brody has been managing the bar and the staff just fine, and it's been a calculated move on Hunter's part to give him that responsibility. It makes me wonder if he's already started the grooming process on Brody, so he can make his escape back to the Tour.

It's crowded for a late-April, Monday night, which is great. Normally the heavy tourist season won't start until after Memorial Day, but I expect Last Call is quite the novelty now that Hunter has taken it over and done a basic refurbish. He had to fire most of Salty's old staff because they were lazy or skimming money, but his new staff is friendly—with the exception of Brody—and efficient. He replaced all the old booths because the leather was dried and cracked, and the Formica top tables went as well, replaced with heavy wood pieces.

The last thing he did before reopening under the name Last Call was to redo the decor by taking down all of Salty's lame-ass fish netting that he used to conceal cracks in the wall, repair the damage, and decorate with a surfing motif. Large photo prints of surfers riding Superbank in Australia, The Bubble in the Canary Islands, or Cloud Nine off Siargao Island hang on the walls, along with surfboards, surf shop prints, and plaques that said things like "If It Swells, Ride It," and "No Waves, No Glory." A huge, life-size print of Hunter taken from inside a wave as it curled over him hung on the west wall, and I found myself staring at that just as often as I stared at him.

He was glorious. His wet hair slapped across his forehead as he crouched on his board, aiming right at the photographer. His right arm stretched out, his fingers dragging through the wave as the barrel rolled over him. He was looking straight at the camera when the photo was snapped and, when I stared at it, it seemed like he was looking directly at me.

It's mesmerizing... just like Hunter himself.

The only reason I'm here on a Monday night is because Hunter is here. Otherwise, I'd be at his house with him. He'd probably either be riding me hard or taking me slowly... you just never knew with Hunter. But he asked me to come out and hang here tonight because his buddy, John, would be showing up soon. He had flown into Raleigh and rented a car to drive in, and he and Hunter arranged to meet here and have a beer or two before heading home.

I pointed out to Hunter that there was no need for me to come out. It's not like we could really interact, at least not without giving away something. And I could certainly meet John another day.

But he had insisted... telling me that even if he couldn't touch me, he wanted to look at me. That warmed me straight through to my toes. Of course, he told me that this morning, just before he pinned me up against the wall of the shower and pushed himself into me from behind. Just the memory of that has me squeezing my legs together to ease the ache

I'm feeling.

Hunter slides his gaze around the room, his eyes coming to rest on mine. He stares at me hard, his eyes burning and needy. I have to swallow twice to get past the lump that is there, because the way he's looking at me right now makes me feel like the most special and cherished individual in the entire world. It makes me want to stand on top of our table and shout out to the world, "Hunter Markham is mine."

But I won't, because even if that was something I had the freedom to proclaim, I'm too afraid that I'm not his and would never get the same sentiment back.

Shaking my head from those morose thoughts, I tear my gaze away from Hunter and watch as Casey carries over our drinks. We decided to go with Bloody Marys this evening because Brody makes a damn spicy drink, and they are on special tonight.

When Casey takes her seat, we all grab a glass and hold it up for a toast. We always do that every time we have a fresh drink, feeling the need to praise something good in our lives.

"It's Alyssa's turn," I point out.

Smiling, Alyssa says, "To Guiseppe… who is the wizened old, Italian man that handpicked the olives that rest inside of our drinks right now. Thank you, dear friend, for making this drink fantastic."

"Here, here," Casey and I shout out, and then knock our glasses against one another while laughing.

"We're starting to run out of things to toast to," I say as I set my glass down.

"Speak for yourself," Alyssa admonishes. "I think Guiseppe was completely deserving of that toast."

"So, did Brody talk to you about doing his community service at The Haven?" Casey asks Alyssa. "Hunter had mentioned it to him."

Alyssa's mouth sets in a firm line. "I stopped by here late last week to grab a sandwich for dinner and asked him about it. He was noncommittal."

Something about Alyssa's tone doesn't sound quite right, and she looks angry. This is something to behold, because it takes a lot to get Alyssa angry. She has the patience of a saint and the disposition of a sweet, fuzzy Golden Retriever.

Casey notices it too and prods her. "You're holding something back. What happened?"

Alyssa shrugs, bringing a smile to her face to hide her discomfort. "It was nothing."

"Alyssa," Casey warns, implying she better cough up the truth or Casey was apt to beat it out of her. Well, maybe hold her down and tickle her, but you didn't want to get on Casey's bad side.

"It's fine. He was just a little... um... rude when I approached him about it."

Brody rude? That surprises me. While he's quiet and withdrawn, and not full of the warm and fuzzies, he's never been rude. Not even prison could do that to him, I'm sure.

"How was he rude?" Casey asks, not disbelieving but interested in hearing more about her brother... the man she was trying to get to know again.

"Maybe it was just my imagination, or maybe I'm too sensitive. But he sort of barked at me that he wasn't interested."

"Oh, hell no," Casey exclaims. "He's not getting away with that shit, especially when you were just trying to help him. I'll talk to him—"

Alyssa sticks her arm out and touches Casey's arm. "No, don't. If anyone has a right to be that way, it's Brody. Just leave him be. I'm sure he was having a bad day or something."

"Who's having a bad day?" Hunter asks as he sits down.

And just like that, my head starts swimming... because Hunter is sitting at our table. His gaze slides over me briefly before landing on Alyssa, but in just that microsecond, a world of meaning was conveyed. I saw it, but I hope no one else did.

He said, *I want to kiss you right now, Gabs, and then I want to take you home and fuck you into tomorrow.*

This makes me yearn deeply because even though Hunter wants me to still stay over at night with him, I'm thinking I should go home to my apartment to give him and John some time to catch up with each other.

"Nothing," Alyssa says quickly, shooting a firm look to Casey to keep her mouth shut. Casey returns a smirk to her but remains silent.

Just then, Hunter's gaze snags onto something behind Alyssa. At first, his face breaks out into a wide smile, then just as quickly, it dims, and his mouth sets into a flat line. I turn slightly to see what Hunter is looking at and notice a man and woman who just walked into the bar. The guy has dark hair that he wears all one length just down to his jawline, and he's dressed casually in shorts and a t-shirt. The woman also has dark hair, which is long and loose. She's wearing a print maxi-dress with gold sandals peeking out. They are a beautiful couple that I assume are tourists, although that doesn't explain Hunter's reaction to them.

The man and woman spy Hunter at our table and start walking toward us. Hunter stands up and steps a few feet away from the table to greet them.

"I'll be damned," Casey says in wonder.

My eyes flick to her. "What?"

"That's John and Sasha Hammer. I didn't realize Sasha was coming."

"Is that John's wife?" I ask.

Shaking her head, Casey says, "No, it's his sister... and Hunter's ex-girlfriend."

Ex-girlfriend? What?

Turning around, I watch as Hunter and John clasp hands and pull each other in for a half-hug, half-back slap, both of them grinning broadly. When they pull away, Hunter turns to Sasha and I watch with my breath stuck in my lungs. As if in slow motion, Sasha moves in toward Hunter, seemingly to give him a hug... which okay, nothing wrong with that.

Hunter's face is impassive, and I'm dying to know what feelings he has going through him right at this very moment. Just as they are getting ready to embrace, Sasha wraps her arms around Hunter's neck, plasters her body to his, and kisses him. And not a friendly kiss on the cheek, or even a quick peck on the lips. Her mouth opens up over his, and I even see her tongue slide into his mouth. Hunter's hands come to her shoulders, and she angles her head in for a deeper kiss.

I wish I could adequately describe the flood of

rage that overwhelms me at this very moment. Rage toward Sasha for kissing Hunter, and rage toward Hunter for kissing her back. And rage against myself for ever even hoping that I could have something with Hunter.

A hazy film of red covers my eyes, and I stand up so abruptly from the table that my thighs hit the edge and cause my drink to topple. Luckily, it flies in the opposite direction of me... straight at Casey for that matter, who also jumps up from the table to avoid having a lap full of Bloody Mary while she yells, "Fuck."

I turn to grab my purse, and I can see from the corner of my eye that Hunter and Sasha have broken apart. As I turn toward him, he's watching me with wary eyes, while Sasha's seem smug and defiant.

Lacing my voice with as much venom as I can, I snarl at him, "You're an asshole."

Turning toward the front of the bar, I stalk across the floor, slinging my purse over my shoulder. I hear Casey call my name, but I don't stop. Brody shoots me a worried glance as I walk by, and then I'm outside in the cool, spring night air.

I stop just outside of the door and take a deep breath, trying to calm myself. I'm seething... beyond furious, and there's no telling what kind of havoc I left back in there with my outburst.

Turning my head left and right, I realize I don't even have a ride. Casey drove tonight, and we were planning to cab it home. No worries... I take off toward the highway, intent on walking home. It's only a few miles.

"Gabby, wait," I hear Hunter call out.

I ignore him and quicken my pace. The sound of his shoes crunching through the gravel start getting louder and before I can even reach the end of the parking lot, he's grabbing my elbow.

Tearing away from his grasp, I snarl, "Get the fuck off me."

He just grabs ahold of me again, this time around the waist, lifting me up and turning me back toward Last Call. I kick my legs out and try to pry his arms away, but he's too strong and sure-footed.

"Let me go, Hunter," I cry out in frustration.

"Not until you settle down and talk to me."

"There's nothing to talk about. You're an asshole." I start really struggling to get out of his bear hug, and he has to set me down and re-tighten his hold. He does this by quickly releasing and re-wrapping his arms around my chest, pinning my arms down at my side.

"Will you just listen?" he shouts when I start to

struggle again. "You're acting like a brat."

That just infuriates me more, giving me the strength to almost bust out of his grip. He surprises me then by letting go but, before I can think to flee, he spins me around and crushes me to him, his mouth coming down hard on mine. For a split second, I kiss him back but then my anger returns. I rip away from him and wipe my mouth, not in a show to dig at him, but because I'm truly disgusted.

"How dare you kiss me after you just kissed another woman?" I say as I stare at him wildly.

"I didn't fucking kiss her," he snarls back at me. "She kissed me, and if you'd waited just a second longer before you jumped up from the table, you would have seen me push her away."

"Whatever," I snap at him. "I know what I saw."

"No, you don't," he says tiredly. "You clearly don't. You're wrong, Gabby."

"What the hell is going on?" I hear Casey from behind me, and I turn to see her furiously stalking across the parking lot toward us. She comes to a stand before us, her arms crossed defensively over her chest. All of my anger toward Hunter gets pushed to the back of my mind, because now I'm dealing with an enraged Casey Markham.

She looks back and forth between the two of us,

waiting for an answer. Hunter sort of turns away and laces his fingers together on top of his head, holding his face up to the sky as if he's praying for patience and serenity.

"I repeat—what is going on?" she asks again, this time with an underlying menace in her voice that makes me cringe. Over her shoulder, I spy Brody walking out of the bar, but he doesn't approach us. Rather, he just stands there, his hands in his pockets, watching all of us carefully.

"Gabby," Casey barks. "Why did you call Hunter an asshole in there?"

Hunter turns toward me, curious as to what I'll say. My gaze falters and falls to the ground, where I kick at the loose pebbles in the parking lot. I can't lie to her... but apparently, I can't look her in the eye either. "Um... Hunter and I have been seeing each other, and I was mad when he kissed that woman."

"I did not kiss her," Hunter grits out, and my head snaps up to his.

"Sure looked like it to me," I throw back at him.

"Whatever," he says in resignation.

"You two have been seeing each other?" Casey asks quietly. "For how long?"

"A couple of weeks," Hunter says.

"And you kept it secret... from me?" The hurt is

evident in her voice, and I feel lower than I've ever felt in my life. Suddenly, the fact that Hunter was kissing—or had been kissed—a few moments ago seems irrelevant.

"Casey," I say as I take a step toward her with apology in my voice. "I was going to tell you. I just—"

"Don't," she snaps at me, holding up her hand. "There's nothing you could say to justify it. You were my best friend…"

Were? As in past tense?

"Casey, I'm sorry," I say urgently.

"Just stop," she hisses. "You're selfish, Gabby… selfish and disloyal, sneaking around… sinking your claws into my brother. You're despicable."

"Now just a minute," Hunter growls at Casey, stepping up to my side. "I went after Gabby, not the other way around."

Casey turns her eyes toward Hunter, blazing bright blue with anger. "Nice to know you were complicit in this, Hunter. You two deserve each other then. Just stay the hell away from me."

Spinning away from us, Casey stomps back to the bar, pushing past Brody, who stands silently, watching it all. Tears well up in my eyes, and I feel so unbelievably helpless.

It appears I've lost my best friend, all because I was too afraid to tell her the truth. And Hunter... well, I've probably lost him too, seeing as how I might have misconstrued the "kiss" situation.

Before the first teardrop falls though, Hunter is pulling me into his arms and tucking my head against his chest. "It'll be okay, Gabs. She's just angry, but she'll come around. She didn't mean those things."

Squeezing my eyes shut to dispel the moisture hanging heavy in them, I nod my head in agreement, although I'm not really sure Casey is going to get over this.

Pulling back slightly, Hunter uses his hand to push my chin up so I look at him. "I swear to you... I did not kiss her. She caught me by surprise, but I pushed her away as soon as I got my bearings. I have no fucking clue what she's doing here."

"I'm sorry," I whisper. "I shouldn't have gotten so mad, and now I've ruined everything. I've embarrassed you, pissed Casey off..."

Leaning down, Hunter kisses me softly, gently holding my head. "Don't worry about it. It will be fine."

Nodding my head, I step back. "Listen, I'm going to head home. You need to go take care of your guests. We can talk more tomorrow."

On the ROCKS

"I'll take you home," Hunter says, understanding it would not be a good idea for me to go to his house tonight. A slight surge of jealousy hits me that Sasha will be staying there with her brother—at least, I assume she will be—but Hunter really hasn't given me any reason to distrust him.

"No," I tell him as I lay a hand on his chest. "I'll get a cab. Go inside and check on Casey... and like I said, you have guests who came in to see you."

Hunter looks unsure, glancing between the bar and me. Finally, he calls over his shoulder to Brody, who's still standing by the door. "Can you take her home?"

"Sure," he says quietly. "Let me go get my keys."

Hunter steps back up to me, reaching a hand up to cup me behind me head. He looks at me, pinning me hard with assurance. "It will be fine, Gabs. Trust me."

I nod even though I completely disbelieve that this could in any way turn out okay.

FOURTEEN

Hunter

Well, if one good thing came out of the fiasco of tonight, at least Gabby and I are out in the open.

Assuming I still have Gabby.

After I loaded her in the car with Brody, I went inside to do damage control. I found Casey in the bathroom crying, while Alyssa tried to talk to her. I walked in there, ordering another customer who was primping in the mirror out, and tried to set things right.

"Casey... please don't be mad at Gabby. She was struggling with what to do, and she was scared."

Glaring at me, she blew her nose while Alyssa patted her on the back and said, "How could you both keep that from me? What does that say about the way you trust me?"

"You didn't react all that well, Case," I point out. "You told Gabby she had 'sunk her claws' in me. Maybe that's what she was afraid of."

"I was madder that she kept it secret, not that she was seeing you."

"It didn't come out that way," I said gently. "But it's done. You need to move past it and forgive her for not telling you. We all make mistakes."

She huffed at that statement, but I ignored it. I gave her a hug, told her I loved her, and suggested she go home and get some rest. They left not long after that.

The more awkward part of the night came from having to deal with Sasha. By the time I finished talking to Casey, Brody had made it back to cover the bar. I headed home with John and Sasha following me in their rental car. The ride was all too short because I was stewing with what to say when we got there.

After giving them a brief tour of my house,

telling Sasha she could have the spare bedroom, and making up the couch for John, I pulled John aside while Sasha was in the bathroom.

"What the hell, man? Why did you bring her?"

"I didn't, dude. Not intentionally. I told her where I was going, and she showed up at the fucking airport this morning. What was I supposed to do, tell her she couldn't come?"

"Yeah, John," I said angrily. "That's exactly what you should have done."

"I'm sorry," he said with genuine remorse. "Do you want us to head back tomorrow?"

My shoulders sagged, and I felt bad for snapping at him. "No, of course not. You can stay as long as you want. But Sasha needs to understand there is nothing between us. And I'm with someone else."

Choosing that moment to join us, Sasha came in wearing a pair of the shortest shorts possible, which could barely still be classified as shorts and not underwear, and a tight t-shirt. She had always been overtly sexual, wearing clothes that showed a lot of skin. I had appreciated it back when we were together... now, not so much.

Turning toward her, I tell her calmly, "That display back at the bar... don't let it happen again, Sasha. I have a girlfriend, and she doesn't take well to that stuff. Neither do I for that matter."

"Oh, Hunter," she said in exasperation as she plopped down on my couch, kicking her long, bare legs up on my coffee table. "Stop being such a stick in the mud. I was just greeting an old friend hello."

"You don't greet friends by sticking your tongue down their throat."

Sasha laughed then, even as she picked up the remote control to turn the TV on, and it was rich, warm, and sexy. It grated on my nerves.

"I got it. No tongue down your throat, but it's your loss," she said with a sexy purr.

"I'm serious, Sasha," I barked at her. "That shit was not cool."

Whatever it was about the tone of my voice finally caused her to turn around to stare at me. At first, her face was hard and her eyes cold. But then it softened and she nodded her head at me. "I'm sorry, Hunter. Really. I promise you have nothing to worry about, and I'm happy for you that you found someone."

She sounded sincere, even as I held her gaze to see if she would avert her eyes and prove to me she wasn't. But she held true, staring straight at me, so I finally gave her a small smile. "Thanks. I appreciate that."

I hoped none of this made John feel uncomfortable, but it was a little too late to take any of it back. Turning to him, I said, "Will you be okay here on your own for a bit? I'm going to go see Gabby."

"Sure," John returned genially. "Take your time. We're good here."

I smiled at him in thanks. "Thanks, dude. Wanna catch some waves in the morning?"

"Absolutely," he said, grinning back at me.

So here I am at Gabby's apartment, knocking on the door. Within moments, it's opened by Savannah. She gives me a warm smile.

"Hey," she says as I walk in. "I thought you might be by."

I raise my eyebrows at her perceptiveness, because she hardly knows me. "Is she okay?"

"She'll be fine, I'm sure. She's in her bedroom."

"Thanks," I tell her quietly as I walk past.

When I reach Gabby's bedroom, I turn the knob and open the door, not even bothering to knock. She doesn't have anything I haven't seen before, but the sight that greets me is unbelievably stellar. I catch her in the midst of changing her clothes. She stands with her back to me, wearing nothing but her bra and underwear. Her panties are nothing but a scrap of cream-colored lace that appears more thong than anything, revealing both globes of her tight ass. Yeah, my dick stands up and takes notice, and it also doesn't miss the fact her arms are bent behind her back, unsnapping her bra. Her back is a work of art unto itself, with her dark hair hanging long and wavy over it and smooth skin for miles below that.

She hears the door open and turns toward me, just as the straps of her bra slide down her shoulders. She's holding the cups over her breasts as she stares at me in surprise.

Gabby is a fucking vision, holding her bra up to cover herself in an uncharacteristic display of modesty, her golden skin complimenting the cream color of her lingerie. I want to tear them off her with my teeth.

But then I notice that her eyes are slightly red, and it's at this moment that I realize she's been crying.

Stepping inside her room, I shut the door and walk over to her dresser, pulling out a t-shirt, and laying it across one of my shoulders to free my hands. She watches me silently, still holding her hands over her breasts, the lace of her bra stuck in between.

Turning toward her, I cup her face with my hands and give her a tender kiss. Then I put my hands over hers and pull them away, the bra falling to the floor at our feet.

She stares at me with wide eyes, blinking slowly over my actions. Her head tilts to the side in curiosity, because I've never been able to keep my hands off her when she's naked and it must be confusing to her that I am doing so at this moment.

I take the t-shirt and slip it over her head, and she automatically threads her arms through. When it's settled over her, I reach to the back of her neck and pull her long hair out.

Taking her hand, I lead her to the bed, pulling her covers back.

"Get in," I tell her.

She follows my orders blindly, crawling onto the sheets, and I pull the covers up over her. As I walk to the other side of the bed, she finally speaks. "What are you doing here?"

I kick off my flip-flops and take off my own t-shirt. "I wanted to come see you. Make sure you're okay."

Quickly shedding my shorts so I'm in nothing but my boxers, I crawl into bed beside her and turn on my side. She does the same, and we just stare at each other a moment.

"You didn't need to come over, Hunter."

"I know," I tell her simply. "It was a matter of

wanting to come over here."

"But you have guests... John and Sasha are staying at your house, right?"

"Yup. But I doubt they'll miss me tonight. I'm sure they're just looking for a good night's sleep after traveling all day."

"I'm sure Sasha will miss you," she says in a small voice.

Reaching my hand out, I stroke my fingers down her cheek and to her jaw. When I reach her chin, I pinch it firmly and say, "Hey... there's nothing between Sasha and me."

"But there was," she points out.

"Yes, there was, but no more."

"Tell me what happened."

Sighing, I reach out to Gabby and pull her into my arms as I roll onto my back. I situate her so her head is on my chest and her body is pressed up against my side. She moves her leg over mine and drapes her arm over my stomach. The warmth and softness of her body immediately both soothes me and causes my blood to race. A contradiction... just like Gabby.

"We dated... pretty seriously, for a while. She was on the women's pro tour and traveled with John and me to the competitions. She took a bad spill though and got injured… wasn't able to compete anymore. Things sort of went south once she moved back home to California."

"The long distance?"

"Yeah. She wanted me to retire, move to California, and marry her. I tried to go there to see her as much as possible while we worked on those issues, but we just drifted further and further apart. I broke things off with her a little over a year ago. It wasn't pleasant."

Gabby is quiet but her thumb is stroking over my ribs as she holds on to me, and I let myself get lulled by the sensation.

"Why did she kiss you?" Gabby's voice floats over the quiet.

"I have no clue. Honestly… our last words were bitter, and I haven't talked to her since. I figured she'd just as soon slap me as kiss me."

"And Casey?"

Gabby's words are hesitant and fearful all at once. I realize suddenly that she could give a rat's ass about Sasha and our history. She was leading up to the information she really wanted… whether or not she had a best friend anymore.

"She's angry we didn't tell her, but she'll get over it."

"But… she didn't seem to care for the fact I was with you. Said I had my claws in you."

"She said that in anger—trust me," I tell her, squeezing her waist where I'm holding on to her.

"But… she sounded so disgusted by it. I don't think she thinks I should be with you. She didn't seem too mad at you."

"Gabs," I murmur to her with patience. "I'm telling you… she'll be fine. She's probably over it already. You guys fight… it happens."

She doesn't say anything for a moment, but when she does, it tears my heart up. "I'm not good enough for you."

I release my hold on her and roll over, pushing her on her back. Hovering over her, I ask, "What? Why would you think that?"

Gabby stares at me a moment, her eyes haunted with insecurity, and it makes me want to strip her naked, slide into her, and fuck the doubt right out of her. But that's not appropriate, nor does it address the issue.

"You are amazing and way too good for the likes of me," I tell her sincerely. "Look what I did to you five years ago… and you gave me another chance."

She shakes her head in denial. "No—don't you see? Casey doesn't think I should be with you. It's why I didn't tell her, because I knew deep down she wouldn't approve. And I can't measure up to someone like Sasha. I mean, geez, Hunter... she was a pro surfer, and she's beautiful. She belongs in your world. I don't."

"Gabby, you're wrong about this. Casey will come around, and as far as Sasha... well, you're just really wrong about that. She doesn't hold a candle to you... I promise."

She doesn't believe me... I can tell.

Which is frustrating, because Gabby is a very smart girl and you can usually appeal to her common sense. Apparently, she's lost every bit that she used to possess, because my words aren't penetrating.

So if words won't make her understand, the only way is to show her with action.

Acting decisively, I move my body over hers, settling against the heat between her legs. My dick starts to grow hard from the contact.

Gabby's eyes go wide. "What are you doing?"

"There's apparently no reasoning with you, so I'm going to show you why we are good together."

I lean down to kiss her, but she stops me dead. "This is just sex, Hunter. It doesn't mean we belong together."

Her words piss me off, and she's in a mindset

that I'm not sure I can change right now, but I still feel compelled to push back. "Wrong, Gabs. It's more than 'just sex,' and you know it. People that just have sex don't sleep together at night, their arms tightly holding on to each other, even in slumber. People that just have sex don't watch morning sunrises together, nor do they go grocery shopping together. More importantly, I've known you most of my life. I've watched you grow up and, once upon a time, I crushed your young heart. Then you forgave my foolishness and invited me inside your body. So you better believe your sweet ass that this is more than 'just sex'. It's a whole lot more and, if you'd just accept that, things would go a lot smoother between the two of us."

With my tirade over, Gabby just stares at me, blinking rapidly. I search for some type of reaction in her eyes… anything to give me a clue if I should kiss her or get dressed and leave.

The reaction I get is not expected. Gabby's lips curl north, and then split into a blinding smile. "That was quite a mouthful, Mr. Markham."

I'm relieved by her reaction, so it is no hardship to smile back at her. "I'm glad you think so. Does that mean you understand and accept what I'm saying?"

"I'm not an idiot," she pouts prettily. I have to

dig my nails into my palms not to lean down and bite her lower lip.

"But do you really mean that... that Casey will get over this?" She's still truly worried about that, and I get it.

"Yes," I promise her. "She'll get over it. You should have seen the nasty look she threw Sasha's way before she left. She may be pissed at us right now, but she's not happy that Sasha kissed me. She considered that a direct slap toward you, not me."

Gabby rewards me with another smile. "You're not just saying that, are you? You know... so you can get laid tonight?"

I flex my hips forward and push my erection up against her. "Oh, I'm getting laid tonight. I'm not worried about that."

She giggles. As I lean down to kiss her, she does something that starts my blood flowing hotly. She brings her hands up against my chest and pushes me off her, flipping me on my back and rolling over on top of me.

Straddling me with her knees firmly gripping my hips and my dick pressed hotly against her backside, she looks down at me and licks her lower lip. Reaching a hand out, she rubs the pad of her thumb across one of my nipples, and I feel it all the way into my groin.

"We're going to be okay?" she asks me while she watches her thumb move against me.

"Yes," I tell her sincerely.

"And we care for each other, right?" She tilts her head slightly, still keeping her eyes pinned to what she's doing to me.

"For almost our entire lives."

"And it's more than just sex?" She asks this last question as she reaches her other hand back behind her, snaking her fingers into the fly of my boxers. Her hand surrounds my dick and she gently squeezes me, causing me to twitch from the contact.

She waits for me to answer, but the words are stuck in my throat because she now takes up a stroking pattern on my cock. When nothing is forthcoming, her eyes slide up to mine and whatever she sees reflected causes her to smile just a tiny bit.

"It's okay," she assures me. "I'm going to expound on the sex thing right now... We can talk more later."

Gabby leans down and flicks her tongue over the nipple she had just been torturing with her thumb, and I can't stop the grunt that comes out. She peeks up at me, giving me a mischievous look.

Then she scoots back down my body, dragging

my boxers down with her as she goes. After she pulls them free from my legs and tosses them over her shoulder, she kneels back with her palms on her thighs and just gazes at me.

"You're such a beautiful man," she says in reverence.

Before I can even compliment her back, I watch, stunned, as she lifts one hand and puts it against her own chest. Then she slides her fingers down her breastbone, down her stomach, and right down into the front of her lace panties. My jaw hangs open as her hand sinks down... way down, and while the lace of her underwear obscures most of my vision, I can tell she just sunk a finger into herself.

Holy. Fucking. Hot.

My dick swells violently and I start to sit up to attack her, when her hand reappears. She bends forward and runs her wet finger across the tip of my cock, and I am absolutely mesmerized by the sight.

"I think I'm ready for you," she whispers as she looks up to me.

"Oh God... that is so fucking hot. I think if you touch me right now, I might come."

She laughs in delight over my proclamation, although I'm not kidding... I can feel a prickle already at the base of my spine, and she has hardly touched me.

Gabby crawls up my body and straddles me, setting down low and rubbing herself against me. The friction of her lace panties, which I can feel are indeed soaking wet, causes me to groan while my hands come up to grip her hips.

I don't know that I've ever been hornier in my entire life, and I ache deeply for her.

"Gabby… get your underwear off… please," I practically beg her.

She looks at me, her eyes gentle with understanding. "It's not needed."

What? Huh? Is she saying we aren't going to have sex?

Oh, hell no.

I start to sit up to roll her over and pound my way inside of her, but she rises up over my lap and takes my cock in her hand. With her other hand, she merely reaches down and pulls her underwear aside before settling down on the very tip of me.

Holding her gaze, not for a moment daring to look away, I'm enraptured by the desire in her eyes as she lowers herself over me, the lace of her panties stretched to the side to accommodate my length.

Both of us can't suppress our moans as she seats herself fully on me, and I have to bite down on the inside of my cheek not to blow inside of her. Thankfully, she holds still for just a moment, her eyes closing while she relishes the feel of me inside her.

When her eyes open up, they are nuclear... flames of lust leaping out. She rises up over me and comes back down slowly, causing my own eyes to roll into the back of my head.

My voice sounds garbled when I try to talk. "Gabby... feels good... don't stop."

"I won't," she assures me as she picks up the pace.

How I hold off my orgasm is beyond me, but I have to make sure she gets there before me... preferably with me. My fears are unfounded though, because the faster Gabby fucks me, the faster I can see her building up. Her telltale signs are a high blush that sits on her cheeks and spreads down her throat to her chest. I know she's close. When I reach out a hand and press it up against the juncture of her thighs, she slams down on me hard and starts to climax. That tips me straight over the edge and I grab her hips again, thrusting up inside her a few more times before I start to come, my orgasm ricocheting through my body almost painfully.

Utterly spent, Gabby falls forward on my chest and I hug her tight to me. After our breathing returns to normal, I shift so we are on our side and tuck her in tighter to me. I know I should head home, so I can be there if John and Sasha need something, but for the life of me, I can't find it within me to care enough to move from this embrace.

FIFTEEN

Gabby

I'm fixing this shit with Casey, and I'm fixing it now. I awoke this morning with my heart feeling lighter, particularly on the heels of Hunter assuring me that Casey was just hurt because we kept this secret, and not because she doesn't want me with her brother. I still have a little fear over that, but there's no way to know for sure unless I go talk to her.

As soon as my alarm went off at six AM, I pushed Hunter out of my bed—yes, he stayed all night—and I grabbed a quick shower because I was eager to start the day. I didn't even bother to dry my hair, letting it hang wet down my back, and I was out the door, munching on an apple for breakfast.

It's almost seven AM by the time I make it to the Markham residence in the tiny town of Avon, which sits on Hatteras Island where we all grew up. The classic stilt house that sits two streets off the ocean is weathered and worn, but you can tell just by looking at it that there's a lot of love inside. You can see glimpses of the Atlantic from the back porch, and the blue waters of the Pamlico Sound from the front porch, making it an idyllic location. Even though Hunter and I live in Nags Head now—which is slightly more exciting than Avon—we still spent a lot of time on Hatteras Island because our parents are still there. In fact, my mom lives just three streets over but she's out of town on a trip to Atlantic City with her poker buddies. Otherwise, I'd be stopping in to pay her a visit, too.

I park my car in the sandy driveway and walk up the long flight of steps to the front porch. When I ring the bell, I'm greeted by Casey's mom, Lillian. She's a nurse at The Outer Banks Hospital, and I wasn't sure if she'd be on shift or not. I didn't expect her dad, Butch, to be home. He's a fisherman and would be out on the water at dawn. Hunter, Brody, and Casey definitely got their coloring from theirmother… golden hair streaked by the sun and glorious blue eyes. They got their love of the water from their dad, just in the form of surfing rather than fishing.

"There's my girl," Lillian says as she opens the door wider, and I step into the warm hug she offers me. "I heard you and Casey got into a spat last night."

I figured Lillian would know, just assuming Casey came home and sobbed on her mom's shoulder. They were very close and shared pretty much everything.

"How is she?" I ask, chewing on my bottom lip in worry.

"Well, I haven't seen her yet, so I'm not sure. I was asleep when she got home, but I'm sure you'll be able to patch it up… no worries."

I blink in surprise. "If you haven't seen her, how do you know about our fight?"

"Hunter called me about half an hour ago to give me a heads up. He said you'd be coming over here to talk to her."

That absolutely amazes me. I never said a word to Hunter that I was going to come see Casey. In fact, I was on my way over to Last Call when I got the wild hair up my butt and decided to just nip this in the bud. The fact that Hunter seemed to know me a bit better than I knew myself freaks me out a bit, but I push that thought aside. I have to deal with Casey now.

Casey and Brody still live at home, which in the grand scheme of things seems pretty lame. Brody actually has an excuse since he just got out of prison and needed to acclimate, but I bet anything he'll be getting his own place before too long. Casey is a different story. She never held down a job long enough to afford to move out, and I didn't have high hopes for that with the way the real estate market is right now.

"So... uh, did Hunter tell you what the fight was about?"

Lillian gives me a knowing smile. "Come on... let's have a cup of coffee. Casey will be up soon, but you and I can talk for a bit."

Oh, just great. Lillian and I were going to talk about my relationship with her son. I couldn't think of anything I'd rather be doing more—which is definitely my sarcastic voice coming out.

I plop down at the kitchen table, while Lillian busies herself with pouring the coffee. My shoulders hunch forward and I sink down into the chair, mentally preparing to shield myself for whatever may be coming.

"What did Hunter tell you exactly?" I ask hesitantly, dreading what she may know.

"He told me everything, Gabby, starting from when he broke your heart five years ago and ending with him staying at your house last night."

My face flames red at the thought of Hunter's mom knowing such intimate details about my relationship with her son. I'm hugely mortified that she knows I had crushed on him and stupidly tried to kiss him—no correction, did kiss him—when I was eighteen. I'm even more embarrassed that she knows we spent the night together. Not that she doesn't know her kids have sex. I mean, hello... we're adults. But I just don't like it so blatantly shoved in her face.

"And you get that look off your face right now, Gabby Ward," she says to me sternly. My eyes snap up to hers, and I see she's giving me the "mom" look, which means she's not going to tolerate something. I'm just not sure exactly what it is she's censuring me for.

I open my mouth to say something, but before I can, she sits down and leans across the table toward me a bit. "Gabby... I'm thrilled you and Hunter are together. You're like my daughter... a part of this family. I cannot think of a better woman for my son than you."

My mouth hangs open, and I stare at her agog. "Seriously?"

"Seriously. And why wouldn't I feel that way? You know I love you, right?"

"Yes, but…" My mind runs amok. It seems so silly that I was concerned about this… about how the family would feel, and that was part of the reason I wanted to hide it.

"But what?" she asks gently.

"I don't think Casey approves," I say in a quiet voice. "And I won't ruin my friendship with Casey over Hunter."

Lillian sits back in her chair and makes a snorting sound. "First… if Casey would make you choose between her and Hunter, then Casey doesn't deserve you as a friend. But I know my daughter, and I know deep down she would love the idea of you and Hunter together. She loves you like I do… more even. Trust me, Casey *will* approve of this."

"Hunter said she's just mad we kept it secret."

"I suspect that's the case." Lillian stands and leans over to kiss me on top of my head. "Now head back to her room and make sure she's up for work… but don't leave out of here without resolving things."

I stand up and give Lillian a smile before I head

down the hall. "Lillian... you know this thing with me and Hunter? It may be nothing. It may amount to nothing in the long run."

She gives me a wise look and an understanding smile. "But it may amount to everything. Just enjoy it, Gabby."

I nod at her and murmur "thanks" before heading back to Casey's room. Knocking softly on the door, I hear her call me in. She's sitting in bed, her back resting up against her headboard. Even though she's still in bed, wearing her pajamas, I can tell she's been up for a while because her eyes are clear and not a hint of grogginess surrounds her.

"Hey," I say softly as I close the door and take a seat on the edge of her bed near her feet.

"Hey," she says, keeping her eyes averted and pinned to her hands, which are clasped in her lap.

"I am so sorry, Case," I begin, laying my hand on her ankle, which rests under the covers by my hip. "I never meant to hurt you, and it was stupid for me to keep that secret from you. You're my best friend. You should have been the first person I told."

She lifts her face and stares at me, her lips drawn downward. "I can't believe you've had feelings for my brother for a few weeks, and I never knew. I must be oblivious."

Her voice isn't bitter or angry, which immediately relieves me. She says it in wonder, questioning the very strength of our friendship that she didn't see it. Which makes what I'm getting ready to tell her that much worse.

"Um… it's actually been a bit longer than a few weeks. At least where I'm concerned."

"What do you mean?"

I take a deep breath and let it out slowly. Pushing her legs aside to give me more room, I cross my legs, leaning my elbows on my knees as I face her. Then I tell her about what happened five years ago, and I catch her up on everything so she knows exactly how the concept of Hunter and I came to be.

When I finished, she just shakes her head at me. "I can't believe you kissed him graduation night. How did I not know that?"

"Because I was mortified and so embarrassed, and I didn't want to relive my humiliation. I only wanted to forget about it."

"No wonder you were such a bitch to him all these years."

"Yeah… I don't have the best coping skills apparently."

There's a moment of awkward silence. Casey's gaze drops back down to her hands while I continue to look at her, waiting to see what else she'll want to know before I beg forgiveness again.

"I'm scared," she finally says, and I jerk in surprise at the small sound of her voice.

"Of what?"

"I'm scared you'll hurt him… or he'll hurt you, and then I might lose one of you."

Oh, my heart breaks and then fills with pain over these words. I don't want my bestie to have these fears, even though I've had the same ones myself. It's my burden to bear though, not hers, so I lean forward, crawl my way up the bed, and flop down beside her, grabbing her in a hug.

"That won't happen, Casey. Our relationship is… um… casual, I guess. Our feelings aren't too deep, but we have years of care and friendship in the mix. We won't hurt each other, I promise. And even if we did, we'd never make you choose between us. You'll always have us both."

She looks at me like I have a neon sign hanging above my head with a bright, glowing arrow pointing down at me that says "Idiot".

"What?" I ask, not understanding the look on her face.

"You're sleeping with Hunter," she points out.

Yes, yes I am, and damn, it is good.

"Your point?" I ask with one of my eyebrows cocked.

"My point is—there's nothing casual about that."

I snicker and then let out a burst of laughter. "Casey... I'm sorry, girl, but you sleep with men all the time and it's casual."

I'm not prepared for Casey's hand when it flies forward and slaps me soundly on my forehead. "You are an idiot. Of course, it's casual for me. That's because I don't have a heart when it comes to men. They're good for two things only, and that's an expensive dinner and an earth-shattering orgasm. But you... Hunter... you are both ruled by your hearts. Once you decided to get intimate, you both went past casual."

Her words hit me like a freight train, because in their simplest form, they ring utterly true. I have an overwhelming sense of dread that maybe she's actually foreshadowing a moment in time where either Hunter or I get hurt... maybe both of us.

"No, no, no, no," she admonishes, and my eyes snap to hers. "Get that look off your face right now."

"What look?"

"The one that just got scared over what I said. The one that said you were going to break it off with Hunter right now to avoid further hurt down the road."

Holy shit. She got all of that with a look? That was exactly the path my thoughts had started to take when she called me on them.

I open my mouth to say something but she cuts me off, grabbing onto my hands. "Don't you dare break it off with him because you're scared, Gabby. I don't want you to break his heart because you're scared."

I'm stunned by her words and by her absolute turnaround from being pissed at me to not wanting me to break things off with Hunter. Her hands squeeze mine painfully.

"Promise me, Gabby," she says urgently.

"I promise," I squeak out, fairly certain she crushed the bones in my fingers. "Does this mean you're no longer mad at me?"

She pulls me forward and gives me a quick hug, thankfully releasing her death grip on my hands. "You know I can't stay mad at you long. Never could."

"And you're not worried that I'll... how did you say it... 'get my claws into Hunter'?"

She snorts. "Hey... we've been besties for almost our entire life. I know how to push your buttons."

"That you do," I agree. "So, we're cool?"

"Cool as an Eskimo's dick when he takes a piss,"

she says with a grin.

I wrinkle my nose in distaste. "All right. I'm out of here. I need to get into work."

"Oh, no you don't," she says. "We need to dish about Sasha."

That's right. I completely forgot about her and her skanky ways when she kissed Hunter last night. Sitting up beside Casey, I cross my legs again, resting my elbows on my inner thighs.

"Okay," I tell her conspiratorially. "Hunter told me a little bit about her and assured me they weren't together. Tell me everything you know."

Casey sits up straighter, and she gets a serious look on her face. We're getting ready to do some five-star gossiping. "I only met her once, about three months before they broke up. Remember when we went out to Huntington Beach to watch one of Hunter's competitions?"

I nod, definitely remembering when Casey and her parents flew across the country to watch him compete. Casey was so excited, as were her parents, because they just couldn't afford to trot across the globe to watch him.

"Well, she was a bitch... couldn't stand her. She was rude to my parents, rude to me, and was a complete bitch to Hunter. I assume their relationship was really on the downswing at that point. Hunter was pretty embarrassed by her behavior. We all went out to dinner that night, and all she did was complain. Complained about the way Hunter surfed, about what clothes he was wearing, about what food he ordered. I swear… he sat through that meal with his teeth clenched so he wouldn't tear into her. The only saving grace was Dad… I mean, you know how easygoing he is, and he could talk for hours with a complete stranger."

This revelation made me feel exquisitely good and made a little bit of the jealousy over their relationship ease in my mind.

"I wanted to knock her teeth out when she kissed Hunter," I admitted. "Then I wanted to kick him in the balls for letting it happen."

"He pushed her away fast, Gabby. I watched the entire thing. You were turned away, grabbing your purse."

"He told me that last night," I add.

"Did you see the look on her face when you approached them? I wanted to knock her teeth out myself. I mean… I knew it. Even before you called him an asshole. I saw the look on your face, the look on his face, and I knew there was something going on between you two. So I looked at her, and she had like this shit-eating grin on her face. It's like she liked causing trouble, you know?"

Sadly, I did know. I hated people like that and had seen plenty in my life. "I really am sorry I didn't tell you about us," I reiterate, just because she's brought up the fact again that she didn't know.

"Seriously, girl... it's fine. I'm over it. I don't even want to talk about that anymore. I want to plot on how we can make Sasha's life hell while she's visiting."

Sighing, I flop back on the bed in frustration. "It's my life that's going to be hell. Hunter said he has no clue how long they're staying, but John had mentioned on the phone he might be here a few weeks. I don't know if I can bear her being in his house that long."

"You don't have to worry about Hunter. He's—"

I cut Casey off. "I'm not worried about him at all. I just hate that we probably won't be spending the same amount of time together that we were before. I mean... it would be awkward me staying over there while she's there, and he certainly can't abandon them to stay at my place."

"You'll figure something out," Casey says as she pats my shoulder. "Now, I need to get in the shower and head in to work."

I roll over and off Casey's bed, telling her I'll see her later, and leave the house. Driving toward Last Call, I hope I can get a few moments alone with Hunter sometime today to talk about our arrangement—how he foresees us being able to spend time together while he has company. Maybe we should just cool it until they leave, but as soon as that thought crosses my mind, my stomach almost cramps with pain at the thought of not seeing him.

Yeah... Casey's right. I can't do casual and the minute I accepted Hunter into my body, I gave him carte blanche access to my heart as well.

SIXTEEN

Hunter

I find Gabby on the back deck of the bar, on an eight-foot ladder, checking the electrical wiring that had been installed the day before by her subcontractor. Walking up to the base of the ladder, I let my eyes leisurely crawl up her body, knowing that while her attention is preoccupied, I can take my time with my perusal.

Not that she minds me looking… I know that for a fact after last night when she put on her own private show for me. Just the thought of her hand skimming into her panties to touch herself threatens to give me a semi, so I have to turn my attention elsewhere. Instead, I choose to focus on Gabby as a whole. The way she confidently stands on the ladder, focused and intent on her work. Her movements are efficient, nothing wasted. When she's concentrating, she tends to chew on her lip and her brow will knit together on occasion.

"You make a mighty fine spectacle, Miss Ward," I say as I reach a hand up and wrap it around her ankle... just in case my words startle her.

As ever, though, Gabby is cool and collected, not even flinching or looking my way at the contact. But she does giggle, which is so contradictory to the general contractor standing before me that parcels out orders and can curse like a sailor when she's pissed about something.

When she is finished to her satisfaction, she finally glances down at me, giving me a welcoming smile. She doesn't seem put out that I'm touching her publicly, but it wouldn't matter if she were or not.

I'm done hiding it. Casey knows... Brody knows... my mom knows, and I'm sure Dad will get an earful when he gets home tonight. All the people whose opinion matters know about it, so there is absolutely no way I'm going to curb my need to touch her.In fact, I think I'll test out her thoughts on the matter right this very moment. Gabby bends slightly to balance her hands on the top of the ladder, so she can start climbing down. I use the opportunity to put my fingers in the back waistband of her jeans and give her a tug backward. She's not prepared for it and immediately starts to fall, giving a small yelp as she does so. But she's easily caught in my hold, and I'm pleased when her arms go around my neck and she smiles at me.

I figure if she's okay with that, then she's okay for this. I lean in and touch her mouth with mine, giving her just a moment of a kiss. She lets out a little sigh from the contact and I feel my heart squeeze inside my chest, so pleased is it from her reaction.

When I pull back, I ask, "So… I'm guessing you're okay now with some PDA?"

She's beyond adorable when she shrugs her shoulders, and her cheeks go red. "I suppose a little can't hurt."

Let's test that little theory. I lean back in and kiss her again, this time hard on the mouth. She opens up to me, warm and sweet. The decadence of the kiss is exquisite, and it fills me up with something other than the normal surge of lust I get when our mouths mate.

Finally, I pull away, because I can't take this any

further... not here at Last Call... in public. Setting her on her feet, I take her hand and start walking toward the front bar. "Got time to eat lunch with me?"

"Sure... but Alyssa said she might stop by and eat here today, so I hope three's not a crowd."

"Oh yeah, because eating a meal with two beautiful women is a complete hardship," I say sarcastically.

When we reach the front bar, both of us take a stool. Brody is there to serve us. He gives me a Diet Coke and pushes a bottle of water across the bar to Gabby, then turns to head back to the kitchen to put our orders in. A BLT for Gabby and a turkey on rye for me.

While we wait on our food, Gabby and I angle our bodies in toward each other and lean against the bar. Her foot kicks companionably against mine, and she has a lazy grin on her face.

"Tell me how it went with Casey," I say to her.

"It was fine," she says after taking a sip of water. "I apologized, she forgave, and then we trash talked Sasha."

I can't help the bark of laughter that comes out of my mouth... the way Gabby just casually told me what they did, including gossiping about my ex. My laughter is apparently appreciated, because Gabby starts chuckling in response.

Grabbing her hand, I pull it onto my lap. Her eyes go somewhat serious, although they still have a hint of mischief in them. "I want you to stay the night with me," I tell her.

"At your house?" she asks, suddenly losing that mischievous light.

"Yes."

She tries to pull her hand back, but I won't let it go. "I don't know, Hunter. I think it'll be just really awkward with your ex there. I'm not feeling very kindly toward her."

"Tell you what... how about at least come over for dinner? I'll invite Casey and Wyatt, both of whom will have your back. Then that will give me time to convince you to stay the night." I try to put on my most devastating smile, and it seems to work because she returns a small one.

"Seriously? Dinner? You want me to sit down and talk to your ex?"

"Well... maybe not one on one to start out, but it will be a group... a get-together... a shindig of sorts. We'll make it casual, grill out... drink a few beers."

Then I go for the kill when I tell her, "Besides...

I want you to get to know John. He means a lot to me, and I want you to see that."

Gabby's eyes go soft at my proclamation, and I do an imaginary fist pump that I got her to agree. "Fine. But dinner is all I'm committing to right now."

"That works for me," I say, leaning in to whisper in a low voice because Brody has come back from the kitchen, "but I know, once I get you there, you won't want to leave... not with the things I have planned for you tonight."

I get the desired effect I wanted because her eyes go from soft and limpid to aroused and hot. "Oh, yeah... what did you have in mind?"

Glancing down at Brody at the end of the bar, assured he can't hear me, I lean in all the way and run my lips along her jawline. "I want to see how many times I can make you come in an hour, just with my mouth."

Gabby pulls back and blinks at me, her mouth hanging open. "An hour?"

"One hour," I assure her. "We'll time it and everything."

"Oh," she says, dumbfounded, but I can tell by the look in her eyes, she's also completely intrigued.

"Hey guys," I hear from behind me, immediately recognizing Alyssa's voice.

I hold Gabby's gaze for just a moment more, and then say in a voice low enough that I'm sure only she can hear, "One hour of pure pleasure."

The pulse in Gabby's throat literally starts beating at my proclamation, and it makes me want to stand up, haul her over my shoulder, and take her home right now to get that hour started.

Instead, I turn to Alyssa and pat the stool next to me, which she takes. Brody walks over and stares at her, waiting for her order. "Hey Brody... can I have a sweet tea and a Rueben?"

He doesn't even respond—which seems to be classic Brody—just walks back toward the kitchen to put in the order. Alyssa stares at his retreating back for a moment before turning toward Gabby and me, shrugging her shoulders at his cold demeanor.

"Did you talk to Casey yet?" she asks Gabby, leaning forward on the bar so she can see around me.

"Yup... this morning. All is right with our world again."

"And I take it you two are now 'out of the closet,' so to speak?" she asks as she points her index finger back and forth between the two of us.

"Yup," I answer, turning toward Alyssa. "In fact, we had a glorious moment of PDA just a few minutes ago, and Gabby didn't slap me, nor did one person raise their eyebrows."

I can hear Gabby snort over my right shoulder. Alyssa chuckles and says, "Oh my God. You two are going to be that couple that everyone hates because they're so freakin' cute together, aren't you?"

Glancing back at Gabby, I see her eyes lowered to the bar and a secret smile on her face. I love how all of this seemingly affects her.

Brody steps out of the back service area with Gabby's and my sandwiches, laying them in front of us. He then fixes Alyssa a sweet tea, pushing it silently in front of her, all while never saying a word. I know Brody has been removed and a bit introverted since getting out of prison, but he never says a word around Alyssa... and I have to wonder why. Does she make him nervous? Or maybe something happened between them one summer when she was visiting? I doubt it, because of the age difference. Brody got arrested when he was twenty-two, so I don't think the time frame fits, but it's possible there could have been something there.

"I'm thinking of putting in a bid to Henry Coursier," Gabby says, breaking into my thoughts.

My head snaps around to hers, and she's looking at me for what I think may be approval, which she'll get. I'm Team Gabby all the way at his point.

"Seriously? That would be awesome."

She smiles at my reaction and picks up a chip, popping it in her mouth.

"For the new store they're going to be opening?" Alyssa asks.

Gabby swallows her food, takes a sip of water, and says, "Yeah... Steve had mentioned it to me when I saw him at Hunter's house a few days ago. I think with this project more than halfway done, and with a good recommendation from Hunter, I stand a good shot of getting it."

"Gabby, that would be amazing. You're first commercial project, which you'll be building from the ground up," Alyssa says with enthusiasm.

"When will you submit it?" I ask her.

"Deadline is end of the week, but I have it almost ready. I started it over the weekend."

My eyebrows shoot up. "When? You were with me all weekend."

She shoots me a smirk. "After you fell asleep, I'd work on it. I didn't have to start from scratch or anything. I looked at some of the ones my dad had done in the past. He built two of their stores. I used that as a template. I just have to get some prices on a few of the materials today, and then I'll be finished."

"I'm proud of you, Gabs," I tell her.

Alyssa echoes that with a, "Me too."

"Thanks guys. I mean… I don't know if he'll even consider it, but it can't hurt to try, right? And Steve said he'd put in a good word for me with his dad."

The thought of Steve Coursier helping Gabby with this burns my stomach. He clearly has interest in her, as evidenced by the fact he asked her out not but three days ago. I don't say anything, however, because it's not my place, and there's no way in hell I'm letting Gabby know that I'm jealous of that douche.

Gabby pops off her barstool and gathers the remainder of her sandwich in her hand. "Actually… do you mind if I use the phone in your office to make some calls, so I can get the bid finished up?"

"Help yourself," I tell her even as she starts to walk by me, to… well, help herself.

She brushes her shoulder against mine as she passes, murmuring to me in a soft, wondering voice, "One hour?"

"Best hour of your life, I guarantee it," I tell her smugly.

"Can't wait," she says, and then heads toward my office.

"One hour for what?" Alyssa asks.

"Um… surfing lessons. I told Gabby I'd teach

her how to surf."

"Cool," Alyssa says with a smile. I note that somehow in the last few minutes, Brody had ambled off and returned with Alyssa's sandwich, which he set quietly in front of her.

"Thanks, Brody," Alyssa says with a smile.

He doesn't respond but starts to walk down to the other end of the bar. Okay, this is just a bit weird. Brody will at least converse with other people. It may only be in one-syllable words, or it may even just be a curt nod of the head, but he literally won't engage Alyssa at all.

"Hey, Brody," I call out to him.

He turns around with eyebrows raised. "What's up?"

"I was thinking about your community service you have to do. You should volunteer over at The Haven. God knows Alyssa could use the help, and I'm sure it will qualify since it's a non-profit."

"I don't think he's interested," Alyssa says carefully.

I look at her in surprise, even as Brody says, "No thanks."

He turns to start walking back toward the end of the bar. I glance at Alyssa, and she's got her head cocked to the side, looking at Brody in curiosity.

"It's really not that hard," Alyssa says with some encouragement. "Helping feed and water the animals, clean cages, some grooming."

Brody doesn't even turn around but busies himself rearranging liquor bottles behind the bar. "Not interested."

"Brody, dude," I interject, because I think this is stupid to turn down this opportunity. "This is right up your alley. You love dogs."

"It's actually fun, getting to play with and exercise the animals," Alyssa chimes in, her voice soft and reassuring. She is smiling at Brody, trying to force the look onto his back, which is turned against us, but there's no way her pretty face is penetrating.

I decide to hit him again, make sure he understands the importance of getting this community service done. "I really think—"

"I don't give a fuck what you think," Brody roars as he spins around, glaring at me. "It's none of your fucking business what I have to do, and I sure as hell don't need any hand-outs from some snotty, rich bitch heiress either."

His last statement is punctuated with a glare toward Alyssa, who gasps over his harsh words.

I'm stunned speechless, having just witnessed Brody going from meek mouse to enraged bull in a nanosecond. Opening my mouth, I start to lay into him for calling Alyssa a bitch but she jumps off the stool, throws a twenty on the counter, and runs from the bar.

"Alyssa," I call out after her, getting off the stool.

As she flees, she collides into Gabby, who has just stepped out of the hallway that leads into my office. She mumbles an apology and sprints for the door. Gabby's eyes turn toward me, and I simply say, "Go after her."

Gabby takes off after Alyssa and, as I hear the front door slam behind Gabby, I turn to Brody with barely contained rage. "What fuck was that? Have you lost your ever-loving mind, talking to Alyssa that way?"

For a brief moment, Brody's eyes go sad and fill with regret, but in a flash, it's gone. Instead, his face is awash with menace and he snarls, "I'm a fucking ex-con, Hunter. I've been in prison... not charm school... the last five years."

His words pierce me, and I sigh. "I know, but you would never have done that to her before you went away. Have you forgotten your basic manners?"

Brody steps out from behind the bar, still holding the rag in his hand. He walks up to me and gets in my face. His voice is arctic when he says, "Yes, Hunter.

I've forgotten all of it. That's a life I don't have any more, so there's no sense in remembering a damn thing about it. This is your brother now. I've been shaped into something else these last five years and if you don't like it… Well, I could give a flying fuck."

Throwing the rag on the floor, he turns his back on me and starts heading for the door. "I'm taking the rest of the day off," he says as he walks away. "Fire me if you want—I don't give a shit."

I follow Brody out the door. Gabby is standing with Alyssa beside her car. Alyssa looks okay, but Gabby has her arm around her shoulder.

"You're an asshole, Brody," Gabby hisses at him as he walks by.

He doesn't even look at her. "Yup. That I am."

Gabby turns to me, her eyes wild and confused. I look back at her helplessly, because I have no clue what the fuck just happened, or whether my brother can even be saved from himself.

SEVENTEEN

Gabby

Casey and I stand on the porch of Hunter's house, looking at each other before we open the door and walk in.

"Who are we?" Casey asks me in a quiet voice.

"We're the two baddest chicks in the Outer Banks," I tell her.

"And where are we?" she asks, her voice getting a little louder.

"We're on the cusp… on the threshold… on the brink of going in," I quickly respond.

"And what are we getting ready to do?" she asks with extreme urgency.

"We're getting ready to show her the way it is."

"And why are we doing it?" she asks with an evil grin.

"Because if I catch Sasha ever trying to kiss Hunter again, I'm going to knock her teeth out... so consider this a public service of sorts for the woman."

"Damn skippy," Casey exclaims. We give each other a high-five, then we take it down low, tickling our fingertips against one another, and then bump our hips together.

Yes, this is our preparation routine we always do any time one of us has a problem and the other one is riding wingman to help solve said problem.

The problem is, of course, Sasha. Hunter insisted on doing this get-together so I could get to know John, but that unfortunately meant I needed to get to know Sasha.

Before I left work for the day, Hunter pulled me aside and assured me that he talked with Sasha, that she was remorseful for what happened, and that it was water under the bridge. He told me everything would be fine, and then he reminded me that he wanted me to stay the night with him. Before I could even decline that invitation again, he made sure to remind me of the one-hour test he wanted to try out on me, which made my blood race hot and my resolve to sleep in my own bed weaken.

So in order to reinforce myself, I had Casey pick me up, purposefully leaving my truck so I would have to go home at the end of the evening.

Back to Sasha. I know Hunter reassured me that she would not be a problem, and that I could expect to have a carefree evening of good food, good beer, and good friends. I wasn't so optimistic, and let me tell you why.

There is something us women have that's called a 'gut instinct'. I can't explain it, I have no clue how it works, and I'm sure there are no scientific studies on it. However, I've had it appear in situations over my lifetime, and I'm guessing at least eight out of every ten times it was spot-on accurate.

My gut instinct told me that Sasha still has it bad for Hunter. I know Hunter says that yes, she may have been thinking that, but the kiss was before she knew he had a girlfriend. Fine… I'll give her that. But when I marched up to Hunter and let myself glance at her, the look on her face was cunning, calculating, and challenging, and she was telling me that it was game on.

I'm also choosing not to give Sasha the benefit of

the doubt, mainly because Casey isn't. That trip out to California sealed the deal for Casey. She felt Sasha's behavior was appalling, but even worse—Casey felt deep down that it was her inherent nature. In essence, based on their interaction, she had a 'gut instinct' about Sasha too, and I was therefore going to trust it as well.

I look at Casey in the eye, take a deep breath, and ask, "How do I look?"

She sweeps her gaze down me, taking in the long maxi-dress I had chosen—a butter-yellow color that set off my tan and made my eyes glow gold. I paired it with silver sandals and left my hair down loose. I was going for casual and carefree, just the way Hunter said tonight's get-together would be.

"You look gorgeous, girl."

"Thanks. Now, let's get this initial awkward part of introductions with her over, so we can drink some beer."

"Amen, sister."

Casey opens the door, and we step into Hunter's foyer. It's quiet, so I assume everyone is out on the deck. We head into the kitchen to put the beer that we brought into the fridge. Before I can even turn around to walk toward the back deck, strong arms circle around me from behind, and I'm pulled back into warm, hard chest muscle.

"There's my girl," Hunter murmurs into my ear.

My eyes immediately go to Casey, who is watching our first display of affection in her presence, and I hold my breath for her reaction. She stares at us, and I can actually feel Hunter grin at her. Don't ask me how I feel it… but I just do.

"Okay, this is wigging me out a little," Casey finally says as she turns and pulls a beer out of the fridge. "I need to ease into these things, particularly with the help of one or seven beers."

"You're driving me home tonight," I remind her, and I feel Hunter's hold tense up a bit.

"No worries," Casey reassures me with a playful smile. "I'll refrain from getting lit up, but how about cool the cuddly shit around me?"

"Get used to it," Hunter says, kissing my temple and releasing me. He goes to the fridge and pulls out a beer for both of us, then says, "Come on… got some people I want you to meet."

Casey and I follow Hunter out on the back deck. I immediately see John, sitting at the outdoor table, his feet kicked up on another chair. Wyatt is standing next to Sasha, leaning against the rail, and laughing at something she said. His eyes go to us, and he tilts his chin up in acknowledgement.

Hunter turns to hand me my beer, saying, "John… Sasha… you know my sister, Casey."

John stands up and gives Casey a hug, and I have to hide a smirk as Casey just looks at Sasha with cold eyes and says, "Hi, Sasha."

Sasha gives her a small smile and quietly says, "Hey."

Hunter brings his arm up around my shoulder and pulls me in close, so I'm tucked up against him. "And this is Gabby."

John leans over and shakes my hand. "Great to meet you, Gabby."

"It's nice to meet you, too," I tell him, and it is genuinely nice to meet him. But then a lead weight fills my stomach as I turn to Sasha. She steps forward and sticks her hand out to me. "Hi, Gabby. I'm really, really sorry about what happened at the bar last night. If I'd known Hunter's girlfriend was there, I never would have done that."

I take hers and give it a firm shake, and it doesn't escape my notice that she said she wouldn't have done that if she'd known Hunter's girlfriend *was there*. Not, she wouldn't have done that if she'd known Hunter *had* a girlfriend. Therefore, that implied to me that she would have definitely made a move on him if he had a girlfriend, just not in said girlfriend's presence.

Yes, my gut instinct is preening right now.

"That's okay," I assure Sasha with a kind voice, although I'm feeling anything but. However, I don't want to cause waves, and I'm secure enough with Hunter that it doesn't really matter if she has designs on him or not. He's not going back to that, I'm fairly positive.

"Hunter tells me you're a general contractor," John says in my direction.

I nod, taking a seat at the table. "Yup… for about three years now. I took over my dad's business when he passed away."

Casey sits down as well, while Sasha and Wyatt remain standing. Hunter walks over to the grill and starts getting it ready. I'm not sure he knows how to cook anything unless it's something he can char over an open flame.

"I'm sorry to hear that," John says in commiseration. "I bet your dad would be proud of you though."

That is such a kind thing to say. I feel my heart immediately open up to John, and I give him a smile and murmur thanks.

Then I'm completely surprised when Sasha says, "I really admire what you do, Gabby. I know what it's like to be in a male-dominated career, always struggling to prove your worth."

I blink at her a few times in surprise, and it hits me like a ton of bricks. Sasha and I actually have something very much in common. I have to give her points for her sudden empathy, and I'm starting to think that maybe I've misjudged her.

"I bet you do understand," I tell her with sincerity. "It's been tough to say the least."

"I sure as hell don't know why," Hunter says from over at the grill. "Her work is fucking amazing."

You know that feeling, when you're on a roller coaster, and it reaches the pinnacle of a long drop, and you're scared shitless, but after you fly over the edge and make your descent, you get a feeling of tingly euphoria?

Yeah, that's what Hunter's words do to me right now, and my cheeks heat up over his public proclamation of his pride in me. My eyes slide to his and he's grinning, because he knows his words have an effect on me.

Maybe I'll rethink staying over at his house tonight.

"More," I moan, even as Hunter surges hard into me with a grunt, knocking the headboard into the wall.

"Jesus, Gabby," he pants against my ear, but he fucks me harder, the headboard now making a steady *thwacking* sound.

With a long groan, he slams into me one more time and closes his eyes tight as he comes… hard.

His entire body trembles, and his breath comes out in a rush as he collapses on top of me, where he lays like dead weight. He's heavy, but he feels divine.

"I think you killed me," he says between heaving breaths.

I giggle and push him off, stretching my body luxuriously. I didn't come… at least not right before Hunter did, but he in no way left me high and dry.

You see… he made good on the promise to work me over for an hour—even timed it with the clock on his iPhone. The get-together tonight ended up actually being… fun. After I found out I had something in common with Sasha, I relaxed a bit and just let myself enjoy. My relationship with Hunter was out in the open, he'd declared to his family and closest friends, as well as his ex-girlfriend, that we were involved, and he was super attentive to me the entire evening.

My skin tingled when I caught him looking at me, warm sometimes, hot others. My belly fluttered when he would laugh… white teeth flashing, his face completely gentled by humor.

And then there were the times when he would touch me. Sometimes it was just casual, sitting beside me and slinging his arm around my shoulder. Sometimes it was intimate… like the time I helped to bring the food into the kitchen, and he backed me up against the counter. I thought he was going to give me one of his passionate kisses, since we were all alone. Instead, he brought his hand up and just skimmed his fingers along my temple, down my jaw, and behind my ear, winding his fingers to the back of my neck. The move caused my eyes to flutter closed over the soft touch, staying closed even as he leaned in and kissed me on my forehead, murmuring, "I'm so glad you came tonight."

It was that touch that caused my heart to stand up and wave the white flag of surrender to him. I realized at that moment, that I hadn't truly opened back up to him since he crushed me years before. But I was open now.

And I opened up to him when our one hour started. I easily capitulated to stay the night, not just because of his one-hour promise, although that played a part. No, it was the kiss to my forehead that got me to change my mind, and I realized I didn't want to sleep away from him.

Ever.

So, yes. I was in deep. I had no clue where this was going, but I was definitely going along with him.

End of story.

As I was saying, the one hour turned out to be mind-blowing but practically impossible for me. Not Hunter… he was strong all the way through, but after he gave me three orgasms in about twenty-seven minutes, I was wiped out. I actually had to push him away from me and beg him to leave me alone, because my sensitive flesh literally couldn't take anymore. He chuckled, pulled me up in his arms, and told me he'd give me a break. We lay there for about ten minutes, talking quietly, about Nascar racing of all things. Neither of us were fans, so not sure why we started talking about it. But when Hunter's iPhone relayed there was five minutes left on his hour time limit, he pushed me onto my back and slid back down my body, his face going back between my legs.

And damn if he didn't get me to come one more time before that hour was up—just before he crawled up my body and slid inside. He was merciless as he fucked me hard. I knew I didn't have it in me for another orgasm, but it didn't matter. I'd had enough, but it still made it no less special the way Hunter made me feel when he was inside of me. His body, his face, the way he touched me, the things he said, the sounds he made, the way he came… hard. Those things were all far more thrilling than the hour he had just spent worshiping me.

"Did you get your bid turned in?" Hunter asks me, drawing me out of my fond memories of Hunter's sexuality and the way he makes me feel.

I turn over on my side toward him, tucking my hand under my chin. He turns toward me, mimicking the move, and our faces are close enough we can look straight into the other's eyes, but not so close as to make our vision blurry.

"Yeah… they wanted the bids by email, so I sent it over this evening. They're supposed to decide next week."

"How long will that project last if you get the contract?" he asks as he scoots his lower half toward me, slipping one of his legs in between mine, and resting his hand on my hip. The move is warm and intimate, made from a desire just to touch our skin together and nothing more.

"Probably six months since we're building ground up. It's a great project. That, along with your remodel, will really help get me to where I want to go."

Rubbing his thumb along my hipbone, he smiles at me and asks, "And where is it Gabby Ward wants to go?"

Good question. Where do I ultimately want to go? It's not something I've let myself think about for the last three years, because I've been so focused on trying to keep my dad's business growing. It's a far cry from where I was three years ago, with a college degree within my grasp and a career as an educator.

This is also the first time, in a very long time, that I've thought about being a teacher. I didn't allow myself to be sad about it when I dropped out of college. I had enough grief over my dad passing to keep me busy. But now... thinking about it, I feel wistful and dejected.

"Where did Gabby go just now?" Hunter asks softly.

I blink hard and realize that my gaze had slid down to Hunter's chest, and my mind had completely drifted off. Dragging my eyes up, I find him watching me with amusement.

"I zoned out," I admit, "was thinking about college."

"Do you want to go back?"

"I don't know. I mean… I never thought I did, but it just hit me a little bit right now… maybe I miss the thought of being a teacher."

"You can always go back to college any time you want, Gabby," he points out.

"Not while running a business, I can't. I mean, I'd want to finish at UNC."

"If you go back to finish your degree, that implies you'd do it to start teaching. If that's the case, you'd give up the business anyway."

It used to be that the thought of letting Ward Construction close up caused acid to bubble up in my stomach. It was such an unpleasant, painful feeling that it prompted me to immediately drop out of school and rush home to continue my dad's work. But thinking about it now… it makes me sad thinking about giving it up, but it doesn't hurt like it used to. I wonder what in the hell that means.

"I've had a job offer," I say, sort of changing the subject but not really, because it's related.

Hunter's eyebrows shoot up in interest. "Oh yeah?"

"Yeah… a buddy of Dad's has repetitively offered me work with his construction company in Raleigh. He does mostly residential stuff, but it would be good income."

"Are you thinking about taking it?"

"No. Not really... I mean, that was my backup plan if I couldn't make Ward Construction work. But with remodeling Last Call, and potentially getting the Coursier's contract, I'm hoping that's moot right now."

"Why was that your backup plan? Why not just go back to school?"

"It was part one of the backup plan," I tell him with a smile. "Go to work and save money. Then part two was to take saved money and finish degree."

"Gotcha," he says as he slides his hand up my ribs. The feeling is nice, calming. He caresses around to my back, and then presses his palm down to pull me in closer to his body. I slide in easily to his embrace, tucking my face into the crook of his neck, and then his arms wrap around me.

Hunter rubs my back softly with his entire palm, soothing me further, causing my eyes to get heavy with sleep. I think to myself, *I don't ever want to give this up*.

"Let me tell you something about the Gabby Ward I know," Hunter says softly, causing my eyes to open back up and my ears to perk with interest. "The Gabby Ward I know can do any of those things she just laid out to me, and she can do them to

269

perfection. You have options, baby, and none of them are bad choices. Follow your heart."

I smile and press my lips against the skin of his collarbone before closing my eyes again.

"Thanks, Hunter," I whisper, just before I fall asleep.

EIGHTEEN

Hunter

Peace.

That is what I'm feeling at this very moment.

It's an experience of complete relaxation of the body, and utter contentment of the mind.

I have it because I'm on my couch, lying on my side, with Gabby tucked in front of me. We're watching a movie—*Talladega Nights*—which she thinks is absolutely hilarious, and I think is pretty fucking stupid. But when I asked her to spend a quiet night at home with me on Friday night, I assured her of two things. First, we would have the house to ourselves because John and Sasha were traveling down to Wilmington to check out the surf scene there, and second, that she could pick whatever movie she wanted.

I remember from the time we were kids, we never really shared the same taste in movies. At first, when she was younger, it's because she was interested in stupid, girlie movies. As she got older, and we would often watch movies together at my house—Gabby, Casey, Brody, Wyatt, and me—she wanted more slapstick comedy, and I tended to want guns and bombs blowing shit up.

It appears, as we are in early adulthood, we've sort of settled into those genres and, since I promised her she could pick, we're watching *Talladega Nights* and not *Mission Impossible: 4*.

But I'm at peace, because even though I can't get into this movie, I can totally get into watching Gabby watch this movie. She is laughing her ass off almost the entire time, twice snorting, which made her laugh even harder. Her body is warm and soft, pressed up tight against me, and her hair smells like clover and honey.

It's nice having her all to myself tonight. We've both been working hard during the day, her more so than me, as her crew has been scrambling to get the covered roof built before this weekend when showers are predicted. Even though the new bar she built is covered with a tarp, she wanted the added protection of the roof. Now all she has left is getting the retractable walls installed next week and the staining done, then she can move on—hopefully to the Coursier's project.

Gabby has stayed with me every night this week. She's developed an easygoing friendship with John and a polite tolerance for Sasha. Oh, Sasha came off nice that first night with a heartfelt apology, but I've noticed she tries to get in little licks on Gabby, which are just subtle enough to be overlooked, but just biting enough that you know she's full of passive aggressiveness.

Just last night, Gabby cooked spaghetti for everyone, which was delicious, but Sasha had to make sure she told her that I wasn't particularly fond of Italian sausage in the sauce. I think it was Sasha's way of reminding Gabby that she had me first and that she knew things about me that Gabby didn't, which let's face it... has got to be tough on the new girlfriend. But before I could even come to Gabby's rescue, she just smiled at Sasha and said, "Duly noted. If he doesn't like it, he can pick it out."

I roared with laughter over that, and so did John for that matter. Sasha just got a pinched look on her face and ate her spaghetti in silence. When I looked at Gabby, she shot me a wink and then slurped a noodle up so fast that it flopped all around and stuck to her chin.

A complete dork, and I loved it.

Gabby howls with laughter at the movie, her body stiffening, and her head thrown back against my shoulder.

"I'm gonna come at you like a spider monkey," she mimics as she wheezes in between laughing. "Oh my God… I think I'm going to pee my pants."

"You're such a dork," I chuckle as I squeeze my arms around her.

Her laughter slows down a bit, but her voice is still buoyant. "Yeah, but I'm your dork."

"Yes, you are," I murmur as I lean over and press my lips to the back of her head.

All of her merriment shuts off instantaneously. It goes not only deathly quiet, but her body freezes in my embrace. Then she rolls to face me, her eyes questioning mine for something, but I don't know what she's seeking.

"Gabby—"

"Shh," she whispers as her fingertips press up

against my lips. She watches me for a moment more, her eyes flickering back and forth between the boundaries of my own gaze as she smiles tenderly. "I'm glad I'm your dork."

Gabby removes her fingers from my mouth and leans in, brushing her lips across mine. Hers are so soft and full, generously covering my own with satin care. When she presses in harder, my mouth opens, gratefully accepting her searching tongue.

It's forever the same, the electric surge of desire that overwhelms me from just the contact of her kiss. My arms tighten around her, returning her passion and claiming her as my own. But it's also different, because Gabby uttered some very important words to me just a moment ago. She released them out into the world, and I accepted them.

She said she was mine.

A weird feeling pierces my chest, painful and warm... like a vice-grip around my heart, squeezing forth the longing and opening it back up for something more peacefully filling.

Gabby said she was mine, and it feels fucking fantastic.

Yes, I'm liking this feeling a lot.

Standing at the bar, I look back over the inventory sheets that Brody had filled out and try to make my purchase list for the upcoming week. It's one of the things I dread about Saturday the most... trying to figure out what shit I have and what shit I need to buy to keep the doors open and my food and drink flowing.

I look up briefly to see Brody stacking new glasses, his head bent... quietly working. Our relationship has been strained this past week, ever since his blow up with Alyssa. I tried to talk to him about it the next day, but he firmly told me it was done, he wasn't apologizing, and he wasn't talking about it. Since then, he's lapsed into being more of an introvert and only speaks when spoken to.

Glancing out the back door onto the deck, I see Gabby out there with her crew, finishing up the final build out of the covered roof. It looks fantastic, and I cannot wait to open that area up to customers... just in time for the start of the tourist season.

My thoughts drift back to last night. When we started kissing on the couch, all thoughts of Ricky Bobby, snorting, and spider monkeys completely obliterated, I reveled in the fact that we just made out for like an hour. Soft kissing, our hands stroking each other, whispery sighs from Gabby... it went on forever and I still could have kept at it, but then Gabby whispered that she wanted to go to bed, and well… that was that.

My feelings for Gabby are deep. I mean, really, really deep. Part of me wonders how it happened so fast, but part of me wonders why it took so long. There was something between us five years ago, something I stupidly froze out. She's been my friend for most of my life. This may, in fact, be the slowest buildup of a relationship in the history of the universe.

I hear banging on the front door of the bar, which is still locked, as we haven't opened back up yet for the lunch hour. That will come week after next, when the roof is completely finished.

Setting my pen down on the bar with the inventory sheets, I head toward the door as I dig my keys out of my pocket to unlock the internal deadbolt.

When I swing it open, I'm stunned to see my agent, Keith Carr, standing there. Pulling his sunglasses off, he flashes me a Hollywood smile and holds his hand out. "Good to see you, Hunter."

I reach out to shake his hand. "Yeah, Keith. Good to see you, too. What are you doing here?"

Keith tilts his head and gives me a disapproving look. "Come on, man. You're stalling and dodging me. You seriously think I wouldn't get on a plane and fly my ass to the east coast to talk to you?"

I step back from the doorway and motion Keith inside. When it boils down to it, I guess I'm not really surprised he's here. He's been pushing me with repetitive calls and emails to accept the new endorsement deals on the table, which will effectively enter me back into the Tour race for the following year. I've been thinking it over, but I haven't been ready to commit.

"Come on in. I was just doing some inventory."

Keith follows me to the back bar, and I motion for him to take a seat on one of the stools. There's no one in here but Brody, and I could care less if Brody hears this conversation. After I settle myself on a stool next to Keith, I say, "Brody... I want you to meet my agent, Keith Carr. Keith... my brother, Brody."

Brody turns and leans across the bar to shake Keith's hand, never saying a word, but at least giving him something less than a glare.

"I sort of figured this was Brody," Keith says with a laugh. "I mean... you two are identical."

"Can I get you something to drink?" Brody asks, taking a swipe at the clean bar top with his rag.

"Nah... I'm good," Keith says affably, and then

turns to me. "So… Hunter, this place looks great. Everything going well?"

"Yeah… going great. Almost finished with some remodels to give me some expanded seating," I tell him as I point to the back glass door to Gabby's crew, who are hard at work.

Keith nods, gives the back door a glance, and then turns back to me. "Have you given any more thought to the endorsement offers?"

"I have. Just like I told you on the phone… and by email. I'm thinking about it, but I'm not sure what to do."

"You know these offers won't last forever," Keith points out. "If you don't make a decision, they'll go on to the next hot surfer and make the same offers."

"I know," I snap, frustrated with the way he's hounding me but equally frustrated I have no clue what to do. "I didn't fall off the turnip truck. I've been in this game long enough to know how the game is played."

Keith holds his hands up. "Easy, dude. You know I'm just doing my job… looking out for you."

"You're looking out for your commission, Keith… at least be honest about it."

Narrowing his gaze at me, Keith leans in and

practically snarls, "Yeah... you take these deals, I'm going to make a lot of fucking money, but don't ever think I'm not looking out for you, Hunter. You screwed the pooch when you walked away at the top of your game, and if you have even the slightest desire to get back on the Tour, you need me to help you do it."

Letting out a sigh, I nod. "I'm sorry, man. And I know you have my back. You always have. I just don't know right now... I have a lot of shit on my plate," I say as I look down the bar at Brody. "How much time can you buy me?"

"A week... maybe two."

"Fuck," I mutter, running my hand through my hair, because I'm not ready to make this decision.

"Look, man. Let's talk this through. What are your concerns? You know I'm your sounding board," Keith says sincerely, and it's true. He's been representing me since the first endorsement deal came to my parents when I was just seventeen. Keith has been a good friend and a trusted advisor.

"Yeah... we need to talk," I tell him, casting my gaze down to Brody again. I left the Tour to come home for Brody, but now I'm not sure that was the best idea. Of course, now I'm saddled with a business I bought, and I just can't walk away from that, either.

I would need someone who I could trust to take it over, and Brody made clear to me that he didn't want a partnership. "Let's go take a ride down the coast, but first, I want you to meet someone."

Keith gives me a smile and then follows me when I head out on the back deck. As soon as I open the door, Gabby's curses hit my ears. "Fuck, Smitty. I told you to move the scrap out to the parking lot. I almost just broke my fucking neck tripping over it."

I grin as I walk toward her, loving the fierce way she stands with her hands on her hips, glaring at Smitty, who is a beast of a man. He just hangs his head in shame and says, "Sorry, Gabby. Got sidetracked."

When I reach her, I take ahold of her elbow and love how she doesn't flinch, because she knows immediately it's me. Turning her around, she hits me with a stunning smile.

"Hey you," she says in welcome.

"Hey," I tell her, giving her arm a squeeze. "Want you to meet someone... This is my agent, Keith Carr. He flew in from L.A. to discuss some offers that are on the table for me."

Looking past me to Keith, Gabby flashes him a full-blown smile as well and gives him a firm handshake. "Good to meet you, Keith. Hope you're taking care of our boy here."

Keith's eyebrows shoot up, and he looks from me to Gabby. "Our boy?"

Slipping my arm around Gabby's waist, I say, "This is Gabby Ward... my girlfriend."

It feels so odd, yet so right, calling her my girlfriend. She claimed she was mine last night, and I took her at face value. I'm sticking with that moniker for now.

"Well, this is a nice surprise," Keith says, and I think I sense an undertone of censorship there, but his face looks completely open and happy for me. "How long have you two been dating?"

I swear I can hear Gabby snort inside her mind, because "dating" isn't exactly how this started out. More like banging each other's brains out, but it's definitely not that anymore. I mean, yeah, we still tear it up in the bedroom, but I think we've both solidly, if not silently, agreed this is way more than just sex.

"I've known Gabby my whole life. She's Casey's best friend. It just sort of happened when I got back into town."

"Ah," Keith says in understanding, but I'm sure he really understands nothing because what Gabby and I have is surreal and unique, and can't be boiled down to a few words.

Leaning down, I give Gabby a kiss on her temple. "I'm going to hang with Keith for a while today. Want to meet us back out here tonight for some drinks? John and Sasha are going to be in some time around eight."

"Sure," she tells me with a smile and a gentle pat on my chest with her hand. "I'll see you tonight."

Gabby starts to turn away, but I reach out and grab her hand. She turns to me, this time with a bit of surprise on her face, and tilts her head to the side. There's nothing I really want to say, so I just step in and skim my fingers under her jaw, just before I lean in to give her a soft kiss on her lips. "See you tonight."

She gives a tiny sigh, which causes that panging sensation in my chest as I pull away. Quirking her lips at me, she winks and turns away.

Looking back at Keith, he's watching me thoughtfully while chewing on the end of his sunglasses. He seems to be almost appraising and then judging my interaction with Gabby, and it starts to get my hackles up.

"What?" I ask as I walk back into the bar, Keith following me.

"Nothing," he says.

"Bullshit… what's the look for?"

"It's just I've never seen you act that way with a woman before, and trust me… I've seen you around plenty of women."

"What do you mean?" I ask, stopping mid-stride and turning around to face him. "You've seen me be that way with Sasha before."

"No, man. Not like that. Never like that."

"Like what?"

"Like you'd never walk away from that," he points out quietly. "Is she why you're having a hard time making a decision?"

My immediate gut reaction tells me to deny, because the reason I'm hesitant is that I'm afraid to leave Brody. But the minute he mentions Gabby in conjunction with me leaving the Outer Banks to go back on tour, I have a sinking feeling in the pit of my stomach, which does not bode well for me.

Shaking it off, I clap Keith on the back. "No, she's not the reason. It's the same reason I left the tour, and you know what I'm talking about. Now, let's get out of here so we can talk about it."

Keith nods, and we head out. I fully intend to discuss with him and use him as my sounding board about my concerns for Brody. Even if I take the endorsements and commit to competing next year, I'm not sure I can just pack up and leave right now to get back on the circuit. I'd need time to get Last Call situated and decide if Brody can handle it. If not, could I sell it... or hire someone trustworthy to manage it.

No, my decision about whether to go back on tour has nothing to do with Gabby and has everything to do with Brody, and whether or not I could leave my brother when he is clearly still so lost.

NINETEEN

Gabby

I hold these truths to be self-evident.

I'm so fucking in love with Hunter, and yes, I know I'm quoting the Declaration of Independence to summarize my feelings at this point, but that's a damn good clause.

Watching him now, the way he laughs, the way he touches me... the way he talks about me. I'm sunk in deep and there's no preventing it, and there's certainly no trying to claw my way out. There's only one thing left to do... and that is give over to the euphoric feeling that courses through my body when I finally admit to myself that I love Hunter Markham.

We're all having a great time at Last Call. I'm sitting at a large, round table with Hunter to my left. To my right is John, looking tanned and windblown, his fist curled around a Budweiser. Sasha sits beside him, intent on talking to Wyatt, who is on her other side. She's wasted no time in latching on to him since she arrived, and I'm completely fine with sacrificing Wyatt to the greater good of the "stay the hell away from Hunter" game plan. Part of me even suspects Wyatt is intentionally keeping Sasha occupied, so her focus stays away from Hunter.

Finally, sitting between Hunter and Wyatt is his agent, Keith Carr. He's staying the night, having checked into the Sand Piper Inn over in Kitty Hawk. He's been busy all night, regaling me with tales about Hunter's career, and I've been enjoying learning more about him. Hunter's not the type that will talk about this stuff unless I push and prod him. He doesn't toot his own horn very well.

So, the reason it became self-evident just now... as we sit in this group surrounded by Hunter's closest friends and advisors—as well as one ex-girlfriend— you know, the people that know him best, you would think this would be a Hunter-palooza—a veritable party to pay homage to the greatness of the numbe two surfer in the world. But on the contrary, even though Keith tries very hard to center the talk around Hunter and how important his career is, Hunter matches him beat for beat in talking about me... in trying to put me to the forefront of the attention.

At first, it was embarrassing, the way Hunter repetitively bragged about my accomplishments and me. I know he just wants his friends to get to know me better, to validate his choice to be with me. By my third beer, and the fact that Hunter had moved his chair close to me so he could drape his arm over my shoulder, I'm feeling more relaxed and willing to let him extol my virtues.

"Hey Sasha... remember that time that Corey Granz cut Hunter off in the third heat of the Bali Pro? You went apeshit on his ass," Keith says while laughing and taking a sip of his fifth Jack and Coke. His voice was getting a little louder, a little more slurred, but we were all here to have a good time.

Sasha laughs, her eyes going warm with the memory, and it makes my stomach clench. It also sort of pisses me off that Keith has now gone down Sasha and Hunter's memory lane, a place I have no wish to journey.

"Yeah," Sasha says, leaning forward against the

table to look at Hunter. "When he got out of the water, I went a little crazy on him."

"A little crazy?" Keith says with a bark of laughter. "You ran up and pushed him so hard that he landed flat on his ass. I thought I would die from the look on his face."

Hunter's hand softly caresses my shoulder, and he says, "It wasn't a biggie. I whipped his ass in that heat, and Sasha acted like a brat."

Okay, this was getting a little awkward, and I sneak a quick glance at Sasha. Her eyes narrow at Hunter but then she shakes it off, even giving me a friendly smile. "Yeah... in hindsight, I guess that was pretty stupid. Hunter can handle himself."

"Exactly," Hunter says in agreement, even as his attention is taken away when someone taps him on the shoulder. It's one of his bartenders... Susie I think, and she leans down.

"The cash register at the front is broken again and won't open. I tried resetting it, but nothing. Brody's too busy at the back bar to look at it."

"I'm on it," Hunter says as he stands from the table. He doesn't leave though, until he bends down and places a kiss on top of my head, which again, is another reason why my heart has flopped over and submitted to love. Because he's always thinking about me.

As soon as Hunter's gone, Keith turns to me. "So Gabby... what do you think about Hunter competing again?"

I take a sip of my beer and appraise Keith. His eyes are almost glittering as he waits for my answer. Somehow, I feel that when said answer comes, he's going to be poised to strike at me in some way. Glancing around the table, I see everyone else is watching me for my answer as well.

"I think it's great... if that's what he wants to do."

"What do you think he wants to do?" Keith asks, and I suddenly feel Sasha's interest hone in on my answer. It could be the way she leans further across the table, practically licking her lips over what I might say.

"He's torn... I think you all know he came back for Brody."

Keith nods sagely. "Yeah... pretty dumb fucking reason, but I get it."

"Shut the fuck up," John snarls next to me. "You have no right to judge his decision."

"Hey," Keith says, picking up his drink and waving it toward John. "I'm entitled to my opinion. Just as you are."

A quick glance around the table, and I see Wyatt with his fists clenched and glaring at Keith, Sasha has her head dipped and a small smirk on her face, and John looks like he's about ready to jump across the table and tackle Keith.

"Listen," I say calmly. "Hunter knows Brody will be okay if he leaves, so that's not something you need to worry about. If he wants to go back, he will, and he'll figure out a way to make it work. All of us sitting here will support him when he does, so everyone just stop worrying about it. Okay?"

Sasha picks up her drink... some fruity concoction. I have no clue what it is, but it's a nauseating pink color, and she holds it up to me in salute. "I agree with Gabby. Hunter will make his decision in good time, and we'll all support it. I think Gabby knows what she's talking about."

Her words are supportive of me, particularly supportive of me as Hunter's girlfriend, but for some reason, they don't quite reach my truth-o-meter. She's holding something back, but I'm not sure what.

Keith raises his glass and slugs back the rest of the contents, slamming it on the table. "To Gabby... may she talk some sense into our boy."

I swear I hear John growl next to me, and I shake my head slightly at him not to say anything more.

Keith is on his way to being drunk, and half of what he says has to be taken with a grain of salt.

"He's a star. He could be a legend, Gabby," Keith says quietly as he stares at his empty glass. "He passes up this chance, he's dried up. It's over for good."

Everyone's heads sort of drop over this proclamation, because it's not something any of us would argue with. We know this is Hunter's only chance if he wants to get back in the game. The endorsement offers won't come again.

"Why is everyone looking so glum?" Hunter says as he walks back up to the table. He doesn't sit down but stands behind my chair, his hands on my shoulders.

No one answers, but Wyatt stands up and says, "It's getting late, and I have to work tomorrow. I'm going to head out."

He glances around the table as everyone says goodbye, and I note that Sasha doesn't look too broken up about it as she gives him a cheerful smile.

Wyatt claps Hunter on the shoulder as he walks by. "Later, man."

Keith stands up from the table, grabbing his glass. "I'm getting me another drink. Anyone want one?"

Sasha and John both raise their hands, and Keith teeters off toward the bar.

"He's going to have a hangover from hell tomorrow," Hunter remarks as he reaches down to my hand and pulls me from my chair. "Now, if y'all will excuse us, Gabby and I are going to take a walk out on the beach so I can have some alone time with my girl."

My heart sighs. Yes, it's evident. I love him.

Leading me by my hand, Hunter weaves his way among the crowd out to the back deck. The area is still closed off to patrons and has a huge sign proclaiming it so, but he walks right through the door and into the cool evening breeze.

We're silent as we make our way down the stairs and onto the sand, our feet sinking in deep until we make our way closer to the water, where it's more hard packed. He leads us south with the water on our left, our hands loosely clasped and swinging back and forth.

"So how long after I left the table before they pounced... tried to get you to choose sides?" he asks me quietly.

"Two seconds," I tell him.

"Have you picked a team yet?"

"Well, let me make sure I know who's playing," I

tell him with a small laugh. "On Team Let's Get Hunter To Surf Again, you have Keith and Sasha for sure. I'm going to take a good guess and say that John and Wyatt are on Team Let Hunter Make His Own Mind Up. Am I right so far?"

"Pretty much. But go ahead and add a third team. There's Team We Want Hunter To Stay. That's comprised of Casey, Mom, and Dad."

"Really?" I ask surprised, because they have always supported Hunter's career as a professional surfer.

"Yeah," he says softly, with a ton of love in his voice. "They love having me home and aren't afraid to say it."

"Where does Brody stand?" I ask hesitantly.

Shrugging his shoulders, Hunter says, "No fucking clue. We haven't talked about it, but we need to. Seeing as how most of my decision has to do with him."

"You're wrong," I murmur.

Hunter stops walking, bringing me to a halt as well. Turning to me, he brings his hands to my shoulders, and then caresses upward along my neck until he's cupping my face. "How am I wrong?"

The moon is bright and I have no problem seeing Hunter's eyes, so I know he can see mine as well. I hope he understands what I'm trying to convey. "It doesn't have anything to do with Brody. It has only to do with what *you* want, Hunter. No one else."

He stares at me a long moment, his eyes full of understanding and appreciation of what I've just said. "You will always put me first, won't you, Gabs?"

"Yes," I answer him simply, because I will. I'll always put him ahead of everything and anyone.

Leaning in, he brushes his lips across mine. When he pulls back, there is something in his eyes that I've never seen before. It is an emotion that is so strong, so powerful, that it makes my legs go weak and my heart start to thrum. It makes butterflies swim in my stomach and causes heat to unfurl throughout my body. I know what that emotion is… it's self-evident.

But to make sure I understand what his eyes are telling me, he says, "I love you, Gabby. I always have. I've loved you like a sister and like a friend. Most importantly and most recently, I love you as a man loves a woman. I need you to know that."

My mind spins back five years ago, to when we stood facing each other, just after our kiss. I was young and naïve, and I wanted those words then. But they weren't right, I realize. Not back then. Because what we had back then wasn't anything like what we have now. It has taken time, maturity, experiences, and work to get to where we are at this moment.

My hands come up to clasp onto his wrists as they still hold my face. "I love you too, Hunter. I've always loved you, and just like you, it's been many different types of love. But what I feel now… this is the type of love I always wanted with you."

The smile Hunter gives me is soul stealing. Then he kisses me and this time, it's absolutely different. Because this time, we've traded the words that have solidified our relationship. We've affirmed to each other that our hearts are mated to one another, and let me tell you, it makes a regular kiss border on the divine. It shakes me to my core, the depth of feeling that we pour into the kiss, and never, ever, in my entire life, have I felt such peace.

Such utter contentment.

Such love.

When Hunter finally pulls his lips from mine, it's to move them to my forehead, giving me a soft kiss and telling me he loves me again. I close my eyes and let his voice wash over me, knowing I will never tire of hearing that from him.

Taking my hand, Hunter resumes our walk, his hand holding onto me a little more tightly. "What team are you on, Gabby?"

"I'm on your team, baby. I'm on the team that makes Hunter happiest."

"Fuck," he grumbles. "I didn't think it was possible for me to love you more, but you just made the impossible happen."

Giggling, I give his hand a squeeze. "Seriously... whatever your gut tells you to do, it will be the right call. And you have my support."

"And you'll wait for me if I go?"

"Of course I will."

"Will you visit me on tour?"

"If I can swing it... I'd love to come watch you and spend time with you."

"It's going to be brutal, Gabby. Being apart from each other... sometimes for months."

"Yes, it will," I tell him honestly. "But we can do it. I'm not going anywhere. I've waited my whole life for you to wise up and love me."

Hunter's quiet for a moment, but then he says, "You have loyalty like no one I've ever known. You dropped out of school without a moment's hesitation, all to keep your dead father's dream alive. Not your dream... *his* dream."

I stop walking and turn to look at him inquisitively. "Hunter?"

"You never put yourself first. You're putting me first right now, and I have to wonder what it says about me that I'm letting you do that."

"It doesn't say anything," I assure him. "This is nothing more than making the best decision for you at this particular point in your life. It's about doing what's right and having no regrets. You're not hurting anyone by this decision, so what's the problem?"

He looks at me skeptically and simply says, "If I go… it will hurt you."

"No. It won't hurt me because there is no intent by you to hurt me. Will I be sad? Yes. Will I be lonely? Yes. That's going to happen. You're going to feel those things too, I suspect. But never hurt."

Hunter pulls me roughly into his arms, gripping the back of my head and pushing me against his chest. I can feel his heartbeat thumping against my cheek as my arms wrap around his waist.

"Thank you," he says quietly.

"For?" I ask, not quite sure why thanks is needed.

"For being you, Gabs. Just for being you."

Yes, it's self-evident.

I love him.

TWENTY

Hunter

At Gabby's insistence, I went ahead and opened Last Call back up for lunch, since all inside work was complete and the outside would be done by the end of the week. But it's extremely slow right now for a Sunday, and not many people know that we are serving lunch again.

No one is sitting up at the bar, and only a few of the booths are occupied, so now is as good a time as any for me to pull Brody aside to talk. I feel like I have to catch him unawares in order to get him to give me ten minutes of quality talk time. He's vigorously avoided talking to me since his blow up at Alyssa.

"Hey Wanda," I say to one of the waitresses as she passes by. "I need to talk to Brody for a minute. Can you handle this area by yourself?"

"Sure," she says with a wink. "It's just Henry Coursier and his cronies. I think I can handle that group for a bit."

I laugh, because Henry Coursier is a big talker and a big charmer. He'll keep Wanda occupied and on her toes. Glancing over at him as he laughs exuberantly at something someone says, I wonder if he's reviewed Gabby's bid and what he thinks of it. I want to ask him, and also put in a good word for her, but I'm thinking that might be stepping on Gabby's toes. Still, it hasn't escaped my notice that he's not called me for a reference, and I hope that doesn't mean he won't consider her bid for some reason.

I'll have to think on that for a bit, and maybe by the time I get done talking to Brody, if he's still here, I'll bring it up in casual conversation.

"Hey Brody," I call out to him. "My office. Need to talk."

By the time I sit down behind my desk, Brody is

walking in behind me, shutting the door. He sits down quietly opposite me, leaning forward to rest his elbows on his knees.

"If this is about that shit with Alyssa last week—"

"It's not," I cut him off, "but I still think that was fucked up. I need to talk to you about the bar."

Brody straightens up and then leans back in his chair. "I'm listening."

"I've been offered some pretty lucrative endorsements if I agree to go back on the Tour next year. I'm considering it. Only problem is that they want me to jump back on this year's tour. Sooner rather than later."

"Can you win this year?"

Shaking my head, I pull a paperclip out of its holder and start fiddling with it. "No, but they want me to go back on Tour now to get the practice and visibility. All in prep for next year."

Brody's no dummy. I can see the wheels spinning in his head. "I don't want a partnership."

"Not offering it again," I tell him, although if I thought he'd take it, I'd gladly give it to him. But I've decided I'm not going to push past the limits of his pride.

"What do you need?"

"I need you to run Last Call and manage it for

me. Take over all the duties I'm doing. I'll hire a bartender to replace you. Keep it going until I return."

"And when might that be?" he asks, although he doesn't really sound all that interested in the answer.

"I don't know. Maybe after next year's tour. Maybe I'll stay on another year... two. Who knows?"

"And you'd need my commitment for that unspecified time period?"

"That's the gist of it. Can I count on you?"

Brody's gaze lowers to the floor. I wait for his answer, fully expecting his support. I'm stunned when he says, "I don't know. I need to think about it."

Okay, I get that. I'm asking him to take on a lot of responsibility, but fuck... I gave up my career to come home and be there for him. I'd think the least he could do is fucking have my back. Still, it's with a calm voice that I say, "Fine. But I need an answer soon. My agent says the deals will be pulled soon if I don't commit."

"So it's a definite?" Brody asks, looking back up at me. "You're definitely doing it?"

"No, it's not a definite. I'm still considering my options, but it would help if I knew you were on board. Help my decision making a bit easier."

"Let me have tonight," he asks.

Taking a deep breath, I say, "Sure."

Brody stands up and walks to the door. I hesitate for a minute, and then follow him. When we step into the hallway, I ask, "Do you want to talk to me about this? Talk through any concerns?"

Shaking his head, Brody gives me an impassive look and doesn't answer my question. "Look Hunter... I know what you've done for me—what you've given up. If I can help you, I will. I'm just trying to sort through some internal shit, and that's best done alone."

"Okay," I tell him. "Understood."

But I don't understand shit about my brother.

Brody starts to turn to head back into the bar area, but then turns around. "How does Gabby fit into your decision-making process?"

"She doesn't, apparently," I tell him. I see his eyes go dark, so I immediately add on, "I mean that she's told me not to factor her in the decision. She fully supports whatever I want to do."

His eyes lighten back up, and he gives me a small smile. "But you're still going to factor her in, right?"

"Of course I am," I tell him with a smile.

Brody just gives me a stiff nod and heads into the bar area. I follow behind him, immediately assaulted with the roar of four men laughing. When I turn the corner, I can tell immediately it's coming from Henry Coursier's table, and I smile internally to myself. The guy is a one-man, walking-comedic show.

As I approach the rear of their booth, I hear Henry say, "…I'd almost consider it, because come on… what a pair of tits."

Shaking my head, I snicker at the man and his dirty mouth.

Then I hear another guy say, "And she has a fine ass, too. Just imagine seeing her bent over a sawhorse every day… you'd walk around with a perpetual hard-on."

Another round of laughter fills my ears, but suddenly, I'm not thinking this conversation is so funny anymore. Suddenly… I have a feeling I know who they are talking about, and I am not appreciating this conversation.

Then Henry Coursier puts a nail in his coffin when he says, "It's all moot. No way am I going to offer that job to a fucking woman. I don't care how great her tits and ass look in a pair of jeans. She's got no business working in a man's field."

Rage such as I've never felt before filters through me. I fucking see a red cape waving in front of me, and I'm a fucking charging bull. I turn the corner to their booth and immediately see Henry Coursier's fat fucking face go pale when he sees me. He's sitting on the inside but that doesn't stop me.

I reach over the man sitting next to him and grab Coursier by his shirt with both fists, hauling him out of the booth and across the table, knocking over glasses and lunch plates in the process. Everyone sitting there is so stunned that they don't even make a move as food and drinks spill onto their laps. I hear Brody behind me say, "Oh shit."

Then I'm dragging Henry through my bar. He tries to rip away from me, so I merely grab him around the back of the neck with one hand, using my other to twist his arm up behind his back. He whimpers like a little fucking girl.

When I hit the front door, I give him a solid push and he goes flying through it, landing on his ass in the gravel parking lot. Henry looks at me in fear because I barrel toward him, again… fucking bull… enraged.

Leaning down, I grab him by the shirt and pull him to his feet. I hear the door open behind me, and people rushing out to the parking lot. I vaguely hear Brody say, "Don't do it, Hunter," but that's the last thing I hear before my arm cocks back and my fists connects viciously with his jaw.

He sags to the ground, and I reach for him again

to pull him up. That's when Brody's arms wrap around me from behind, pinning my own arms to my sides. He growls in my ear, "Let it go, man."

"Get the fuck off me, Brody," I yell. "I'm going to murder him."

Henry Coursier starts to sit up, rubbing his jaw. His lip had split with that one hit and blood dribbles down his chin. When he sees Brody has a hold of me, he decides to man up and sneers, "What's wrong, Hunter? Can't handle a little truth about your piece of snatch?"

"You fucking piece of shit," I roar and pull free of Brody, lunging toward Henry, who starts to crabwalk backward to get away from me.

Brody tackles me from behind, grabbing around both of my legs, and we both go crashing into the gravel. Rocks dig and cut into my skin, but I barely feel them. Fury is still blistering inside of me, and I can only think of getting to Henry and beating the shit out of him for what he said about Gabby.

"Stop it," Brody hisses in my ear as I try to throw him off me. "If you keep going, those other guys are going to jump in. Then I'm going to jump in, and then I'm going to get my parole revoked. You want me to go back to prison?"

And just like that, I go still. Brody's words hit me

hard, and there's no fucking way I'll ever put my brother in danger like that. Besides, I can get Henry Coursier on his own some other time and kick his ass.

"Okay," I say. "I'm done—now get off."

Brody stands up hesitantly and offers me a hand. When I reach out to take it, I see my hand is pouring blood from a gash on the side of my palm, presumably made by a rock.

When I stand, I wince and look down at my legs. There's a hole in one knee, and I can feel there's a cut in there somewhere too.

Looking down at Henry, I say, "Get the fuck off my property and don't ever come back around. I catch you alone at any time in the future, you best be sure I'm going to finish what I started."

"Fuck you, Markham," he says as his buddies help him up from the ground.

I don't even respond but reach into my pocket and pull my Jeep keys out.

"Where are you going?" Brody asks.

"To go see Gabby," I tell him, sick to my stomach that I need to tell her exactly what happened. This shit will be out over the gossip waves in about five more seconds, and she needs to hear it from me. I need to be there when she finds out about this… because it is *not* going to go over well.

"At least go home and get cleaned up first," Brody says. "You look like a nightmare."

I don't respond but throw myself into my Jeep, peeling out of the parking lot before Coursier and his crew even make it to their cars. But Brody's right... I need to get cleaned up first before I go see Gabby.

Gabby opens her door, smiling at me brilliantly. I soak it in, knowing that look is not going to be around much longer.

"What are you doing here?" she asks brightly. "Not that I'm complaining."

I step inside but before I can say anything, she sees the bandage on my palm. Taking my hand gently, her fingers trace the outside edge. "Oh my God. What happened to you?"

"Got in a bit of a fight," I tell her quietly. "Got a minute to talk?"

"Sure," she says with worry as she leads me over to the couch. She sits down, patting the seat beside her, and turning to face me after I plop down.

I don't know any other way to say this other than to just say it. "You're not going to get the Coursier project."

Gabby blinks hard, and her mouth draws down. "Oh."

She's silent for a moment, chewing on her bottom lip, and her gaze drops to her hands, which are clasped in her lap. My fingers itch to take her in my arms, and I will, but I need to get the rest of it out first.

"He's not giving you the bid because you're a woman. No other reason than pure bigotry."

I watch her carefully as what I say sinks in. She stares at her hands, her thumbs twirling around each other, and I'm poised to grab onto her if she breaks down.

Instead, she looks up at me, her eyes sorrowful. "Is that how you hurt your hand?"

"Yes," I tell her. "His jaw hurts more, I can guarantee you."

"You hit him because he's not giving me the job?" she asks in wonder, along with a little bit of censorship. I start to relax, because Gabby seems to be taking this better than I expected.

"No, I hit him because he's a pig, and he was talking about your tits and ass to his friends."

"Oh," she says again, and her gaze drops once more to her hands. I'm prepared... at the first sign of a teardrop, or a tremble of a lip, I'm lunging for her.

Her mouth opens slightly, and she... snickers? Loudly.

Then she snorts with laughter and claps her hand over her mouth as her eyes raise up to meet mine, crinkled in amusement. Then she lets loose, falling back against the armrest of the couch, laughing hysterically and clutching her stomach with her hands.

My jaw hangs open, and I think to myself, *That's it. Gabby's gone off the deep end. Time to pull out the straightjacket.*

She sits up after a few more chortles, wiping the back of her hand across her eyes, which are now indeed wet with tears... from fucking laughter.

"What's so funny?" I ask her in confusion.

Gabby leans forward suddenly, crawling across the couch to me, and slithering her way right onto my lap, where she straddles me. Wrapping her arms around my neck, she leans in and kisses me, giggling once more. "I just think it's fucking adorable that you would get in a fight to defend my honor."

"Seriously? You think that's fucking adorable?" I ask as my hands come up to grip her waist.

She nods her head with her bottom lip pulled between her teeth, staring at me intently.

"I don't want to be adorable," I tell her. "I want to be fucking macho... like a knight in shining armor."

Gabby giggles again, and it's the best sound in the entire world. She leans in and kisses me, sweetly at first, but the minute my fingers sink into the flesh at her hips, she opens up and gives it to me hot and wet.

I groan, then she groans, and then I flip her on her back, settling in between her legs. I kiss her hard while I clasp her tight to me, ignoring the dull ache from the cut in my palm and the gash on my knee. She responds just as hard, pushing her hips up into me and moaning into my mouth.

"I love you," she says against my lips, and my entire world flips upside down over her sweet words. She pulls slightly back to look at me. "I love that you defend me, and that you were worried about me, and that you wanted to come and tell me in person, because I know you, Hunter. You wouldn't want me to hear it elsewhere. Only while you were here in front of me so you could hug me if I took it badly."

I stare at her, awash with love, and fucking hot as hell with desire at this moment. But mostly love for my girl.

"Are you really okay about that?" I ask as I lean down and rub my cheek along hers.

"Yes," she whispers. "I'm fine. It's nothing I haven't heard before, and I'm sure I'll hear it again."

"You're amazing, Gabs. Most women would have been in a dither over that."

"A dither?" she asks incredulously. "That's fucking adorable."

Laughing, I push my hips against her so she gets another taste of the hard-on that's about ready to bust out of my pants. "Let's see if you think I'm fucking adorable when I'm making you scream in pleasure."

"Bring it on, baby. Bring it on."

So I do.

TWENTY-ONE

Gabby

Knock, knock, knock.

Vaguely, it comes to me through the darkness that someone is knocking. On the wall? On the door?

"Fuck," Hunter groans beside me and I come awake, realizing I'm in his bed. The knowledge that I'm naked and wrapped in his arms makes me feel warm and snuggly, and I push back against him, wiggling in closer.

"Stop doing that," he growls in my ear.

"Someone's at the door, and I don't want to have to answer it with a hard-on."

After kissing me on the back of my head, Hunter releases me and rolls out of bed. I can hear him in the dusky gloom of early morning, pulling on his pants. I open one eye and look at the clock. Six in the morning, so it must be important.

"Want me to get up with you?" I ask groggily.

"No. Go back to sleep, baby."

"'Kay," I say as I roll over into the warm spot he just left and curl my hand under my chin. I hear the bedroom door open briefly, then shut again, and I nestle down under the covers to go back to sleep.

I let my mind drift to last night with Hunter. It was an ordinary night. He worked at Last Call until about eight, and then I met him here at the apartment, where we shared a late dinner with John and Sasha. They are going to be leaving in a few days, and I know Hunter wants to spend as much time with John as he can. We stayed up until about midnight, drinking beer and shooting the shit.

When it was time to go to bed, Hunter stood up from the couch and pulled me up by my hand. "We're heading to bed, guys. See you in the morning."

John and Sasha both gave us smiles. John's genuine as he softly said, "Goodnight," and Sasha's accommodating.

When we were in the privacy of Hunter's bedroom, he wasted no time in peeling my clothes off. As my shirt came over my head and his hands worked at my bra strap, he asked, "Are you sure you're okay about not getting that bid with Coursier?"

As often seems to happen around Hunter lately, my heart just melted over his continued concern. "Yes, baby. I'm fine. It's not the end of the world for me."

"Okay," he said as he nuzzled my neck. "Just wanted to make sure."

We were silent after that as we both helped the other undress, softly kissing and stroking in between broken breaths and whispered sighs. Hunter made love to me last night, so very slowly, the only measure of our excitement was the quickening of our breaths as he moved leisurely in and out of me. Our hands were clasped together tight and, when he wasn't kissing me, he was looking down at me with love and tenderness. We came together and it was shattering, even as it was quiet.

And then Hunter was pulling me into his arms to go to sleep, as I murmured to him that I loved him.

Smiling, I realize that my thoughts didn't cause me to drift back to sleep. Rather, I'm wide awake. Just thinking about Hunter excites me, and I'm not talking sexually, although last night was blistering hot in a sweet way. But I'm talking about excited as in I hate to spend a single moment away from him. I've never felt more alive than I do right now, and even though I got smacked down by Henry Coursier yesterday, I feel like I can pretty much accomplish anything I set my mind to.

Throwing the covers back, I roll out of bed and pull on my jeans and a t-shirt. I can hear the murmuring of voices from the kitchen and assume Hunter's talking to his early morning visitor.

When I open the bedroom door, the voices filter in clear and I realize it's Brody in the kitchen. His words stop me in my tracks. "You need to do this, Hunter."

I hear Hunter sigh and can actually envision him raking his hand through his hair. "I don't know, man. I thought I had it figured out."

"Well, just so there's no hesitation on your part as relates to the bar, I've got your back. I'll handle it while you're gone and gladly hand it back over to you when you get back. Whenever that may be."

My breath freezes, and I realize they're talking about Hunter leaving for the Tour. I immediately consider heading back to the bedroom, because I'm so eavesdropping right now, and I have no clue if this is a private conversation. I'm hesitant to walk into the kitchen, because let's face it… Brody isn't the most loquacious person in the world, and I don't want to impede upon him finally talking straight to his brother.

So I hang in limbo, hiding in the hallway, and listening in on their talk.

"Thanks, Brody. That means a lot."

"So when will you leave?"

"If I accept, probably within a week."

"What do you mean 'if I accept'? Isn't this a done deal?"

"Fuck no," Hunter says in exasperation. "I'm just not sure."

"Something wrong with the offer?"

"No."

"Something wrong with your ability to surf?"

"Of course not."

"Something wrong with me watching Last Call while you're gone?"

"You know there's not," Hunter growls.

"Then it's Gabby," Brody says emphatically.

"Keep your voice down," Hunter hisses. "She's in the bedroom sleeping, and of course it's Gabby."

My heart starts pounding as I realize that Hunter

is very much factoring me into the equation as to whether or not he stays or goes. A rush of feelings plow through me from extreme love that he cares for me enough to walk away from fame and glory, to sickness over the fact he might actually walk away from fame and glory for me.

"Dude… you know I like Gabby, but don't fuck this up over a woman. Nothing is more important than this shot you're being handed."

Well, we both wondered which team Brody was going to be on, and he's clearly in the same corner as Sasha and Keith.

"Brody… I love her. I don't know that this shot is more important than Gabby is. I think she might be the most important thing that's ever happened to me in my life."

I can hear a low whistle coming from Brody, and then he says in a low voice, "If she loved you the way you love her, she wouldn't hold you back."

"That's just it… she's not holding me back. She'll support me if I go."

"Then what's the fucking problem?"

"I don't know," Hunter says in a tired voice. "It's just not sitting right with me. I think I need to talk this through with Gabby some more… see if I can get some better perspective."

I hear chair stools scraping on the floor and realize that Brody must be getting ready to leave, so I hightail it back to Hunter's bedroom. Quickly shucking off my clothes, I crawl back under the covers with my heart racing.

Hunter is considering not going back on the Tour because of me. I'm floored, stunned beyond belief, and I'm really not quite sure how I feel about that. On the one hand, I've been dreading the thought of being away for him for so many months out of the year.

On the other hand, we're both young and have all the time in the world to be together. This opportunity for Hunter is fleeting. It could be the biggest regret of his life if he passes this up. And there's no way in hell I want to be tied to that.

When the bedroom door opens, I think about feigning sleep but realize my heart is still beating far too erratically to pull it off well. So I roll over and say, "Hey".

"Hey," he whispers as he pulls his clothes off and slips back into bed.

"Who was that?" I ask as a means of giving him a lead in to talk to me. That's what he told Brody... that he wanted to talk to me about this more.

"Just Brody," he says and offers no more.

Instead, he rolls to the side and pulls me into his body, my backside resting flush against his front. He curves an arm around my waist and squeezes. "Let's go back to sleep for a bit."

"I'm not tired," I tell him so he knows I'm available to talk.

Just lay it on me, babe. I'm right here.

"I'm not tired either," he murmurs, while nuzzling into my neck with his mouth.

"So what do you want to talk about?" I prod, opening the door wide open for him to walk through into conversation land.

"Don't wanna talk," he whispers, the arm that's around my waist now loosening so his palm lays flat on my stomach. Heat courses through me at his touch… the tone of his voice, because I know damn well what he wants to do, and God help me… I want it too.

I try one more time, part of me hoping it's in vain, as his hand starts to graze down my skin south. "What did Brody want?"

Hunter's fingers dip into the edge of my underwear, at the same time his teeth grab ahold of my earlobe and gently bite down. Then he gives it a lick as he releases it. "Don't want to talk about Brody right this minute, babe."

"But—" I start to say, and then gasp as he sinks a finger into me.

"Still want to talk right now?" he murmurs in my ear.

Shaking my head, I push my hips against his hand, demanding more. Because we can always talk about Brody later.

"This is soooo what I needed," I say as I lean over and slurp from my straw. I'm halfway into my third Pina Colada of the evening, and I'm feeling no pain.

Casey grins at me, leaning over to slurp her own drink. "You definitely needed a girl's night out."

Yes I did. Hunter and I never did get to talk about Brody, because after he fucked me silly this morning, we both had to get ready to go to work. I stewed about my dilemma all day and realized that what I really needed was another woman's advice. So I called Casey, invited her for a girl's night out, and here I am.

Swallowing the creamy, coconutty goodness, I look at her seriously. "Will it freak you out if I talk to you about Hunter?"

"You're not going to talk about sex with Hunter, are you?"

"No way. That's sacrosanct."

"It's what?"

"Sacrosanct... you know."

"No, I don't know, or I wouldn't ask."

"Sacrosanct... like... you know, sacrosanct."

"Oh my God," Casey says while laughing. "You're spouting words you don't even know what they mean."

"I do too know what it means. I just can't express it right now but I'm sure it applies in this situation," I say, leaning forward for another icy sip of coconut love. "Besides, we're agreed we're not talking about it, so moving on."

"Okay, moving on," Casey agrees. "So what's up, pup?"

"I'm in love with your brother," I tell her, mentally bracing for her reaction.

"Holy shit! That's huge," she says with excitement, literally bouncing up and down in her chair while clapping her hands. "When are you going to tell him?"

"I already did."

"What did he do?" she asks with trepidation.

"He told me he loved me too. Well, he told me

322

first and then I reciprocated."

"Fucking right on, Hunter," Casey exclaims with a fist pump. Waving her hand in the air, she catches a waitress' attention. "Two more Pina Coladas. We're celebrating!"

"So… do you think it's weird?" I ask her softly.

"No way, Gabby. I mean… it was weird when I thought you were just banging my brother, but I can definitely see you two in love. Oh my God. We'll be real sisters when you get married."

"Whoa, whoa, whoa there. No one's talking marriage," I say firmly, pulling another dose of liquor up my straw.

Casey doesn't even hear me, and then lets out a huge squeal. "Holy fuck me standing… you know what this means, right?"

"What?" I ask, excited, and yet fearful to hear her answer.

"It means Hunter will stay here. He won't go back on tour."

Averting my eyes down to my glass, I think carefully on how I'm going to continue this line of discussion with Casey. It's the exact thing I wanted to talk to her about when I suggested having a girl's night out, and she just gave me the opening. However, I need to be careful because Casey is on

Team Get Hunter To Stay, and I'm now a floater, not sure which team I'm on.

"So… you want him to stay, huh?"

"Of course, silly. My brother has essentially been gone for the last ten years. I love having him home, and I don't want him to leave again."

"Yeah… but, this is a shot he probably shouldn't pass up," I point out. "It could set him financially, and he still has a lot of career ahead of him."

"I know," Casey says with a shrug of her shoulders. "And if he goes, I'll support him. But that doesn't mean I want him to go. You don't want him to go either, right?"

"Of course I don't… I mean, I do… but I don't. You know?"

"No."

"I mean… I want him to be happy, and if surfing is what makes him happy, then he needs to do that."

"Agreed," Casey states emphatically. "But there's something else, so spill."

"It's just… I'm going to be miserable if he goes, but there's no way I can ever push him to stay. In fact, I'm feeling like I need to push him to go, so he won't have any regrets."

"That's natural to feel that way, girl."

"Yeah… but… I overheard him talking with

Brody this morning, and he specifically said he's thinking about not going because of me. I can't let him do that."

"You said there's no way you could ever push him to stay, right?"

I nod, slurping up the last remaining bit of my drink, looking at the empty glass sadly, and then smiling big when the waitress magically appears and sets a full one in front of me. "It's not my place."

"Exactly," Casey says and slaps the table. "Just like it's not your place to push him to stay. Take the pack off, Gabby. He'll come to the decision that's best for him, and we'll just both secretly hope that he'll stay."

"I feel bad that I'm secretly hoping he'll stay."

"It will be our little secret, okay?"

"'Kay," I tell her and take a deep drink.

And just like that, my problems seem to be solved. I'll fully support Hunter in his decision, but I'll secretly hope, pray, light candles at church, and offer up a virgin sacrifice, if only he'll stay here with me.

And I also pray that if he does stay, he doesn't come to regret it, and he most specifically doesn't come to regret staying because of me.

TWENTY-TWO

Hunter

"Five ball, corner pocket," I say as I line up my shot. Drawing my cue back along the valley between my thumb and forefinger, I focus on the orange ball, drawing an imaginary line from the pocket, straight through the ball, across the table, and to my stick. Pulling back, I release a gentle tap on the cue ball and watch as it smoothly rolls toward the five. Knowing without a doubt my shot was perfect, I don't even stay to watch the five sink into the pocket, but start moving my way around the table to line up my next shot.

"You still haven't lost your touch, dude," John says in reverence.

"Yeah, well, owning a bar does have its perks. I get to practice a lot more."

John laughs as he leans on his own pool cue, scratching at the beard on his face. "Remember that little bar in Peniche we were in, and they had that beat-up, old pool table that had a huge groove right in the middle. And we had to structure all our shots around it?"

Smiling, I nod, "Seven ball… side pocket."

Sinking the shot with ease, I stand up and look at John. "And remember that Portuguese girl that came in, betting us ten euro a ball? She kicked our asses. Knew every way around that damn groove in the table."

Chuckling, John says, "Yeah… those were good times."

"The best," I affirm.

Leaning over to take my last shot, I tap the far bumper with my cue, indicating a bank shot, and then nod to the bottom left pocket. Just as a draw my stick back, John says, "Let's make a bet on this shot."

Cocking an eyebrow at him, I ask, "What do you

have in mind?"

"How about if you miss it, you really tell me what's on your mind as far as surfing again? None of this wishy-washy shit you've been handing everyone."

"And if I make it?"

John shoots me an evil grin. "Then you still tell me honestly what's on your mind."

Bending over, I do a quick line up, pull my stick back, and give a short punch to the cue ball. With perfection, it hits the eight ball, banks off the back bumper, and rolls cleanly in the bottom pocket.

I throw my stick on the table, indicating I'm done, and glance across the bar. Sasha is engaged in a game of darts with a few of the locals, so I have some time to talk to John privately.

I walk over to a corner table and sit down, waiting for John to follow. Sipping at my beer, I look out across the bar again and watch Sasha. John follows my gaze but patiently waits for me to talk.

"I loved your sister," I tell him candidly.

"I know," he says softly. "But not enough."

"No," I agree with him. "Not enough."

John has always been the type of friend that I could lay anything on... without fear of judgment or reprisal. When I was eighteen, I competed in a pro event in Australia, and the waves were massive. The competition was the fiercest I had ever been among. Part of the sport of professional surfing is trying to beat your competitor to the wave. It takes determination, aggression, and power, something that I usually didn't have a problem with at eighteen, because I was just cocky enough to have all of those qualities in spades.

I remember watching the heat before mine, trying to get my head into the zone. I watched as a young newcomer...fuck, I can't even remember his name now, snaked his opponent by cutting in on his wave, and then doing a vicious cut-back, causing the fins of his board to hit the other dude and slice into his ankle. It was an egregious move that got him disqualified and ended the other dude's career because it severed his Achilles tendon.

It was at that moment that I realized I was in the big leagues, and I had a wave of uncertainty crash through me, causing my heart to skitter out of control and my stomach to cramp tight. John was standing beside me, and I didn't even have to say anything, but I did... because I knew I could and I knew he'd understand.

"Fuck," I told him, my voice quaking. "I don't know if I'm ready for this."

He brought his hand up and clapped it around

my neck, giving me a slight shake. "You're ready. Doesn't mean it's not scary, because it is. Use that fear to make you smart."

He affirmed my fear, didn't hold it against me. That empowered me more than anything did, because he taught me to embrace it and use it to my advantage. Any other person out there would have called me a pussy and probably destroyed whatever healthy ego I had at that young age.

Not John though. He mentored me through it and showed me I could trust him. Over the years, he's been there for me time and again, handing out sage wisdom, slapping me on the back of the head if necessary, and generally being there to pull my head out of my ass when warranted.

"Gabby's different though," John says softly, breaking into my ruminations.

I look at John, taking in the understanding bend in his eyebrows, the way his eyes are non-judgmental and accepting.

"I love her more than surfing. She's more important than surfing. You can throw all the money in the world at me, you can guarantee that I'd win every competition... none of it is better than Gabby. I can't leave her, John. I don't want to leave her."

"Then don't," he says simply, as if it were really

just that simple.

I mean, it really is just that simple to me, and it's nice to know that John sees it the same way. I'm not sure why it's so complicated for everyone else that has weighed in with their opinion.

So that's that.

I'm not taking the deals; I'm not going back on the tour. I'm going to stay here, run Last Call, and be with Gabby. Taking a deep breath and letting it out, I feel like the weight of the world has been lifted from my shoulders and it feels fucking fantastic.

I search deep within... look for signs of uncertainty, fear, or regret.

I come up empty.

All I feel is excitement about my life with Gabby, back home with my friends and family. I don't even feel a pang of sorrow for leaving my surfing career behind.

This is absolutely the right thing to do.

Turning to John, I grin. "I'll call Keith in the morning and give him the bad news. He's not going to be happy."

"Bad news about what?" I hear from behind, and see Sasha sauntering up to our table. She takes the seat to my left and looks at me with curiosity.

"I'm not going back on tour," I tell her, still

smiling with mega wattage on the inside.

Sasha's brows furrow, and her lips flatten out. "You got to be fucking kidding me. You're going to give all of that up?"

"Looks like," I tell her lightly.

"You're a fucking idiot. And let me just guess... you're giving it all up so you can be with your precious Gabby, right? Un-fucking-believable."

"What the hell is your problem?" I snarl at Sasha.

At the same time, John says, "This is none of your business, Sasha... stay out of it."

Her head flips back and forth between us and she chooses to address me instead, her voice venomous. "I'll tell you what my problem is... I tried to get you to leave the tour for me, and you wouldn't even consider it. But you'll do it for her? Gotta tell you, Hunter... it fucking stings a little."

I stare at her incredulously. "You mean your opinion on this comes down to jealousy? You want me to leave this all behind and go back on tour, just so you don't remain the one woman I wouldn't give it up for? You want to lump Gabby in with you? Well, I'm sorry, Sasha... but Gabby *is* different from you. My feelings for her are different."

Sasha reels backward, and she looks like I just slapped her in the face. Instant regret washes over me, because while I'm angry with her, I don't want to hurt her. I know I've done that enough.

"But… but… you've not been with her that long. You and I were together for almost two years. Why would you risk your career for such an unknown?"

Reaching across the table, I grab Sasha's hand. "I've known her most of my life, Sash. Far longer than I've known you. But that doesn't have anything to do with it. It's just a feeling I have… that this is the right thing for me at this moment in my life."

She stares at me for a moment, disbelief coating her face. Then she pulls her hand away and stands up from the table. "Excuse me… I'm going to go to the ladies' room."

As she walks away, I turn my head to John. "That went well."

"Sorry, dude… that was bound to come out. Sasha's been carrying some bitter feelings obviously."

"You know I don't want to hurt her, right?"

"I know, man," he says as he stands up. "I'm going to go hover like a big brother and catch her as she comes out… talk to her a bit."

"Sure," I say, my thoughts already leaving Sasha and John behind, wondering what Gabby's up to.

As John walks away, I pull out my phone and dial my girl. She answers on the fourth ring, just as I was about to hang up.

"H-e-e-e-e-y babe," she drawls.

Oh, yeah... she's tanked.

"My Gabs is drunk tonight, huh?" I laugh into the phone.

"Just a little... more like really, really buzzed."

"Having a good time?"

"Would be better if you were here," she breathes into the phone. "I miss you."

My heart constricts pleasurably just from the longing in her voice. "I miss you too, baby."

"So... you were going to talk to me this morning about why Brody came over... but you never did. And now that I have a good buzz going on, I wanted to ask you about it."

Chuckling, I tell her, "It wasn't much. He just wanted to let me know that he'd watch Last Call for me if I wanted to go back on tour."

"I have a confession to make," she whispers into the phone and, for a split second, I think she might be getting ready to talk dirty to me. Which I'm totally up for, by the way.

Instead, she says, "I overheard your conversation with Brody."

"You did?" I tease her. "Skulking in the hallway?"

"Yeah... something like that."

My brain scrambles around to remember exactly everything Brody said, and it suddenly hits me why Gabby brought this up. "Don't give what Brody said another thought."

"I'm not thinking about what he said. I'm thinking about what you said. I'm not more important than your shot at this."

"Gabby," I say... my voice soft and reassuring. "My decision's made. I'm staying here because it's what I want. I want that more than I want the money and fame."

She's silent on the other end, and I can envision her chewing on her lip as she considers what I said. Her voice is hesitant when she says, "I'm afraid you'll come to regret it, and then hate *me* for that."

"What?" I exclaim loudly. "That's ridiculous. Gabby... this is my decision. Mine alone. You've not pushed me one way or the other, so this will never blow back on you. You hear me?"

She's silently digesting what I say, so I wait her out. When she doesn't respond, I push at her. "Are you picking up what I'm putting down?"

I hear her giggle on the other end, and then she says, "Yeah... I'm picking it up."

"Good, baby... Now, we can talk about this

more tomorrow. I'll see you at the bar in the morning."

"Want me to come stay with you tonight?"

"Nah… enjoy your night out, and then get home and get some rest."

"But, I'll miss you," she whispers into the phone, and I can tell she's doing that so no one else hears her.

"I'll miss you too, honey… but it's just for tonight. Besides, sounds like you'll be too drunk to let me take proper advantage of you."

"Okay," she sighs into the phone. "We're going to be out for a while still."

"Cabbing it home, right?"

"Right."

"Drink lots of water before you go to bed… take some Ibuprofen."

"Got it."

"And Gabby?"

"Yes?"

"I love you."

"I love you, too."

I disconnect the call and tap the phone against my chin. Today is the start of the rest of my life with Gabby. Hundreds of thoughts and desires of all the things I want to do with her flood my mind.

I want to travel with her... take her around the world and show her all the amazing things I've seen so far. I want to see new things with her, so we can share them together for the first time.

I want to spend lazy afternoons lying on the couch, while I watch football and maybe she reads a book.

I want us to go grocery shopping together, and fight over whether or not to buy fat-free or skim milk. I want to make her breakfast in bed, and I want her to make me chocolate chip cookies when I'm feeling down.

I want to do all of this now, so we still have time for the important stuff. Like building a life together. I'm not sure exactly what that means, but I'm guessing there is going to be a moment where we move in together, get engaged... get married... have kids.

Yeah... I see it all, and I know without a doubt I've made the right decision.

TWENTY-THREE

Gabby

    Slipping the key in the lock, I quietly turn it and push Hunter's door open. I had called about ten minutes ago, first his cell phone, then his landline, but he didn't answer either. I left a whispered message on his answering machine that I was going to swing by, hoping that if John or Sasha were up, they wouldn't be prancing around naked or something when I walked in.

    I swung by the local donut shop and picked up a

dozen donuts, which I take into the kitchen and set on the table. The house is quiet, but I'm not surprised. It's just a little after six in the morning, and I wanted to get an early start over at Last Call. I think I can get the staining finished today, tomorrow will be about tiny touch ups, and then the job will be complete.

What I'll do after that, I have no idea, but I'll figure it out.

The mere fact that Hunter has decided to stay, has put a lot of things in perspective. I feel like I have the fortitude now to keep pushing forward with Ward Construction, because the one thing I know for sure… Hunter believes I can do it.

I leave the kitchen and turn into the hallway that leads to Hunter's bedroom. As soon as I make that turn, I sense something out of place, and I glance up. His bedroom door opens, and for a split second, I think he might walk out.

Then my jaw drops open as Sasha steps out, wearing a robe that hits the top of her thigh, and I'm guessing not much else. Her hair is wet, and I'm also guessing she just took a shower. She looks me directly in the eye, and doesn't seem the least bit surprised to see me standing there.

In fact, her lips curl upward in a smirk as she

quietly shuts the door behind her, and she has the brass balls to say, "Oops. Busted."

"Seriously?" I ask in disbelief.

Sasha walks toward me and says in a whisper, "Gee... I'm sorry, Gabby. I heard some noise out here and came out to investigate. I never in a million years thought you'd be standing out here."

"Seriously?" I ask again.

She just smiles at me in a simpering sort of way, and actually twirls a lock of her wet hair around her finger. "This is a little awkward, huh? Maybe you should go ahead and just leave. I think Hunter's made his choice."

"Seriously?" I ask one last time, acting like I'm in disbelief at what is going on here, but on the contrary, I know damn well what is going on here, and this bitch just met her match.

"You step out of Hunter's bedroom, and you want me to believe that you were in there doing what? Having sex with him? You want me to believe you slept in there last night?"

"Isn't it obvious?" she purrs, and I don't miss the fact that she's still trying to whisper.

Okay, time to put an end to this charade.

I step past Sasha and make my way to Hunter's door, relishing that she gasps and makes a grab at my arm. "What are you doing?"

"Exposing you," I tell her.

Pushing the door open, the hall light bathes Hunter's bed in a warm glow. He's lying on his side, the covers pulled up tight over him. It's clear by the way the covers are smooth on the other side that he slept there alone, but that's exactly what I expected to see.

I make a glance behind me and see Sasha standing in the doorway, her arms crossed over her stomach and a sick look on her face. And in that moment, I have a brief flash of pity for her fill me. I don't know what her motivation for doing this was, but I suspect it stems from the fact that she loved him at one point, and I know how mighty fine that feels.

Turning, I face Sasha and stare at her a moment. Then I softly shut the door on her, enclosing me in the room alone with Hunter, relishing the look of fear on her face because she knows not what I'm going to do.

I crawl onto the bed and fit my body up to his back, wrapping my arm around the lump that is him under the covers. He's breathing deeply in his slumber and I just hold onto him a while, basking in the love I feel. It's like nothing I've ever felt before, and I realize what a lucky woman I am. To have been given the love of her life... the one I have wanted forever.

Leaning up on an elbow, I bend over and kiss the side of his neck, just below his ear. "Morning, baby."

He gives a slight groan from the touch, and then he turns over, pulling his arms out from under the covers to wrap around me. "Gabby?"

"Now, who else would it be?" I tease, all the while thinking to myself... just a few minutes ago, Sasha was in here.

I made a split-second decision when I closed the door on Sasha's face not to tell Hunter about this. She and John are heading out early this afternoon for an evening flight out of Raleigh. I don't want to make waves, and I certainly don't want to do anything that can potentially come in between John and Hunter's relationship. Sasha will be Sasha and, maybe one day, I'll tell Hunter what she did, but for now, it doesn't serve any purpose other than to get everyone riled up.

When I saw her walk out of his room, there was not even a second of doubt in my mind that she was staging this. I knew... without a doubt... that she must have heard my message on the answering machine, and knew I was coming over. I didn't need to see the smoothness of the covers of Hunter's bed to know she hadn't been in it, and I bet if I walked in his bathroom right now, the shower would be bone dry, even though she made it look like she had just come out of there.

Hunter has my absolute trust and loyalty. There was never a moment that I felt he would betray me with another woman. That is how secure I am in my love for him, and in his love for me.

And fuck if this high road doesn't feel good.

Hunter pushes the covers down so he can pull my body in closer to his, and the heat emanating off him burns through my clothes. He snuggles in deep, pulling my face into the crook of his neck, and wrapping both arms and legs around me.

"You feel good," he murmurs sleepily, squeezing me tight.

"And you smell good," he adds as he takes a deep sniff of my hair.

One of his hands drifts down my back and over my butt, grasping me tightly there.

"I bet you taste fucking divine, too," he says, his voice now a little less groggy and a whole lot more alert.

Giggling, I hug him tight. "Bad man, and while I'd love to let you find out exactly how I taste, I don't have time. I just wanted to drop off some donuts for you, John, and Sasha, and give you a good morning kiss before I started work."

He makes a sound of disgruntlement deep in his throat, but then he pulls away slightly to grin at me. "You sure you don't have like five minutes to spare? No, wait… ten minutes to spare?"

Pushing out of his hold, I swing my legs off the bed. "Sorry, babe. Duty calls."

When I turn back to look at him, my breath catches in my lungs. He's beautiful… lying on his back with his hands propped behind his head. His smile is magnificent, showing me all the kind and lovely things I know to be deep inside this man. He looks so happy, and that makes me happy.

Leaning over, I sweep the hair off his forehead and give him a kiss. "See you later."

"Love you," he says as he turns over in bed to go back to sleep.

"Love you, too."

I tiptoe back through the house, because I assume John is still sleeping, and I pray that I don't run back into Sasha. The coast seems clear, and I literally trot down the stairs high on life.

But when I get to my truck, I come to a dead stop because I see her standing there. She's still in her robe and leaning up against the passenger door. Gone is the smug look on her face, and rather, I see an interesting array of confusion and earnestness.

"You didn't tell Hunter what I did," she says matter-of-factly. "How come?"

I walk up to stand before her. "Because it was unnecessary. I didn't believe you, and I didn't want to get Hunter upset."

She appraises me a moment and, for the first time, I don't feel like she's looking at me like a bug that she wants to crush. Instead, her face gets softer and her voice is genuine when she says, "I misjudged you."

"I think so," I tell her. "I'm just not sure what you hoped to accomplish by that. You had to have known you might have driven me away if that little scheme had worked, but there's no way Hunter would have ever taken you back. Not after what you did."

Sasha gives me a sad smile. "Gabby... I didn't do that to get Hunter back. I did it only to push you away."

I blink at her, stunned by her words. "Why? I don't understand."

Gabby looks up at Hunter's house, a wispy smile on her face, and then turns back to me. "I care for him a great deal. I may not have shown it all that well, and I screwed things up with him when I demanded he leave the tour to be with me. I know that, and I accept that. And while I may have misjudged you, I have never misjudged Hunter. I see how in love with you he is. So I've known from the get-go that Hunter would never go back on the Tour. There was no way he was going to leave you."

"You tried to drive me out so Hunter would go back on Tour? I still don't get it... what do you stand to gain?"

"Nothing. I'd gain nothing, but Hunter would gain everything. And I still care for him. Always will. I don't want to see this opportunity slip past him, and while John is too laid back to push Hunter one way or the other, I'm not."

I move past Sasha and lean up against my truck, staring at the ground while I digest what she said. I sort of believe her... that she doesn't want anything for herself, but wants him to have another shot at the world title.

"Gabby, you don't know Hunter the way I do... at least not the Hunter that is a professional surfer. And you don't know what it's like... to be out there in the heat of competition, never knowing what type of wave Mother Nature is going throw your way. It might be a small set, making you hone in and focus on your skills. It might be a massive barrel, so big it could crush you on the coral below, and your heart is in your throat as you coast it out. Either way, the adrenaline high when you drop in to ride that bitch is like nothing you can imagine. It's like touching Heaven with your fingertips. Forget for a moment the fans screaming his name, and forget the money that will fatten his bank account. Hunter was born to be a legend. This opportunity, to walk away from a career and then literally be begged back by all the biggest surfing retailers in the world, this isn't offered to everyone. It's not even offered to the number one guy right now. It's Hunter they want, because it's Hunter that has the ability to hit the top, but more importantly, he has the ability to stay at the top. This is a once-in-a-lifetime opportunity and trust me, he will regret this until the day he dies if he passes it up."

Her words slam into me hard, and even though I've heard plenty of talk of endorsement deals and seven-figure paychecks, no one has made me consider the intangibles of what this might mean to Hunter. No one until his ex-girlfriend, who stands before me and explains to me how truly special this offer is.

"He's made his mind up," I whisper. "I've not pushed him either way."

"Then get him to change his mind," she says.

"I can't," I tell her, casting my eyes to the ground.

"You can't, or you won't?"

Her words are hard but not overly harsh. I look up to her and say, "I can't. I want him to stay, trust me. But not at the expense of him passing up an opportunity that could haunt him later in life. I'd never want that. I think... no, I know... I really want him to take this shot."

"Then get him to change his mind."

Shaking my head, I push away from my truck. "I don't know how, Sasha. I overheard him talking to Brody. He said I'm more important than the Tour... than surfing. I don't know how to change that."

Sasha steps toward me, angles her head in, and says in a quiet voice, "Then you make yourself less important."

The power of her words overwhelms me, and my body jerks. The only way I could possibly make myself less important is by breaching our trust... our loyalty... our love. The thought of it makes me want to vomit, because I'll be sacrificing myself and hurting Hunter immensely. He'll ultimately get to go back to his surfing career, but I'll be a wreck when he's gone.

Part of me wants to cry out to the Heavens that this isn't fair. It shouldn't be up to me to be the sole bearer of responsibility when it comes to Hunter's welfare and happiness. But then I realize that it is not a responsibility that I would entrust to anyone else either. The one thing that is more important than how this will affect me… is how this will affect Hunter and his future.

Sasha may be full of herself, and she may be catty and scheming, but one thing I trust her on, for some odd reason, is that this shot for Hunter is far more important than I originally gave it credit. I think my own selfishness in not wanting him to leave, prohibited me from truly recognizing how special this opportunity is for him. As such, I need to do whatever it takes to give him that shot, because he won't take it for himself if I'm involved.

It's time for me to step up and make sure that Hunter is taken care of.

"All right," I tell her as I step back and start walking around my truck to get in. "I know what I can do, but it will have to wait until after you and John leave town. I'll talk to him tonight."

"What are you going to do?"

"Don't worry about it, but you can help out. The rest of the day until you leave, I want you to try to avoid Hunter. Don't engage him in talk, stay out of his way, and be aloof if you can. Got it?"

She nods her head at me and softly says, "Sure."

Sasha and I stare at each other for a moment

over the hood of my truck. I wait for a look of triumph to enter her eyes, but it never comes. She just gives me a sad smile, tips her head at me, and heads back toward Hunter's house.

Opening the door to my truck, I watch her as she walks up the stairs and disappears inside. I stare at Hunter's cottage for a few more moments, sadness welling up inside of me that my times locked inside of there with him are coming to an end.

I try not to be bitter, but I can't help it. It seeps in.

I finally got what I've wanted my whole life, only finding out that I don't have the power to keep it. Moreover, I have the power to push it away.

The only thing I can do… the only way I can soothe the ache that has already started in my chest, is to remember that Hunter is getting what he needs and deserves and, God willing, maybe our time will come back around one day.

TWENTY-FOUR

Hunter

After opening my fridge and grabbing a beer, I check my watch for like the tenth time in the past hour and wonder where the hell Gabby is. I haven't seen her since that unbelievably sweet moment this morning when she came over to bring donuts and snuggle with me for just a bit. Of course, I wanted to do more than just snuggle but I have a dick between my legs, so sue me.

Still... it was a side of Gabby that I very much

liked seeing. The woman who used to be the girl that crushed on me, who is now very much the woman that sees this as way more than just a good time in bed. I'm not sure when I became this reflective, mushy kind of guy, but I'll certainly blame Gabby for that.

I think today may be the first time since we've been together that I haven't seen her for such a long period of time. She wasn't at Last Call today, her crew saying she was off running errands while they worked on staining the outdoor area. I've tried calling her a few times, but just get her voice mail. For some reason, that just doesn't sit right with me.

I distracted myself with packing John and Sasha off to the Raleigh airport. I hated to see John go. Sasha, not so much. While she was on good behavior for most of the visit, it was still just awkward. Even more awkward today for some reason, as she would barely look me in the eye. If I asked her a direct question, she would mumble a response while staring at the floor. So very weird, so I'm glad she's gone.

Wandering into the living room, I twist the cap off my beer and take a healthy pull. For not the first time in the last few weeks, I wonder what it would be like if Gabby moved in here with me. It was something I had thought about a lot, especially when

John and Sasha were here. Mostly because their presence meant that I couldn't have much alone time with Gabby, and it made me think of all the things we could do together once they were gone.

Yeah, I thought of all the ways and places I could fuck her in this house, but mostly, I thought of stuff that would completely have my man card revoked if anyone knew about it. I thought it would be only fair that if she cooked dinner, I would do the dishes. And I wondered if we would fight over the TV at night, knowing that if a football game were on, I would win that argument. I tried to figure out if I had enough counter space in my bathroom to hold all of a girl's necessities, and I smiled to myself thinking that I would get to wake up every morning to her beautiful face.

Fuck, I'm not sure what I am turning into, but I'm not fighting it. No, I'm surrendering to it.

The minute I made the absolute decision to stay here, I made the decision in my mind that Gabby was the only one for me, and that there was no sense in slowing down where she was concerned. While I don't believe the last five years without her were wasted, because let's face it, I've had a pretty amazing career, I don't want to waste another minute.

A knock at my door causes my adrenaline to

spike, because I immediately know it's Gabby, although for the life of me, I can't figure why she doesn't just walk in. She has a key.

Setting my beer on the coffee table, I hop the back of the couch and open the door with almost giddy excitement, man card be damned.

There she stands… golden-kissed skin, hazel eyes, and chocolate hair, framing the most beautiful face I've ever beheld.

"Hey baby," I murmur as I snag her by the hips and pull her into to me. She steps forward, caught off guard, her hands coming up to my biceps. I bend down to touch my mouth to hers, but her head turns to the side and I end up grazing her cheekbone.

Pulling back, I look at her in curiosity because she turned away from my kiss, and now I am very much aware that she is pushing back from me. I drop my hold and she steps by me, walking into my house.

"What's wrong?" I ask, closing the door and turning to her.

Her shoulders are tense as she walks into the living room, so I follow behind in trepidation. When she turns, her face isn't one I recognize. It's hard and her eyes are cold, causing my stomach to bottom out.

"I repeat. What's wrong?" My voice sounds oddly detached and fear-tinged.

"We need to talk," she says, her eyes firmly rooted to the carpet.

Taking three long strides around the couch, I walk right up to her, placing my hand under her chin and lifting her face to mine. "So talk, but do it while you look me in the eye."

Her eyes fill with sadness for a moment, a light sheen of moisture coating the green-gold brilliance. It kills me to see that look and I start to wrap my arms around her, but she's having none of it. It happens so quickly, I'm sure maybe I even imagined it, but the sadness is gone and replaced by a hard glint as she steps away.

"We're over," she says.

Of all the things I thought she might say, that never crossed my mind. Blinking at her hard, because surely I heard wrong, I say, "What?"

She takes a few more steps to put distance between us, coming to stand in front of the TV. Crossing her arms over her chest, she says, "We're over. It's done."

"You're breaking up with me?" I ask incredulously.

"Yes."

Her words are tinged in ice, her backbone ramrod straight. Defiance pours out of her eyes, daring me to argue with her.

Fuck that… I'm arguing.

"Want to clue me in on why we are over? Because as far as I remember, this morning you were crawling into my bed, telling me you loved me." My words are just as icy as hers, my anger building fiercely inside.

"Does it matter?" she asks with aggression.

"Fuck yeah, it matters," I snarl at her. "You break up with the person you supposedly love, you better have a fucking good reason."

Her eyes dart away from mine, once again sad and uncertain. I can't put my finger on it, but there's something going on inside of her that is fueling this ridiculousness. If I can figure out what it is, grab ahold and pull it out of her, I can salvage this fiasco.

Taking a step toward her, I soften my voice, "Gabs… please tell me what's wrong. We can fix it."

It's still there… for just a brief moment, the look of uncertainty and sorrow, but then it's gone— vanished. When her eyes meet mine again, I know it's gone for good. In its place is resolve and determination, such as I've never seen on her face before, and dread overwhelms me.

"You slept with Sasha last night," she throws at me, and it's a blind side I didn't see coming, hitting me so powerfully I physically jerk backward.

"Are you fucking nuts?" I bellow, outraged that she would even make such an accusation.

"No," she says quietly. "Sasha told me. She was waiting for me outside by my truck when I left you this morning."

My mind starts spinning, frantically searching for clues as to what the hell is going on, and how in the world I landed in this mess. It hits me hard… the way Sasha was acting today. Refusing to meet my eyes, mumbling responses. She acted as if she couldn't get out of here fast enough today when she and John were leaving.

"Son of a fucking bitch," I yell, clasping my hands on top of my head and looking in vain up to my ceiling in a silent plea for some type of help from God above.

Dropping my hands, I spin to Gabby and pin her with a hard stare. "And you believed it?"

"Yes," she says, her hands now clasped and wringing together.

"You fucking believed it?" I shout, taking a step toward her.

She takes a step back but tilts her chin up at me. "Yes."

Fury such as I have never felt flows like lava

through my veins. Some of that rage is for Sasha, for being spiteful enough to outright lie to Gabby and jeopardize my relationship. But most of that anger is reserved for Gabby, because she should have never believed it of me. She should have trusted me and, moreover, she should have come to me the minute Sasha filled her head with those lies.

Turning away from Gabby, because looking at her right now is not causing my rage to subside, I start to pace back and forth, racking my brain for a solution to this madness.

Stopping suddenly, I turn to her. "It's a lie."

"Maybe," she says, her hands wringing hard against one another. "But it's given me enough doubt that I can't continue on with you."

I stare at her in disbelief. "I don't believe this. I really can't fucking believe this. You've known me your entire life. You gave your body to me... you gave your fucking heart to me. And you believe Sasha over me?"

"She sounded convincing," she says lamely.

"And I don't sound fucking convincing?" I roar, thumping a fist against my chest. "Do I not sound like I'm telling you the truth?"

She flinches and I instantly regret yelling at her, but I'm spinning so fast out of control that I can't rein it in. Then she practically drives me to my knees when she says, "It's my experience that the man who protests the loudest is usually hiding the most."

My jaw hangs open as I look at her. The woman that I thought that loved me... she's gone. Vanished.

In her place is someone I don't recognize. Because the Gabby Ward that I love, the one I've known most of my life, would never believe a practical stranger over someone she loved. It's not possible.

I take a step back and fall onto the couch, hopelessness coursing through me. I'm beaten down, no way to defend myself, no way to reach through her thick skull.

"You're wrong about this, Gabs," I whisper, looking up at her with pleading in my eyes.

She stares at me a moment, sorrow filling her gaze. "I'm not."

Leaning my head back against the couch, I close my eyes and rub the bridge of my nose. I open my mind up and beg for something to come to me... for an idea on what to do next.

I'm empty. Completely, fucking empty.

"I talked to Keith this morning," she says, and the statement is so out of place in the context of our conversation, I know I must have heard wrong.

Lifting my head up, I narrow my eyes at her. "You talked to Keith?"

"Yes. I'm sure you know, but there's a pro event in Fiji at the end of next week. He's booked you a ticket. You're flying out of Raleigh in two days."

I stare at her, my eyes searching her face hard to try to figure out what the hell she's talking about. "Why the fuck would I go to Fiji?" is the only thing I can think to say.

"Because there's no reason for you to stay here anymore," she says simply.

"You're here," I tell her to point out the obvious. "Why would I go when you're here?"

"Because we're no more."

"Maybe I'll work to change your mind. Maybe I'll fucking drag Sasha's ass back here, and we'll confront this lie head on."

A brief flash of panic flitters across her face, but then I think I must have imagined it because steely resolve sets in stone once again. "You can do that if you want, but I won't be here."

"Why not?" I ask with dread.

"Because I accepted that job in Raleigh. I start next week."

Utter hopelessness washes through me, and suddenly I feel tired to my very bones. My voice is low, quiet... ironically calm. "This is really happening, isn't it? We're really over?"

"Yes," she whispers.

I stare at her, letting my eyes roam her face. The face I've seen a million times… in laughter, in sorrow, in pleasure. Now… it's looking at me impassively, her eyes cold and distant. I stare at her hard, letting that look burn into me, willing it to replace all those other images. She tries to hold my gaze but eventually it's too much for her, and her eyes slide down to the carpet.

I wait for her to look back up at me. For her to tell me that this whole fucked-up scenario is some terrible joke gone awry.

But she doesn't.

"Get out," I tell her softly, watching her eyes fly back up to me.

She just stands there, looking like a deer caught in the headlights. I'm not sure what her hesitation is, because she's flayed me down to my soul. The longer she stares at me, the hotter the acid burns in my veins.

"Get. The Fuck. Out," I repeat, and the menace in my voice shocks her back to reality. She spins away and runs to the door, throwing it open and hurling herself outside. When I hear the door slam shut, I close my eyes once again and try to figure out what all I need to do to get ready to leave for Fiji.

TWENTY-FIVE

Gabby

My phone rings, bringing me out of my stupor. I roll over in my bed and pick it up, seeing the word "Casey" on the screen. I want to ignore it, but I can't. Casey's worried sick about me, and it pains me to be the cause of that.

"Hey Casey," I say softly as I connect the call.

"You're still lying in bed, aren't you?" she demands.

"Yes," I tell her, because I'm in exactly the same

spot I was yesterday when she called me. Today's the day Hunter's flight left for Fiji and the knowledge has me so mired in despair and darkness, I can only manage to pull myself up to go to the bathroom before tumbling back down into the comfort of my bed.

After I broke up with Hunter two days ago, I immediately went home, put on my pajamas, and crawled into bed. I told Savannah that I didn't want to be disturbed, and I locked my bedroom door.

Within less than an hour, Casey showed up and was banging to gain entrance. I ignored her, even as I could hear her sit down on the floor outside my bedroom and talk to me. She told me that Hunter had called her, told her that he was leaving, and that we had broken up. She was freaked... I get that. But I ignored her and, after about half an hour, she left. I rolled over and went to sleep, not waking up until the next morning.

Then the calls started. Repetitively. Casey was the worst, calling me at least every fifteen minutes. My mom called. Hunter's mom called. Alyssa called. Even Brody called once, but only that one time. I was shocked as hell when Sasha even called, but I ignored that too. Savannah knocked on my door a few times, offering to bring me food, but I politely declined.

Finally, last night, I answered Casey's call, mainly because I knew I was worrying the hell out of everyone, and I didn't want to do that. Her first words were, "Oh honey... tell me everything," and then I started sobbing.

I couldn't talk for almost five minutes, so Casey filled me in on what she knew, which was next to nothing. Hunter had apparently called her and told her that we had broken up, but not the reason why, and that he was going to Fiji. My heart ached mostly, that we were over and he was leaving, but there was a tiny part of me that was happy that he was taking his shot to get back on the tour.

When I calmed down enough, I basically told Casey the same thing, that for reasons I didn't want to discuss right now, that Hunter and I were indeed over. I did not tell her about my lie to make Hunter leave, nor did I tell her that I lied to him about me taking the job in Raleigh. I figured I would handle that duplicity at a later time, when my brain was more alert and not mired in depression.

Casey then cooed and soothed me over the phone, assuring me that it would be all right. But I knew it would never be all right again. My heart was broken, and there was nothing that would ever put it back together again.

"How are you feeling today?" she asks, jarring me back to the present.

Sighing, I say, "Like shit."

Laughing, she says, "Well, the only way to get past that is to come hang out with your bestie today."

"No way," I tell her adamantly. "I'm lying in bed and refusing to brush my teeth. My goal is to let a fur carpet start to grow."

"That's gross, Gabby, and completely unacceptable. If you don't get showered, get your teeth brushed, and get your ass down to Last Call in one hour, I'm coming to get you. And don't think that a locked bedroom door will keep me out. I could have had that lock picked the other day in about five minutes flat, but I was respecting your need to grieve."

"I'm still grieving," I grumble.

"That may be so, but you're going to stop that process as of today."

"No," I pout. "I'm not coming."

"One hour," she says ominously, and then disconnects the call. I stare at the phone, blinking, and disbelieving she just hung up on me. My first reaction is to thumb my nose at her, roll back over, and go to sleep, but then my stomach rumbles and I realize it's been almost two days since I've eaten.

Then my heart rumbles, and I realize that maybe what I really need is to get stinking drunk to help ease the ache that has been lodged in my chest since I broke up with Hunter.

Taking a deep breath, I let it out slowly and then pull myself up off the bed. I decide I need to get on with my life, and the first step is to indeed go hang out with my bestie and get rip-roaring drunk, so I can toast the end of my relationship with Hunter.

It doesn't take me long to shower, but I go ahead and put the extra effort into shaving because it's hot as hell outside and I'll be wearing shorts. My teeth are already a bit furry, so I spend extra time brushing and flossing. After a quick rub of moisturizer, I do a quick dry of my hair and pull it up into a ponytail holder. Throwing on a ratty t-shirt, a pair of cut-off jean shorts, and my flip-flops, I open my bedroom door for the first time in two days.

The apartment is silent and as I walk by Savannah's room, I see it's empty. Stopping in the kitchen, I pull a bottle of water out of the fridge and drink half of it, hoping to stop a little bit of the ache in my stomach because I'm hungry. Noticing a note on the table, I bend over and see it's from Savannah.

On the ROCKS

Gabby,

Hope you are feeling better. I'm off on a quick assignment. I'll see you tonight, and we can do dinner together if you're up for it.

Hugs,
Savannah

I smile at her kind words, and it's the first time my lips have quirked upward in two days, the feeling foreign and slightly weird. But it reminds me that although I may not have Hunter, I still have some awesome friends, who will just have to sustain me.

Speaking of awesome friends, I grab my truck keys off the pegboard on the kitchen wall and head for the front door. Time to get my Casey on.

I open my front door and immediately turn to my left to grab the mail out of our box, which is mounted on the wall. I lean into the foyer and throw it on the small table, content to look through it when I get back home. Pulling the door shut, I lock the deadbolt with my keys and then turn to walk down the stairs.

And I come face to face with Hunter.

He's leaning back against the railing of the walkway, his arms folded over his chest. His hair is typically surfer-esque, sun streaked and windblown.

His facial scruff is at the perfect length, not too scratchy and not too soft. His blue eyes are glinting as they look at me, but I can't read the look on his perfectly tanned face.

He is utterly the most gorgeous man on the planet, and after I get over being blinded by his brilliance, it finally seeps into my addled brain that he's standing here in front of me rather than sitting on a plane to Fiji.

"What are you doing here?" I ask in disbelief.

"We need to talk," he answers simply.

"No, we don't," my brain automatically denies, thus pushing the words from my mouth.

"Yes, we do."

"No, we don't."

"Gabby… give me the courtesy, please."

Oh, fuck that shames me, and while I have no desire to talk to him, because I am completely out of sorts with the fact he's standing here when I just had accepted the fact I'd never see him again, my shoulders sag and I nod my head in capitulation.

"In your apartment if you don't mind," he urges, nodding towards my door.

My heart starts hammering as I turn around and unlock the door, pushing my way inside. I hear Hunter follow me in and close it behind him.

Glancing around... I'm not sure where to go. Kitchen? Living room? Bedroom? Definitely not, because that's not a place we'll ever be in together again.

So I opt for the living room, walking to the center of the room and turning to look at him. It's reminiscent of just two nights ago when I stood in his, telling him that we were over, and breaking both of our hearts in the process.

I carefully watch Hunter as he walks around the living room, casually looking around, one hand tucked in the pocket of his shorts. The silence is deafening, causing my anxiety to ratchet up a notch.

He reaches down to one of the end tables and picks up a small sandpiper figurine sitting there, examining it briefly before setting it down.

The waiting... wondering what he is doing here, is killing me, so I say, "Um... I'm on my way to meet Casey, so... uh... this isn't a good time."

"Casey's not meeting you," he says softly, picking up a small photo of Savannah and me that sits beside the sandpiper.

"She's not?" I ask stupidly.

"No," he says as he sets it back down. "She called you with that ruse to get your mopey ass out of bed, so I could talk to you."

I blink at him… once, twice. "Mopey ass?"

"Yeah. Heard you've been locked in your room for two days, pining away for me."

Okay, that is exactly what I've been doing, but the smug way he says it rubs me wrong.

"I have not been pining after you," I assert, raising my chin up in the air.

He then turns to look at me, his face bland. "Do you think I'm stupid, Gabby?"

"What? No… I mean… that might be debatable right now," I say, torn between confusion and anger. "Hunter… what in the hell are you doing here?"

In two steps, he's standing in front of me, and the nearness of him nearly has me sobbing from the sensation. As he looks down at me, his eyes roam over my face as his fingertips come up to trace the outline of my jaw.

"You must think I'm stupid," he says softly, "if you think I was going to fall for that line of horseshit you fed to me the other day."

"Hunter—"

"Terrible lie you told me… about Sasha," he murmurs, his fingers sifting through my hair to cup the back of my head.

"Hunter—"

He leans down, his nose almost touching mine.

"Pushing me away… trying to make me leave so I could have my shot at the world title."

"Hunter—"

"Sacrificing what we have together, because *you* thought it was what was best for *me.* "

This last statement is laced with anger and bitterness, yet his touch remains soft.

"Hunter," I say, begging him to listen to me.

"Don't ever lie to me again, Gabs," he says with warning as his lips come closer to mine. "I don't like it, and it has no place in our relationship."

Then he kisses me… roughly, his fingers sinking into my scalp and holding me tight. His tongue pushes in between my teeth, swiping at my own, causing my head to spin and my hands to involuntarily latch onto his rock-hard biceps.

His kiss is demanding at first, forcing me into submission, making sure I understand I fucked up and he's here to take control of the situation. I don't even think to fight him; instead, I open myself up and return the kiss as if my very life depended on making him understand that I know I fucked up.

Eventually, his movements soften against me, and I sigh against the gentleness with which his mouth moves across mine.

When he pulls back, I open my eyes to see him

staring intently at me. "Tell me you love me," he demands.

"I love you," I answer quickly, assuredly, most definitely.

"Tell me you will never push me away again."

"I'll never push you away again."

"Tell me you know I love you, the way you love me."

"I know it, Hunter," I say quietly, tears starting to fill my eyes.

"Baby," he says with care, pulling me into his arms. He tucks my head into his chest, stroking the back of my head, while I start to cry into the soft cotton of his t-shirt. "What am I going to do with you?"

"I'm sorry," I mumble through my wet tears. "I'm so sorry. I didn't mean to hurt you."

"I know," he whispers. "I figured it out quick enough."

Pulling back, I ask, "How?"

Hunter releases his hold on me and takes my hand. Leading me over to the couch, he sits down, pulling me onto his lap so I straddle him.

Running his hands up my legs and onto my hips, he looks up at me. "Baby, I was devastated when you left my house. Was like a fucking zombie... walking around, packing my shit up to leave. But something was bothering me... a look on your face... a moment of uncertainty when you told me about Sasha. I kept coming back to that, and then it hit me... you were making it up. I don't know how I knew it, but I just did. So I called your little cohort, Sasha, and got the truth."

"You called Sasha?"

"Yeah... after I reamed her a new one for filling your head with bullshit, she told me about your conversation by the truck. She also told me about her coming out of my bedroom that morning, trying to get you to believe that we had slept together. My baby didn't believe that though, did she?"

"No. I knew you wouldn't do that."

Hunter's hands leave my hips and come up to hold my face. "Gabs... you cannot unilaterally decide what's best for me. This whole charade was stupid and nearly destroyed both of us."

I close my eyes, shame coursing through me. My hands come up to grip onto his wrists, not to remove his hands, but to hold him in place. When I open them back up, I look at Hunter intently. "I'm so sorry. I thought I was doing the right thing. I just didn't want you to pass up something that you would regret later. I know how special this opportunity is."

Hunter pulls me forward and gives me a swift kiss, then pushes me back again so I can look at him. "It is a special opportunity, Gabs. But it's not as special as my opportunity with you. Trust me when I say… this is the right decision, for me to stay here, because of you."

"But I don't want you to regret it… maybe come to hate me for it later."

Smiling at me with censure, he says, "Not possible. Listen to me… I have had an amazing surfing career. I reached all my goals I ever aspired to. But when I made the decision to leave and come back here for Brody, I didn't have a moment of regret. That told me that I was ready to leave, that I had nothing more to accomplish."

"Really?" I ask, hoping beyond hope he truly means that.

"Really. My goals right now are very simple. Want to hear what they are?"

I nod at him.

"Okay, and these are in no particular order. I'd like to take you back into your bedroom, strip you naked, and make you come with my mouth. Then I want to fuck you… hard… so you never forget the passion we have between us. I want you to move in with me, so I can wake up every morning with you wrapped up tight against me, and I want to take you around the world... and share with you all the beautiful places I've been. One day... I want to have children with you, and God willing... they'll give us grandchildren. I want it all, and in no particular order, but if you agree, we should probably start with the fucking thing first."

"No, with the making me come with your mouth first," I tell him as I lean in to give him a kiss.

He returns it, hot and wet, his arms wrapping around me and pulling me in tight.

I pull back briefly, causing him to growl at me. His eyes are hot and needy, and I can feel his thickness pulsing between my legs as I straddle him.

Softly, I bring my hand up to his face and lay it against one cheek. "I love you, Hunter. I'm so sorry I did that to you, and I promise I'll never push you away again."

"You already told me that, baby."

"I thought it bore repeating," I whisper. "And I want to help you accomplish all those goals you set out."

He smiles at me then, wide and brilliant, as he stands from the couch with me wrapped around him. "Let's start in the bedroom, and then we can work on getting you moved in with me."

"Sounds like a plan," I tell him, my heart filled with more happiness than I've ever known in my entire life.

Hunter walks back to my bedroom, carrying me in his strong in his arms, toward a future that I had always dreamed of with him.

Now… that future is a reality.

EPILOGUE

Brody

Walking into Hunter's kitchen, I deposit the large box I was carrying on the counter. It's taped shut and has the word "Dishes" written in black Sharpie. There's a lit candle on the counter and subtle wafts of cinnamon apple hit my nose. I expect that's Gabby already putting her touches on Hunter's house.

I close my eyes and inhale the scent, relishing in the sweetly tart smell. It's something I do every time my nose encounters a pleasing aroma.

I savor.

And I ruminate.

And I am thankful for such a smell.

I sniff again, deeply, because it helps to drive the smell of incarceration out of my memory. For five years, I smelled the inside of a prison. It's a distinctive odor that I never got used to... a combination of toilets overflowing with shit, sweaty armpits, with just a hint of bleach underneath. The bleach was used to scrub away the shit, or even sometimes bloodstains from the floor, but it never really eradicated the underlying stench. The gritty lump of soap we were given certainly did nothing to erase away the sweat and grime of prison life.

"Hey man... give me a hand here?"

I open my eyes and see Hunter struggling with three boxes, which he's stacked one on top of the other, the top one getting ready to slide off. Within three strides, my long legs eat up the distance. I grab the top package before it can topple over.

"Where do these go?"

"My bathroom," Hunter says. "I'm almost afraid of the fact that Gabby has three boxes of shit to put in the bathroom."

"I heard that," Gabby grumbles as she comes in, carrying a DVD player that she sets on the living room floor near the TV.

Walking up to me, she takes the box from my hands. "Do me a favor, Brody? Will you switch out my DVD player for Hunter's? Mine's Blu-ray, and I want to bring him into the twenty-first century. I'll just head to the bathroom to put away my three boxes of shit, as Hunter so fondly called them."

Shaking his head with a smirk on his face, Hunter follows Gabby back to the bedroom. I smile internally, truly happy for them. I know I wanted him to leave her behind so he could have another shot at getting back on the ASP World Tour, but I have to trust that my brother knows what's best for himself. I'd never give up something that important for a woman, but to each his own.

I turn toward the DVD player to swap it out. Sitting down on the floor, I pick up Gabby's unit and examine it. Blu-rays had come out a few years before I started my incarceration, but I never had one. It wasn't something I could afford as a struggling med student at Duke. Still, it looks simple enough. There's an HDMI cable hooked up to the back of it already, and after getting to my knees so I can peer around the back of Hunter's TV, I see there's a corresponding plug for the other end.

Within two minutes, I have Gabby's Blu-ray hooked up, and I start to head back out to her truck for another load. As I walk by the mantel, a photograph catches my eye. Reaching out, I take the frame down so I can see it more clearly.

It's of Hunter and me... taken the summer before I got arrested. It's out at Cape Hatteras, I believe, and Hunter had been in for a quick visit. We decided to head out and catch some waves, even though that was what Hunter did for a living. He was always happiest in the water, so that's where we hung. I sort of remember this day and, if I'm not mistaken, Casey had been out there with us and took the photo.

Hunter and I are happy and relaxed, our arms slung around each other's shoulders and our free hands giving the "Hang Ten" sign. His hair is still the same today as it was then... medium length and with choppy layers... light brown with streaks of gold from the sun. Mine back then was much shorter than his was, but the coloring was the same. After a few weeks in the hot Carolina sun for my summer break, my hair had lightened up pretty quickly.

We were the best of friends, but I think that's natural for identical twins. Our bond boiled down genetically to matching strands of DNA, but it was fortified by the fact that Hunter and I had a pretty deep mental connection.

Always had growing up, sometimes even knowing if the other was sick or in pain.

Not kidding.

As I look at this photo, I start to feel a twinge of something inside my chest. Like an ache or a hollowness. Maybe I'd even call it a yearning. It's the same feeling I had when I first went to prison... when I was aching for my family... for my life. But that ache eventually went away, and I didn't think on it too much. Over time, I started slowly shutting those things I missed away in a little compartment... and then I buried it deep. I found it made the pain go away and let me focus on my new life as a felon.

I'm the first to admit... my family never let me try to lock them away for good. Mom and Dad came to visit me often, as did Casey. Hunter came when he could while on tour and, in between visits, they all wrote to me frequently. I tried to write back, but honestly... what would I tell them?

Dear Mom and Dad,

Life here is good. I managed to survive another day without getting shanked, beaten or raped. I met a new friend. He's in for armed robbery but he seems really nice. I even ate an entire meal without a single bug in it, and I managed to actually get three whole hours of sleep last night. Miss you both.

Love,
Brody

Yeah, I wasn't about to share the painful details of my life with them, but since that was the only thing I knew, there just wasn't anything to write home about.

Putting the frame back on the mantle, I give it one last look and yeah, it's a bit wistful. Then I make myself push that ache aside, and I head out the door.

Back out to help my brother move on with his life with the woman he loves, while I have no choice… not really… but to stay behind.

Next up...

Make It A Double

Book #2 in The Last Call Series.

Brody Markham has endured a nightmare, spending the last five years in prison and losing everything that was dear to him. Now he's back home, trying to survive in a world he doesn't recognize anymore. While his family and friends desperately try to reach through to him, he shelters himself further and further away from their love.

Alyssa Myers has worked her entire life to distance herself from the luxurious and privileged lifestyle in which she was raised. Running her non-profit agency, The Haven, she is content to spend her days helping abused animals find sanctuary, which fulfills her in a way that money just can't buy.

Maybe it's that she recognizes in Brody some of the same characteristics she sees in her homeless wards, or maybe it's the way he looks at her sometimes with a look warring between desire and disgust, but Alyssa is powerless to stop her personal quest to make Brody whole again.

While Brody struggles to surface from the darkness, Alyssa tries to protect her heart in case he's not willing to accept the light that she has offered him.

About the Author

USA Today Best-Selling author, Sawyer Bennett is a native North Carolinian and practicing lawyer. When not trying to save the world from injustice, she spends her time trying to get the stories she accumulates in her head down on paper. She lives in North Carolina with her husband, Shawn, and their three big dogs, Piper, Atticus and Scout.

Connect with Sawyer online:

Website: www.sawyerbennett.com
Twitter: www.twitter.com/bennettbooks
Facebook: www.facebook.com/bennettbooks

Made in the USA
Middletown, DE
11 February 2017